FUNNY MONEY

ALSO BY JAMES SWAIN

Grift Sense

FUNNY MONEY

A MYSTERY FEATURING TONY VALENTINE

JAMES SWAIN

ATRIA BOOKS

NEW YORK LONDON TORONTO SYDNEY SINGAPORE

Copyright © 2002 by James Swain

Library of Congress Cataloging-in-Publication Data

Swain, James.
Funny money : a Tony Valentine novel / James Swain.
p. cm.
ISBN: 0-7434-3686-5 (alk. paper)
1. Private investigators—New Jersey—Atlantic City—Fiction.
2. Swindlers and swindling—Fiction. 3. Atlantic City (N.J.)—Fiction.
4. Blackjack (Game)—Fiction. 5. Gamblers—Fiction. I. Title.

PS3569.W225 F86 2002
813'.54—dc21   2001058761

First Atria Books hardcover printing

10 9 8 7 6 5 4 3 2 1

ATRIA BOOKS is a trademark of Simon & Schuster, Inc.

For information regarding special discounts for bulk purchases, please contact Simon & Schuster Special Sales at 1-800-456-6798 or business@simonandschuster.com

Printed in the U.S.A.

For Margaret and Charles Swain

Acknowledgments

Thanks to George Lucas, my editor, Chris Calhoun, my agent, and my friends Steve Forte and Shawn Redmond, for their help and guidance.

Above all, thanks to my wife, Laura, my partner in writing, and in life.

My father always told me

never to bet on anything

but Notre Dame and the Yankees.

But for anyone not willing to

take my father's advice,

I now declare this casino open.

–Governor Brenden Byrne
at the opening of Caesars
Palace, Atlantic City
May 26, 1978

1

Heat

"Crossroaders see the world differently than the rest of us," Tony Valentine was saying to his neighbor over dinner in his kitchen. Buttering real butter onto his roll, he took a healthy bite. "Don't remind me, bad for my heart, but I've got to have the real taste now and again. Makes life worth living, if you know what I mean."

"What's a crossroader?" Mabel Struck asked.

"A crossroader is a name for a hustler or a cheat. It comes from the Old West practice of cheating at saloons that were located at the crossroads of one-horse towns."

"I presume so the cheater could make a hasty getaway."

"Exactly. So where was I?"

"You were painting an altogether ugly picture of the people you put behind bars," his neighbor said sweetly.

"Right. Crossroaders live a lie twenty-four hours a day. You know the worst thing that can happen to a crossroader?"

Spooning a forkful of homemade lasagna into her mouth, Mabel shook her snow-white head no.

"Getting heat."

"Is that like getting hives?"

"No. When you get heat, it means someone suspects you. And

once someone suspects you, you can't move in a game. So crossroaders do everything imaginable not to get heat."

Mabel, who had never gambled, was slow to catch on. She was more impressed with his colorful stories of celebrities he'd met during his twenty-plus years protecting Atlantic City's casinos than the nuts and bolts of his profession.

"Give me an example," she said.

Valentine scratched his chin, trying to think of an example that would not confuse her. "Have you ever played poker?"

"My late husband used to hold Friday night poker games at the house. I didn't play, but I understand the rules."

"Good. Let's say a crossroader is playing in your late husband's Friday night game. Between hands, he secretly palms out a pair of kings, and sticks them under his leg. A minute later, another player takes the deck and counts the cards. 'This deck is short,' he says. What does the crossroader do?"

Mabel gave it some serious thought. "I know. He says, 'Let me see those cards!' And he grabs the deck and adds the two kings."

"Very good."

She clapped her hands. "Am I right?"

"You most certainly are. What does he do then?"

"He counts them."

"Right again. Now for the big test. What does he say after he counts them?"

Mabel hesitated, clearly stumped.

"What would *you* say?" Valentine asked her.

"I'd say, 'You must have counted wrong. There are fifty-two.' " Mabel brought her hand to her mouth. "Wait. That would narrow it down to the two of us, wouldn't it?"

"It would," Valentine conceded.

"And that would bring heat, to use your expression."

"Precisely."

"All right, I give up. What does the crossroader say?"

"He says, 'You're right, there are only fifty cards.' And he pushes the deck to the center of the table. By agreeing with the first player, he takes the heat off himself."

"What does he do then?"

"He waits," Valentine said.

"For what?"

"Another player will inevitably pick up the deck and count them, and he'll say, 'Wait a minute, there's fifty-two.' And that will put all the heat on *him.*"

Mabel made a funny face.

"No wonder you like putting these people in jail," she said.

Valentine escorted Mabel home. It was a beautiful place, this town on the west coast of Florida they'd both retired to, the breeze filled with the Gulf of Mexico's warm spirits. As they walked the hundred yards that separated their New England–style clapboard houses, they stopped to inspect a brand new Lexus parked in a neighbor's driveway, the sales sticker prominently displayed in the side window. They were of the generation that were greatly fascinated not only by the astronomical cost of things these days, but also by people stupid enough to fork out the money.

At Mabel's house they stopped again, this time to smell the seductive night-blooming jasmine in her front yard.

"Are we a couple of squares or what?" she said.

"I like being a square," he said.

"You could have fooled me."

"What do you mean?"

"Your life is *exciting*. I envy you."

Going inside, he did a quick tour of the downstairs, then checked the back door and windows. Being old made you a target, and he feared that Mabel would one day lose her valuables to a burglar. He found her waiting in the foyer.

"Everything's shipshape," he said. "You know, you really ought to consider getting a dog."

It was a conversation they'd had many times. Mabel was going to get a dog when she was good and ready. She gave him a peck on the cheek. "Thanks for the fun evening."

"You're welcome. Listen, I've got a proposition for you."

"What's that?"

"How would you like to come work for me? I need someone to answer the phone and act as a buffer with clients. You could even help me with some cases."

Mabel hesitated. She liked Tony and sensed that he liked her. But he lived in a different world, one that she was not sure she'd be comfortable in.

"But I don't know anything about casinos or cheating."

"No, but you're one of the best judges of character I've ever met, and that's half the battle when it comes to spotting crossroaders. I'll teach you the basics. It'll be fun."

"You think so?"

"I do."

He was making it sound easy. If Tony had impressed anything upon her, it was that crossroaders weren't like other criminals. They used sophisticated sleight-of-hand, cameras, and hidden computers to commit their crimes. They were smart people, and it took even smarter people to catch them.

"Do you have any books I can read, so I don't sound too stupid answering your phone?"

"I've got a whole library."

"And you promise to help with the technical stuff?"

"I will."

Mabel hesitated and saw him smile. *He was going to make it fun,* she realized. She gave him another peck on the cheek.

"It sounds wonderful," she said.

◆

Valentine was settling into the La-Z-Boy in his living room when the phone rang. He never answered the phone, preferring to let the caller go into voice mail and leave a message. He considered it one of the great perks of working for himself.

The ringing stopped. He waited a minute, then dialed into voice mail. The message was from Doyle Flanagan, his ex-partner in Atlantic City. He dialed Doyle's cell number and caught his friend as he exited a McDonald's drive-through.

"Don't you ever go home?"

Doyle had retired from the force six months after him. Finding it impossible to live on his pension, he'd gone to work as a private investigator. "I wish. You have a chance to look at the surveillance tape I overnighted?"

"Sure did."

"Aw, for the love of Christ," Doyle said.

"What's wrong?"

"The bitch shortchanged me."

Valentine listened as Doyle went back through the drive-through and argued with the cashier, letting his hamburger go cold over twenty-five cents. Doyle's tape was still in Valentine's VCR, and he picked up the remote and hit play.

The tape was from The Bombay, the largest casino in Atlantic City. It annoyed him that New Jersey Gaming Control let its casinos record at extended play in order to conserve tape. It made the tapes hard to view and was a strain on the eyes.

6

The Bombay tape showed six people sitting at a blackjack table. The player in question—who Doyle had identified in a note as being European—was in his late thirties and had hair that stuck out at odd angles, like electricity was playing with it. He was winning big, his nervous mannerisms suggesting his play was not on the square.

"You think he's cheating?" Doyle asked.

"He sure *acts* guilty," Valentine said.

"Guy sweats a lot, doesn't he?"

"Like a whore in church."

Doyle dropped his cell phone. Picking it up, he said, "I've broken so many cell phones Liddy finally bought me one made of stainless steel. Any idea what he's doing?"

"I've got a couple of theories."

"I really want to bust this joker," Doyle said.

His partner was challenging him. Valentine watched the European play a few more hands. He heard his partner humming along to a song on his radio. Van Morrison's "Tupelo Honey."

"Got it," Valentine said.

"What's he doing?" Doyle said.

"I've been watching the way he places his bets. When he bets big, he's very direct. It's like, *bam*, here's my money. He knows he's going to win the hand."

"How's he doing that?"

"He's got a partner at the table marking the high cards," Valentine said. "The European is at first base, which means the top card for each round is his first card. Whenever he sees a marked card at the start of a round, he bets heavy."

"But he doesn't know what his second card will be," Doyle said.

"No, and he might lose sometimes. But over the course of an evening, he'd have an unbeatable edge."

"Who's marking the cards?"

Valentine stared at the other five players at the table. Marking cards is a felony in New Jersey and punishable by four and a half years in prison. His eyes locked on a chain-smoking beauty that reminded him of a young Audrey Hepburn.

"The lady at third base," Valentine said. "She's as tight as a drum."

"You're a genius," Doyle said.

"How much is The Bombay into these crooks for?"

"Six million."

"Come on, be serious."

Doyle coughed into the phone. Valentine sat up straight in his recliner. Casinos got ripped off every day—Las Vegas lost a hundred million each year—but it went out the door in dribs and drabs. Big scores happened, but mostly through card counters. As far as he knew, no hustler had ever stolen six million from any single casino. It was *too much* money.

"You're positive about this," Valentine said.

"The casino confirmed it. Uh-oh," Doyle said, starting his engine.

"Something wrong?"

"Looks like I've got company."

"Who?"

"The European. I made his white van yesterday when he was leaving The Bombay."

"Get the hell out of there."

Doyle's tires screeched as he threw the car into reverse. "Shit, the passenger window is going down . . ."

"Get the hell out of there!"

"Someone's pointing something at me. Looks like a transistor radio. . . ."

Valentine started to say something, then heard a loud *Boom!*

that sounded like a thousand doors being slammed. He yelled into the phone, but his partner did not reply. He could faintly hear people screaming inside the McDonald's. He waited for someone to come outside, pick up the phone, and tell him what in God's name was happening.

Then Doyle's cell phone died.

Valentine called every cop he knew in Atlantic City. After ten minutes he found one who was on duty, and got put on hold. He began to pray. In his mind, he knew what had happened. Could picture it as clearly as the hand in front of his face. Yet it took hearing the cop coming back on the line and saying, "Tony, I'm sorry," before he accepted the fact that his best friend of forty years was dead.

The cop stayed on the line, trying to console him. Valentine struggled to say something, but the words weren't there. His eyes started to burn. Then the room got very small.

Then he put the phone down and cried.

2

Cold

The cemetery was called Sunset Gardens, the manicured grounds new and horrible. The atmosphere was not serious enough, the place better suited for a happy-clappy John Tesh concert, with thirtynothings sipping overpriced wine and talking on cell phones. Getting out of the limo, Valentine heard another pall-bearer mumble that Doyle wouldn't have been caught dead in a place like this, ha, ha.

Grunting, the six men lifted the coffin out of the hearse and walked solemnly to the freshly dug hole that would serve as Doyle's final resting place. The cold February air blew hard on their backs. Old-timers called Atlantic City the lungs of Philadelphia, the easterly winds often cruel and punishing. Depositing the coffin on a gurney, they filed out under the funeral director's watchful eye.

Valentine walked with his head bowed, disgusted. Who wanted to be buried in a place that looked like a golf course? He'd buried his wife eighteen months ago and come away hating the business of death. *Would you like the thousand dollar pine coffin, Mr. Valentine, or the two thousand dollar polished maple?* What was he supposed to say—*put her in a cardboard box, she won't care and neither do I?* But his grief had been too great, and he'd gotten hosed every step of the way, from the flowers to the tombstone. When he died, he was going to be cremated, his ashes spread on the Atlantic City shore. Simple and efficient, the way death was meant to be.

10

He stamped his feet to stay warm and listened to Doyle's brother, Father Tom, read to the crowd from the New Testament. Cops and pols and every judge from the past thirty years had come to pay their respects. You couldn't have worked law enforcement in Atlantic City and not known Doyle, and there wasn't a dry eye on the lawn.

He stole a glance at Liddy, Doyle's widow. She looked stricken, like she still could not believe it. A cop's wife for so long, she must have thought that when Doyle retired the risk of his getting killed would end. She'd dropped her guard, and now she was paying for it. Her two sons, Sean and Guy, were doing a good job holding her up. Sean, a redhead, was his old man's spitting image. Guy was more like Liddy, a musician, reflective.

Behind them, confined to a wheelchair, was Doyle's mother Sarah. Back in '74, Sarah had spearheaded the Casinos–No Dice campaign. She'd done such a good job convincing New Jersey voters that gambling was a bad bet that when a referendum did pass four years later, it was isolated to Atlantic City, a town nobody cared about. He remembered the last time he'd seen her. It was the night Doyle had gotten shot, twenty years ago. She'd come into the emergency room to thank him for nabbing Doyle's shooter, who lay dying next door.

Father Tom asked the crowd if anyone wanted to speak in Doyle's memory. Valentine stepped forward.

"Doyle was my best friend. And my partner. I know he's looking down on us and not liking all the long faces. I know a lot of stories about Doyle. This one's my favorite.

"Once, Doyle and I caught a chip thief. The thief's name was Thurman, and he wasn't very smart. Thurman would put his coffee cup on the table next to another player's chips. When the player wasn't looking, Thurman put the cup on the chips and stole one with gum stuck to the cup's bottom.

"Doyle and I caught Thurman and ran him in. Thurman swore he didn't know how the twenty-five dollar chip got stuck on his cup. We realized we didn't have any proof except a used piece of gum, and it was going to be Thurman's word against ours in court.

"Finally, Doyle had an idea. He went into the station house's kitchen and found a metal colander. He put the colander on Thurman's head and connected it with wires to a photocopy machine. While I distracted Thurman, Doyle wrote the words *HE'S LYING* on a sheet of paper and put it in the copier.

"Doyle had me do the questioning. I said 'Thurman, did you steal that man's twenty-five dollar chip?' Thurman said, 'No, sir!' and Doyle pressed the copy button. The piece of paper came out, and Doyle held it up and said, 'Uh-oh!'

"So I said, 'Thurman, you've been doing this for a while, haven't you?' And Thurman said, 'No, sir, not me.' And Doyle pressed the copy button again. This time when the copy came out, it was enlarged to twice its size. Thurman started trembling, and Doyle said, 'I think we've got our man!'

"Thurman confessed a short while later."

Among the sea of mourners there were a few sad smiles. Returning to his place with the other pallbearers, Valentine bowed his head. Father Tom finished with the Lord's Prayer, and then the crowd dispersed.

◆

Doyle and Liddy lived in a split-level ranch house in the suburb of Absecon. Cars lined the street, and Valentine parked his rental on the next block. He hadn't talked to Mabel all day, so he turned on his cell phone and dialed his office.

His call went straight to voice mail, which meant Mabel was talking to a customer. "Hey, kiddo, it's me. Hope everything's okay. I'm leaving my cell phone on. Call if you need anything."

He got out of the rental and hiked it, the cold making him shiver. Finding the front door ajar, he went inside.

The living room was smoky and filled with cops, and he shook hands and slapped backs as he made his way over to a corner where Father Tom was tending to his mother, Sarah. Kneeling, Valentine kissed the elderly matriarch of the Flanagan clan on the cheek.

"It's been too long, Mrs. Flanagan," he said.

"Mother had a stroke last summer," Father Tom told him. "She can't speak."

Valentine stared into the elderly woman's withered face. In her chestnut-colored eyes he saw the old sparkle, all systems on go. Rising, he pumped Father Tom's hand. Ten years Doyle's junior, he'd given up a football scholarship to Notre Dame to do the Lord's work. The priest said, "Mother and I were just looking at an old picture of you and Doyle. Weren't we, Mother?"

The old woman blinked. Valentine swallowed hard.

"I'd like to see it," he said.

In the middle of the living room, a table had been arranged with old photographs of Doyle. Father Tom removed one and handed it to him. It was a black-and-white snapshot of Valentine and Doyle in their septic cleaner uniforms, their first real jobs.

"I was trying to remember the slogan on your uniform," the priest said.

"We're number one in number two," Valentine replied.

That got a smile out of him. Sarah blinked some more. Valentine put the photo back and excused himself.

In the kitchen he found Liddy tending to several guests who sat around the breakfast nook. Putting the coffeepot down, she threw her arms around him.

"Oh, God, Tony," she cried softly. "When Lois died, I couldn't imagine how you felt. Now I know."

No you don't, he thought, holding her tightly. *You haven't woken up for a year and a half saying good morning to someone who isn't there.*

"How the boys holding up?"

"So, so," she sniffled. "We celebrated Sean's thirty-fifth birthday last week. You know what he told me? He said, 'I can't believe it's taken me this long to appreciate my own father.'"

Valentine thought of his own son, whom he'd been warring with forever, and wondered if those same words would ever leave Gerry's lips. He doubted it.

"Where are they?"

"Out on the patio."

"I want to talk to you later, if that's okay."

She smiled bravely. "I'll be right here."

He found Sean and Guy sharing a cigarette by the brick barbecue. He hugged Guy first and felt the younger boy's heart beating wildly out of control. Guy pulled away and walked to the other side of the yard.

Hugging Sean, Valentine said, "Is he all right?"

"I think it's just sinking in," Sean said.

Valentine edged up to the younger boy. "Hey."

Three generations removed from the motherland, Guy looked more Irish than either of his parents. He popped a cigarette into his mouth and offered Valentine one.

"Didn't know you smoked," Valentine said.

"Seemed like a good day to start."

It was a good line, and Valentine gave in and took one. He'd quit the day he'd made detective and never found anything to

replace the sensation of nicotine. They shared a match, and he
filled his lungs with the great-tasting smoke.

14   "During the funeral, all I could think about was Dad's killer,"
Guy said. "How he got up this morning, had breakfast, read the
paper, and did all the things that my father will never do again. It
made me so . . . angry."

Guy started to cry. He was going to miss his old man for the
rest of his life, and there was nothing that Valentine could tell him
that was going to make it any easier to deal with. They finished
their cigarettes, and then Valentine's cell phone rang.

◆

It was Mabel. Guy and Sean went inside. Standing on the edge
of the patio, Valentine said, "How's it going?"

"I've got a panicked customer on the other line," she said.

"Who?"

"Nick Nicocropolis in Las Vegas. He called up and yelled in my
ear for five minutes. Said he's getting ripped off by some slot
cheats. He's rude and *very* crude."

Valentine was paid monthly retainers by a dozen casinos, and
in return provided advice when the casino suspected it had been
ripped off. Nick, owner of the Acropolis Resort & Casino, was a
hardheaded little jerk who'd refused to sell out to the big hotel
chains and was struggling to stay alive.

"Did Nick describe the scam?"

"Yes. He said a cleaning lady found thousands of silver dollars
in a room and thought it suspicious. A husband and wife were
staying in the room, so security watched them. The couple were
playing one slot machine exclusively. Security detained them but
couldn't find anything. Nick's holding the couple, and they're
screaming lawsuit."

Guilty people usually did. "Call Nick up and have him describe what security found on the couple when they grabbed them. I'll wait."

Mabel put him on hold. Slot cheats were limited in their methods of stealing coins and rigging jackpots, and he had a feeling Nick's security people were missing something obvious. His neighbor came back a minute later.

"Nick said the couple both had money, credit cards, and their ID. Oh, and both were drinking glasses of iced tea."

"Nothing hidden up their sleeves?"

"No. And Nick said they frisked them."

"Huh. Let me call you back."

Shivering, he walked around the patio a few times. Eighteen months ago, he'd helped Nick nail another gang of cheaters, and the Acropolis's layout slowly came back to him. Nick's joint was ancient and still had many old-fashioned Bally's cast-iron slot machines. Cast-iron slots could be manipulated much easier than the new computer-chip models, and he realized what the couple was doing. Taking out his cell phone, he punched in Nick's number from memory.

Moments later, Nick was on the line. Nick was many things—sex fiend, loudmouth, ex-drunk—and also the squarest casino owner in Las Vegas. Valentine spelled it out to him. "The couple you arrested are a couple of old-time slot cheats. In one of their glasses of iced tea—which I hope you didn't throw out—is an extra-long spoon. When they hit a jackpot, one of them blocks the machine from your surveillance cameras, while the other sticks the spoon up the coin slot so more coins will come out. It's called spooning."

"How the hell do I prosecute?" Nick growled.

"Check the spoon for marks, and check the inside of the slot machine for similar marks. If they match, that's all the evidence you need to convict."

"You're sure about this," Nick said.

"I'd bet my reputation on it."

16

"You're a smart guy," Nick said, "even if you are from New Jersey."

"Good-bye," Valentine said.

♦

The crowd thinned out around five; by six, it was just Valentine and Liddy and the boys. Tying on an apron, he filled the kitchen sink with hot water and attacked the dishes, Guy drying and Sean putting away, Liddy fixing another pot of coffee. The stereo played one of Doyle's dixie jazz albums, Jack Maheu's seductive clarinet floating through the house, Doyle's easy laugh haunting every other note. When the dishes were done they sat at the kitchen nook with their cups.

"Tony," Liddy said, "did you talk to Doyle recently?"

Valentine shook his head. He had not told anyone about his last conversation with Doyle. "No. Why?"

She stared into the depths of her cup. "Something was troubling him. We went out to dinner last week, and Doyle was grumpy and out of sorts. Finally, I asked him what was wrong, and he said, 'If I told you, I'd have to kill you.' He was trying to make a joke, but it didn't come out that way."

Valentine had a senior moment and dribbled coffee onto his shirt. He got a sponge from the sink and blotted it out before it turned into a stain. Then he said, "He must have said something . . ."

Liddy shook her head. "I tried. But he wouldn't open up."

Valentine finished his coffee. When Doyle was a cop, he'd talked to Liddy about the cases he was working on–Liddy had told Lois and Lois had told him–and Valentine had never seen any harm in it, Liddy not being the type to blab. So why hadn't Doyle talked to her about *this* case?

The stereo played its last song and the house became silent. After a long moment, Sean spoke. "Yesterday, I met with a detective named Davis who's working on the case. I asked him if he had any leads, and he told me that nine out of ten murders are committed by people the victim personally knew, or were friends with. I said, 'Detective, you obviously didn't know my father.' He didn't get it."

"No one who was Doyle's friend would have killed him," Liddy said, wiping her eyes.

"Amen," Valentine said.

3

Sparky

It was dark enough for the street lights to have come on. Walking to his rental, Valentine saw a black mini-Mercedes pass by, a familiar face behind the wheel. It was Frank Porter, head of The Bombay's surveillance department. Porter got out of his car, and the two men shook hands.

"You look good," Porter told him.

"So do you. Still telling jokes?"

"Yeah. Now I just need to find an audience."

Atlantic City was filled with busted dreams. Porter's was in show business. When he wasn't catching cheats at The Bombay, he told jokes at open mike nights in comedy clubs. He was an overweight, jovial guy who looked like he should be as funny as hell. The only problem was, he wasn't.

"That was a nice thing you did at the cemetery," Porter said. "What story are you going to tell when I kick the bucket?"

Valentine had to think. "How about Superman?"

That made Porter smile. Right after gambling had come to Atlantic City, a wacky guy in a Superman costume had appeared in several casinos. Jumping on a chair, he'd shouted, *I can fly!* and started flapping his arms until security escorted him out. One day, the guy had appeared at the casino Porter was working in.

Smelling a rat, Porter had detained him. Under interrogation, the guy had broken down and admitted that while he was "flying," his partners were switching a blackjack shoe on an unwitting dealer. The case had drawn a lot of attention and led to all blackjack shoes in Atlantic City being chained to their tables.

"Listen," Porter said, "I shouldn't be telling you this, but Doyle was doing a job for me before he got killed."

Valentine started to say "I know," and bit his tongue.

"We've had this European guy ripping us off at blackjack," Porter said. "Bleeding us for months."

"How much?"

Porter stared at the ground. "Six million bucks."

Valentine whistled. "You tell the police?"

"No."

"Why not?"

"We didn't have any proof."

"You think the European killed Doyle?"

"He sure had a motive."

"Want me to get involved?"

"You're not going back to Florida?"

"Not right away."

"Yeah, I'd love for you to get involved," Porter said. "You were always the champ when it came to doping out scams."

Valentine realized his toes were freezing. He agreed to come by The Bombay the following morning and have a look at their surveillance tapes. He shook Porter's hand and started to walk away. Then he came back and said, "Is Sparky Rhodes still in town?"

"Sure," Porter said.

"Does he still live over on Jefferson?"

"Yeah. You thinking of paying him a visit?"

"I sure am," Valentine said.

A knowing look spread across Porter's face. They shook hands again. Then Porter said, "Do you know why marriage changes passion?"

Valentine told him he didn't.

"Because you're suddenly in bed with a relative."

"See you tomorrow," Valentine said.

♦

Valentine drove back to the beach in his rental. Atlantic City is laid out in a grid, with hardly a bend or curved road, and soon he was cruising down streets named after the first twenty-six states. New Hampshire, Vermont, Rhode Island. He wondered how many kids had learned their geography in the backseats of their parents' car, like he had.

He passed a two-story brick house on Fairmont Avenue where the local mafioso had once hung out. Being Italian, the "boys" had never hidden their faces. They'd gone about their business in the open, their ethnic pride getting in the way of good old-fashioned common sense. By the mid-seventies most of them had gone to prison or were mulch. Then the casinos had opened, and a whole new breed of criminal had descended upon his hometown.

He parked in an alley next to Sparky's house and got out. Sparky lived in a slum, the block lined with tenement houses, the fences that surrounded them all chain link. Sparky's own house hadn't changed. Peeling paint, a dead lawn, shades darkening every window. He rapped three times on the front door. Moments later, the dead bolt was thrown and the door swung in. Sparky Rhodes sat in a wheelchair in the foyer, his long silver hair tied in a ponytail, a .38 Smith and Wesson tucked into the folds of his camouflage vest.

"Hey, Sparky. How's it going?"

"Having the time of my fucking life. How's life in sunny Florida?"

"Fine. Can I come in?"

"Sure." Sparky turned his wheelchair on a dime and started rolling down the hall. "I had a feeling you'd be coming by."

"Why's that?" Valentine said.

Sparky wheeled himself through the poorly lit house and beckoned for him to follow. There were piles of fast-food wrappers in every corner and stacks of yellowing newspapers. On the walls, photographs of Sparky as a cop, before a juvenile delinquent's bullet had taken him down. The pictures of his wife were long gone.

"You and Doyle were partners," Sparky said. "Partners get close. Sometimes, they promise each other things."

"Sometimes they do."

Twenty years ago, Doyle had taken a bullet so Valentine could shoot a murder suspect. In the hospital he'd told Doyle he'd repay him the favor one day. Groggy from pain killers, Doyle had said, "I should hope so."

"You have anything particular in mind?" Sparky asked.

"Something with some bark," Valentine said.

Going into the hall, Sparky threw open a yellow door. A ramp descended into the basement. The rubber wheels of his chair hit it with surprising force. Valentine followed him down, holding the railing for support.

A naked bulb hanging from the ceiling came to life. Sparky went to a padlocked door and used a small key hanging from a chain around his neck to open the lock. They went in.

The room was a perfect square and housed Sparky's vast collection of firearms. On the floor sat a footlocker. Sparky flipped open the lid. "These are all clean. No serial numbers, no history. Something for every man's taste."

Valentine knelt down and examined Sparky's wares. There was a silver-plated Mac II, a Cobray M-11, a Tec-9, a Colt .45 with a Buck Rogers laser scope, a .25 caliber Raven, and on the bottom of the footlocker, an Uzi nine, a shorter and easier to handle version of the Uzi submachine gun, with a magazine capacity of twenty rounds.

"That's my favorite," Sparky said.

Valentine stood up. "I was looking for something I could keep in the pocket of my jacket. Small, but with a good punch."

"You're talking a Glock pocket rocket," Sparky said. "Leaves an exit wound the size of your fist."

"That sounds about right," Valentine said.

Backing up his wheelchair, Sparky took a Glock off the shelf and held it up to the light. It was a small gun, the barrel lovingly polished. He turned it over several times in his hands, then handed it to him.

Valentine reached for his wallet.

"It's yours," Sparky said.

He started to say something about not coming here for charity, but Sparky cut him short.

"He was my friend, too," the paralyzed cop said.

Valentine pocketed the Glock.

"He was everyone's friend," Valentine reminded him.

4

Gerry

Valentine awoke the next morning at seven, the sunlight streaming into his motel room. Wrapping himself in a blanket, he went and cracked a window, then sat in a chair listening to the waves pound the shore while remembering how he and Doyle had often ended their shifts by walking the beach. Sometimes, they kicked off their shoes and stuck their feet in the water, two flatfoots cooling off. The memory was made vivid by the lingering taste of yesterday's cigarette, and he cursed himself for smoking it.

For breakfast, he ate the remains of last night's Chinese take-out. Out of nostalgia, he'd picked a cheesy motel off Pacific Avenue to stay in. The Drake. Efficiencies, rooms by the day, week, or month; HBO and Showtime; no dogs. What more could a man want?

The banging on his door was loud and frantic. Taking the Glock off the night table, he slipped it into the pocket of his overcoat hanging in the closet. Then he went to the door with the blanket hanging from his shoulders.

Through the peephole he spied his son, his hair peppered with silvery flakes of snow. Physically, they had a lot in common, but that was where the similarities ended. He went and hid in the john. The banging continued.

"Come on, Pop," his son bellowed through the door. "I saw you looking at me."

"Who's me?"

"Gerry."

24   "Gerry who?"

"Gerry your fucking son, the apple of your eye, the product of your loins."

Valentine opened the door. Gerry smiled, stuck his hand out. He was dressed in a somber three-piece suit and a tie. He'd lost the annoying little earring and shaved away the stubble he called a beard.

"The funeral was yesterday," Valentine informed him.

♦

Gerry had cried all the way from New York, or so he said. Doyle had been like an uncle to him, Guy and Sean like brothers, Liddy his surrogate mom. He made it sound like he'd spent every weekend at their house, and not with the dope-smoking lowlifes Valentine remembered so vividly.

"So how'd you find out where I was?" Valentine asked over pancakes at the IHOP down the street.

His son made a face, his mouth dripping maple syrup.

"I'm just curious, that's all," Valentine said.

Gerry kept eating, the look becoming a frown. The restaurant was deserted, the snow keeping everyone home. In the kitchen a radio was playing Sinatra, New Jersey's favorite son.

Valentine said, "You want me to figure it out by myself?"

"Go ahead."

"Mabel told you. Now, I didn't give her my number, but I did call her, and since she has caller ID, she must have scribbled the number down. You called, and she gave you the number. Bingo."

"Why you making a federal case out of it," his son said belligerently.

"You could have called my cell phone."

"I wanted it to be a surprise."

"I hate surprises."

"Even when it's me?"

Especially when it's you, he almost said. "If I'd known you cared so much about Doyle, I'd have called you. But unless my memory's fading, the last time Sean came over to the house, you bloodied his nose."

"I still wanted to pay my respects," his son said. "Hey, you going to eat your bacon?"

Valentine glanced at the grisly strips on his plate. During his last checkup, the doctor had heard a swishing in his neck and determined his carotid artery was getting clogged. Someday, he would need to have it scoped, which sounded like no big deal, except two percent of patients had a stroke on the operating table and never came back.

"Why, you still hungry?"

Gerry frowned again. Valentine could never get him to admit anything, not even what day of the week it was.

"No," his son said.

"Then why do you want my bacon?"

"I just don't want it to go to waste, that's all."

"You still sending money to those starving kids in Africa?"

"Aw, Pop, for the love of Christ . . ."

Their waitress slapped the check down, then gave Valentine the hairy eyeball. She'd been lingering by the cash register eavesdropping. No doubt she'd figured out the bloodlines, and was now painting Valentine out to be a jerk for playing rough with his son.

Valentine removed his wallet. "Can you break a hundred? It's the smallest I've got."

"Hey, Harold," she yelled into the kitchen, "can you break a C-note for Donald Trump?"

A bullet-headed man stuck his head through the swinging kitchen doors, said, "Nuh-uh," and disappeared.

Valentine laid his Visa card atop the check.

"We don't take credit cards," she said.

He slid the check toward his son. "Cover this, okay?"

Gerry dug his wallet out. It was made of snakeskin and looked like something Crocodile Dundee might have owned. He dug around in the billfold, then said, "No."

"You don't have ten bucks?"

"No," he said again.

"Where's your money?"

Meeting his father's gaze, he said, "I lost it, Pop."

Gerry owned a bar in Brooklyn, did a brisk business running a bookmaking operation in the back. He always carried a fat bankroll. Better than a ten-inch prick, he'd told his father, who'd slept with two women his entire life.

"How much?" Valentine asked.

"Fifty grand."

Their waitress had dropped all pretense and was hanging on every word. Her name badge said *Dottie.*

"Dottie, how about a little privacy?"

She ignored him. "Did you really lose fifty grand, kid?"

Gerry lowered his head shamefully. Valentine slapped a hundred onto the check.

"I'll come by later for the change," he told her.

♦

Snow had hooded the cars, and they walked to the corner of Jefferson and stopped at the light. A half-block away, the surf pounded the desolate shoreline.

"Okay," Valentine said. "Let's hear it."

Gerry stared straight ahead as he spoke. "Last Saturday, I get a call from a guy named Rico Blanco—you don't want to know what he does for a living—and he invites me over to a club called the Spanish Fly in lower Manhattan. I've known Rico since high school, so I say, what's the harm?"

"Isn't that club in Alphabet town where all the drug deals go down?"

"Alphabet town got cleaned up," his son said. "Studio apartments go for two grand a month, bathroom down the hall. Anyway, I meet Rico at the Fly. There's a bartender named Sid. He starts serving us drinks. Then this gambler comes in named Frankie Bones. Frankie is all flash and cash. I've heard Frankie is a made guy, but he's always seemed okay to me, you know what I'm saying?"

"Look at me," Valentine said.

Gerry turned sideways and looked into his father's eyes.

"Get to the goddamned point, I'm freezing my nuts off."

"*I am,*" his son insisted. "Sid turns on the TV. Next thing you know, we're watching football, Boston College playing East Bumfuck. BC is winning and Frankie starts hollering. Seems he got tossed out of BC for selling dope, nothing major, just nickel bags to guys in his frat house, only the cops got wind—"

"Get on with it!" his father roared.

"Right. So Frankie starts betting on East Bumfuck—"

"And you started betting on BC."

"How could I not bet on them? It was like watching a scrimmage."

"And you started winning," Valentine said. "Let me guess. By halftime, you were up ten grand."

Gerry's expression turned sullen. All his life, his old man had been a mind reader, knowing exactly where and how he'd screwed up. "Twenty," he said.

"You took a drunk for twenty grand? Shame on you."

"Pop, cut it out."

28 Valentine bit his lip. He was trying to be civilized about this and let Gerry present his case, but it was hard. He loved his boy more than anything in the world, but it did not change who his son was.

"So what happened?"

"Start of the fourth quarter, East Bumfuck's quarterback gets knocked out. The coach sends in some red shirt. Frankie pulls out this monster wad and throws it on the bar. He says, 'Seventy grand says BC is going down.' Then he goes to the john. I ask Rico and Sid what they think—"

"And they told you to do it," Valentine said. He could no longer feel his toes and decided to finish his son's tale before he got frostbite. "So you bet the farm against a loud-mouth drunk on a game that was a sure thing. But then a crazy thing happened. The red shirt starts throwing the ball like Dan Marino. He runs BC's defense up and down the field. One touchdown, two touchdowns, three, then four. Of course, your buddies are feeling terrible. And when the game's over and BC loses, well, they're downright miserable that you've lost all your money. Weren't they?"

"You're really enjoying this, aren't you?"

"It was a setup, Gerry. The game was a tape. It's the oldest hustle in the world. Didn't you see *The Sting?*"

The clouds had opened up like a busted feather pillow. Snowflakes stuck to everything they touched, the two men turning white before each other's eyes.

"So what happened?" his father asked.

"I wrote Rico a marker," Gerry said. "Rico sold the marker to these hoods named the Mollo brothers. They tracked me down to Yolanda's apartment. They slapped me around, then Big Tony made a move on Yolanda. I'm sorry, Pop, but I caved in."

"Meaning what?"

"I gave the Mollos the bar."

Gerry had borrowed fifty grand to buy the bar, plus gotten Valentine to put the place in *his* name, his own history with the law a major deterrent in gaining a liquor license. On paper, the bar was Valentine's, even though he'd visited the joint only once.

"How the hell did you give them something you don't own?"

"They think I own it, Pop."

Valentine thought about his clogged artery, wondering if the pressure building inside him might send a piece of plaque to his brain. "What do you want me to do?"

"I know this is going to sound stupid . . ."

"Try me."

"Lend me another fifty grand so I can buy the bar back."

"What?"

"Come on, you've got the money. What's the point of sitting on it? You're just going to give it to me eventually."

"I am?"

"Sure. Have you ever seen a Brinks truck at a funeral?"

Valentine's jaw tightened. His son had come here to put the squeeze on him. He placed his hands on Gerry's chest, and gave him a shove.

Gerry slid backward on the slick sidewalk. Then he took off at a dead run. Crossing the street, he entered a wooded park.

"Come back here."

Puffing hard, Valentine entered the park and followed Gerry's footprints until they disappeared beside a brick wall. Did his son think he was born yesterday? Standing on tiptoes, he peeked over the wall. Gerry sat in a frozen flower bed, cell phone in hand.

"Will you listen to me? My father said no. That's right. *N O*. Well, you're just going to have to move."

It was Yolanda, Gerry's third-year med-school girlfriend whom Valentine hadn't met but had a low opinion of anyway.

"Hey, stupid . . ."

Seeing his old man climbing over the wall, Gerry started to run, his butt caked with brown dirt and leaves.

"Come back here!"

"I'll figure out something," Gerry told Yolanda, fleeing through the woods toward a frozen pond.

"I said come back here!"

Kneeling, Valentine packed a snowball between his gloveless hands, then hurled it with all his might. He'd always had a strong arm, and the snowball arced gracefully in the air, then returned to earth and hit the back of his son's head. Gerry fell like he'd been shot.

An invisible knife pierced Valentine's heart. Years ago, Lois had made him promise never to fight with his son when he was in a bad mood. "You'll hurt him," she'd warned.

He ran through the forest in a panic. What if he'd scrambled Gerry's brains, turned the worm into a vegetable, could he live with that? No, no, of course not. He loved him; that had never changed. Coming to the forest's end, his eyes fell on the spot where his son had fallen.

Gerry was gone.

5

The Great One

Cursing, Valentine climbed into his rental. Buying Gerry the bar had been an olive branch, his way of trying to make peace. And now Gerry had given it away to a bunch of hoods. His son could screw up a wet dream.

The engine whined but did not turn over. The car was made by Ford and called a Probe. Naming a car after a surgical procedure seemed pretty dumb. Through the snowy windshield he saw a white van with tinted windows pull up to the corner.

The light changed, but the van did not move. Rolling down his window, Valentine stuck his head out and remembered that Doyle's killers had been driving a white van. He reached into his pocket for the Glock, then realized how stupid that was.

Get out of the goddamn car.

He had the door open when he heard a gunshot. A bullet cracked the windshield dead center. He hit the pavement hard, struggling to draw his gun, when he heard the van speed away.

He lifted his head. Without his bifocals, he couldn't see worth a damn, and the van's license was a blur.

Blue gunpowder smoke hung in the frigid air. He got up, then popped the hood of the Probe. The main wire to the distributor cap hung down. He reconnected it, then got in and tried the engine. Soon the heater was blowing and his teeth had stopped chattering. But his heart would not slow down.

♦

Valentine drove back to the Drake wondering why the European had come after him. Had he been at Doyle's funeral, and heard Valentine's eulogy? Back in Sicily, where Valentine's family was from, it was common for killers to murder their victims' best friends to avoid retribution later on. Which meant the European would probably try again. He needed to start being a lot more careful. And switch motels.

Frank Porter's mini-Mercedes sat idling in front of the Drake. He parked on a side street so Frank wouldn't see his windshield, then hiked over. Porter hit the unlock button.

"How'd you find me?" he asked, climbing in.

"I called your office," Porter said. "Mabel told me."

Valentine made a mental note to tell Mabel not to do that anymore.

"I need a favor," Porter said.

"What's that?"

"I told Archie Tanner about your offer to help. Archie says, 'Screw that. Hire him.' I told Archie I'd have to ask you. Archie says, 'It's your ass if he says no.' "

Archie Tanner owned The Bombay and was one of the richest men in New Jersey. He was also a mean, foul-mouthed thug and disliked by everyone in the casino business.

"Your ass, as in your job?" Valentine said.

"That's right," Porter said.

Normally, Valentine would have said yes, just to help Porter out. Only this was Archie Tanner, a man he'd never trusted.

"I need to talk to him first," Valentine said.

"About what?"

"My terms."

Porter blew out his cheeks. "Okay."

Soon they were heading north on Pacific Avenue, and Valentine noticed that Porter looked pale. He'd recently gone through a bitter divorce, with his ex getting everything but the house.

"So how's the joke-telling business?"

Porter smiled thinly. "I heard a joke which sums it up pretty well."

"What's that."

"Do you know the difference between a comedian and a pizza pie?"

"No."

"You can feed a family of four with a pizza pie."

◆

Twenty minutes later, they were sitting in Archie Tanner's penthouse office atop The Bombay. Archie knew how to live, and the room's panoramic view was the best in town. To the east, cruise ships dotted the churning black waters of the Atlantic; to the west, a private Lear jet landed at Bader Field, the airport's crisscrossing runways forming a black cross in the snow.

And then there was the office itself. Burnished mahogany book shelves, polished wood floors covered with Persian rugs, a marble desk the size of a sports car. On the walls, framed photos of Archie clowning with Frank Sinatra, sparring with Muhammad Ali, kissing the Pope's ring.

Porter picked up a book on the coffee table. It was Archie's ghost-written autobiography, *The Great One: The Life and Times of Atlantic City's Living Legend.*

"Archie send you one?"

Valentine nodded. Archie had bought several thousand copies

and sent them to everyone in town. The inscription on his copy had read *To the squarest guy in Atlantic City.*

"So, what did you think?"

"I read ten pages and threw it in the garbage."

Porter rolled his eyes. In the adjacent office they could hear Archie chewing someone out. The brunt of his assault was either a dopey fuck or a fucking dope, and when the door opened and the great one marched in, Valentine was surprised to see three attractive young misses in tow. One blond, one brunette, one African-American, all dressed in stylish leather miniskirts and black leggings. The blond had been crying, her cheeks still moist. Valentine rose from his chair.

"Sit down, sit down," Archie said, pumping his hand. For a punk, he cleaned up well, and wore a handsome blue Armani suit and silver necktie that accentuated his deep tan. When Valentine remained standing, he bristled.

"What's the matter, you got piles?"

"There are ladies in the room." Facing them, he said, "Name's Tony Valentine. Nice to meet you."

The ladies introduced themselves. Gigi, Brandi, Monique. Hardly any makeup, no jewelry, Monique sporting a little rose tattoo on her bare shoulder. They were a far cry from the rough-and-tumble females that had worked in the casinos twenty years earlier. Archie stood behind his desk, not enjoying being upstaged. "I call them my Mod Squad," the casino owner said. "One blond, one brown, one black. Get it?"

Valentine eyed him the way he would any other blow-dried moron. "You know, Archie, with all this dough you ought to consider buying yourself some class."

Archie's face grew red. He looked like he wanted to bust

Valentine in the mouth, only Valentine knew that wasn't going to happen. Thirty years ago, he'd ticketed Archie for speeding and found bootleg cigarettes in the trunk of his car. He'd let Archie go because he knew his old man, and that single act of kindness had let Archie later obtain The Bombay's gaming license, his record clean as a whistle.

"Ladies, if you don't mind, we have business to discuss," the great one said.

The Mod Squad filed out, with Brandi catching Valentine's eye. She winked.

"Pleased to meet you," Valentine said.

◆

"So how's retirement treating you?" Archie asked, sitting at his desk sipping Evian out of a Waterford tumbler.

Valentine swirled the ice cubes in his soda. Life had been treating him crummy, but he didn't think Archie really cared.

"I opened a consulting business. It keeps me busy."

"Still catching hustlers, huh? You were always the best, wasn't he, Frank?"

Porter nodded. "Tony's the best."

"That's what I said. I remember when The Bombay first opened. We were getting killed at blackjack. *Everybody* was beating us, even little old ladies. I didn't know my ass from my elbow back then, so I tell another casino owner, and he says, 'Call Tony Valentine. He's the best at catching cheats.' Now, I've known Tony a long time. How long has it been, Tony?"

"Since I busted you," Valentine said.

Archie burst out laughing. "What a kidder. Anyway, so Tony comes in, takes a stroll through the blackjack pit, and comes up to me. He says, 'Hey, Arch, were you born yesterday? You're using playing cards with a one-way back design. I said, 'So?' And he says, 'If a card gets turned around, every player at the table can track it.' So we replaced the cards, and our problems vanished."

Valentine sipped his soda. He didn't remember the incident, which he attributed to the fact that so many casinos had gotten ripped off back then. Atlantic City hadn't known what it was doing, and hustlers from around the globe had come running.

Rising, Archie crossed the spacious room and stopped at the floor-to-ceiling window that faced the ocean. "You and Doyle were buddies, weren't you?"

"That's right."

"I was down in Florida when he got killed. I would have come to the funeral, but business had me tied up."

"You buying Disney World?"

Archie took a big fat cigar from his pocket and fired it up. "I'm buying hotels, Tony. Hotels that I'm going to turn into casinos. Florida isn't going to let the Indians have a monopoly forever. Gambling generates taxes, and taxes build roads and schools, two things Florida desperately needs."

Valentine nearly stood up and walked out of the room. He'd retired to Florida because it didn't have casinos. Biting his tongue, he said, "Okay."

Archie picked up on his hesitation. He stared at him in the window's reflection. Then said, "How would you like to finish doing Doyle's job?"

"Depends," Valentine said.

The great one's eyes turned into slits.

"My rate's a thousand bucks a day, plus expenses. I also need access to your surveillance control room. And your library of surveillance tapes."

Archie turned to look at Porter. New Jersey law strictly forbids outsiders inside a casino's surveillance area, and Archie would be disciplined and fined heavily if Valentine was discovered where he didn't belong.

"We'll have to risk it," Porter told his boss.

"Okay," Archie said. To Valentine he said, "Anything else?"

Valentine was about to say no, then saw something sparkling on his shirt. He removed a tiny shard of glass that had been part of his rental's windshield.

"A car," he said. "My rental's shot."

Archie went to his desk, picked up a key ring, and tossed it to him. "This is my spare. It's in the basement. I'll call the guard, tell him to let you out."

Valentine glanced at the keys. They were for a Mercedes. He'd planned to go looking for the European anyway; now he was going to get paid for it, and drive a rich man's car.

He picked up his overcoat from a chair, then went over to the window and stuck his hand out. Archie shook it, the way business had always been done in Atlantic City.

"Nice to have you onboard," Archie said.

Valentine stared downward. He saw kids sledding on the Boardwalk, just like Gerry had once done. And the two guys walking on the beach, that was him and Doyle just off work, going to get a burger. *You move away,* he thought, *but you never leave.*

"Nice to be onboard," he replied.

6

Funny Money

"You're brutal," Porter said as they descended in Archie's private elevator.

"Just being honest," Valentine replied.

"Is this what I have to look forward to when I retire?"

"They say it gets worse."

The elevator's walls were made of glass, and Archie's vast empire lay below. The Bombay's casino was the length of three football fields, and its Arabian Nights architecture was as gaudy as any neon-soaked building on the Las Vegas strip.

Valentine watched a tour bus pull up to the entrance and disgorge a mob of white-haired geezers. Atlantic City's casinos preyed on the elderly, who squandered their pensions and Social Security checks playing slot and video poker machines. The elevator doors parted and they got out.

"How does Archie think he can get gambling passed in Florida," Valentine said. "The voters have rejected it twice."

"Archie's talked Florida's governor into passing special legislation so counties can decide whether or not they want casinos," Porter said.

"So Archie's trying to rewrite the law."

"You got it."

"Good luck."

"He's already spent a fortune buying up hotels in Miami and St. Petersburg. Trust me, Arch knows what he's doing."

They walked the casino floor. The Bombay's interior decor was one part faux India, one part Arabian Nights, the rest New Jersey schmaltz. Cocktail waitresses wore skimpy *I Dream of Jeannie* costumes, the dealers and croupiers silk shirts and satin bow ties. Every seat at every slot machine was taken, the room a sea of polyester and blue hair.

"I need a cup of coffee," Valentine said.

"Sinbad's is our best bet," Porter replied.

Valentine followed Porter through the blackjack pit. Passing a table, he stopped to watch a young female dealer shuffle the cards, then deal a round. Porter edged up beside him.

"Something wrong?"

"She's new, isn't she?"

"Started last week," Porter mumbled. "How could you tell?"

"Her hole card is a red nine."

"Don't screw with me."

"Bet?"

"With you? Never."

"Then watch."

The players at the table played their hands. Then the dealer turned over her hole card. It was the nine of hearts. Porter pulled Valentine away from the game.

"How the hell did you know that?"

"She flashed a corner when she slid it under her face card," Valentine explained. "Inexperienced dealers do that sometimes. Hustlers call it front loading."

Porter cursed under his breath. Every day, hustlers walked through his casino, looking for flaws in his games, or green dealers who didn't know all the rules. For every problem he didn't fix, he lost thousands of dollars, sometimes more.

"I'll pull her off the floor right now," he said.

◆

They met up in Sinbad's ten minutes later. A harem girl served them coffee in elephant-shaped mugs. Blowing away the steam, Valentine said, "So, tell me how The Bombay lost six million bucks, and you managed to keep your job."

Porter spit coffee on himself. "That's not funny."

"It wasn't meant to be funny."

Grabbing a handful of paper napkins from a dispenser, Porter wiped his chin. "I didn't get canned because it wasn't my fault."

"Why's that?"

"I don't know if you noticed it, but The Bombay's changed."

Valentine had noticed. Walking through the casino, he'd gotten lost several times.

"Back in November, Archie launched a new promotion," Porter said. "Every customer gets a pail of special coins, called Funny Money. People gamble with it and win prizes."

Valentine sipped the scalding brew. He'd seen a lot of cocka-mamie promotions in casinos over the years, and they'd always produced the same results: the casinos lost money.

"Who's idea was this?"

"The Mod Squad's. They run the marketing department. At first I thought it was stupid. Casinos aren't supposed to give stuff away. But it worked, so they obviously know something."

"Worked how?"

"It changed people's perceptions of us."

"Right," Valentine said.

Porter whipped out his cell phone. Five minutes later, the Mod Squad were sitting in Sinbad's, with Brandi enthusiastically explaining the promotion to him. Up close, she was what guys of his generation called a dish, with green bedroom eyes and a soft Southern drawl, and he found himself staring a little harder than he probably should have.

"Ninety-eight percent of people who play in a casino lose," she said. "They have a good time, but they go home broke. The idea behind Funny Money is to let people go home thinking they won something."

"Change the perception," Valentine said.

She flashed a smile to melt your heart. "That's right. Last October, we put Funny Money slot machines in the casino. It meant reconfiguring the floor, but sometimes you have to take risks in this business if you want to succeed."

How old was she? Thirty-two? She talked like she'd been in the business a hundred years. Gigi, the beautiful blonde, took over. "Funny Money coins only work in the Funny Money slots, which pay out at a rate of twenty percent. The prizes are remainders we buy from the Home Shopping Network. Some of the stuff we get for free, it's so bad."

The three women shared a giggle. Being around them felt like a TV sitcom. Valentine laughed along, just to humor them.

"Funny Money machines also have a jackpot," Gigi said, "which is a new car. General Motors gives us that for free. For the publicity."

"So the prizes don't cost you anything," he said.

It was Monique's turn. She looked like she pumped iron, and jumped right in. "But the guests are winning *something*, and that's what counts. They go home happy. We're changing the experience for them."

"And they tell their friends," Gigi said.

"And their friends come to The Bombay," Brandi said.

Their synchronization was uncanny. It still sounded dumb, but what did he know? Mencken once said that no one had ever lost money underestimating the taste of the American public, and this sounded right up Mencken's alley.

Brandi's cell phone rang. Taking it from her purse, she flipped it open. "Yes, Archie."

"Where's Gigi and Monique?" the casino owner bellowed.

"With me."

"Break time's over! Get your tight little asses up here, on the double."

Brandi dropped the cell phone into her purse. The three women's smiles faded.

They filed out of the coffee shop, leaving Valentine to wonder how modern women liked being treated like little girls. If it bothered them, they were doing a hell of a job not showing it.

◆

"So this is the culprit," Valentine said, standing next to a gleaming, six-foot-tall Funny Money slot machine, the handle glowing like a *Star Wars* laser saber.

"Not so loud," Porter said. "We've got a customer."

A woman wearing a jogging suit jumped on the stool and began feeding coins into the slot while jerking the handle. Physically, she was not much to look at, except for her right arm. Her pulling arm. A cross between Popeye's and Rod Laver's.

"Having a good time?" Porter inquired.

"You bet I am," the woman said. "I've already won a K-Tell orange peeler *and* an electric foot massager."

"Ask her how much she lost at the tables," Valentine whispered in Porter's ear.

"Shut up, will you?" Porter said through clenched teeth.

Even the best game would eventually beat you, and the woman soon ran out of coins and left. Taking her stool, Porter pointed at the ceiling. "See that eye-in-the-sky camera? Well, it used to watch one blackjack table. When we added the Funny Money slots, we had to rearrange things. Now, that camera watches *two* tables."

The practice was called double-duty and frowned upon in the gaming industry. Valentine said, "Let me guess. These are the tables where the European ripped you off."

Porter nodded. "Somehow he knew which tables had double-duty cameras. He waited until the other table had heavy action before starting to play. He ripped us off for months, but we only caught him on film a few times."

"Didn't someone notice the take was off?" Valentine asked.

"The take *wasn't* off," Porter said. "The promotion has been such a boon for business, it didn't show."

Something wasn't adding up. Valentine said, "If the take wasn't off, why did you hire Doyle?"

"Having the floor rearranged bugged me," Porter admitted. "I would look through a camera and not know which table I was seeing. So I hired Doyle to bird-dog for me."

"And he spotted the European."

"First night on the job," Porter said.

An elderly man with a walker shuffled over. His liver-spotted hands cradled a bucket filled with Funny Money. Porter helped him onto the stool.

The gods of chance were smiling down. On the elderly man's first pull, the reels lined up six elephants. A buxom hostess appeared and presented him with a sixties lava lamp.

"I always wanted one of these!" the elderly man exclaimed.

◆

They found an empty booth in the back of Sinbad's. Porter waved away the waitress.

"Okay, so what do I do?"

"A couple of things," Valentine said. "First, accept that you've got a mole in the casino. The mole told the European which tables had cameras doing double-duty."

"Jesus," Porter said. "Why didn't I think of that."

"Second, accept that the European will show up again. Most hustlers skip town when they get made. The European killed Doyle instead."

"He thinks we're easy pickings."

"That's right."

"If he does, we'll jam him."

Jam meant having someone arrested. Valentine lowered his voice. "For what? You can't prove he killed Doyle, and you can't prove he ripped you off. The police will let him walk, and Archie will fire you."

"So what do I do?"

Valentine wrote his cell phone number down on a napkin and slid it across the table. "Call me."

"No police?"

Valentine slid out of the booth and put his overcoat on. Sinbad's was empty, and he slipped the Glock out of his pocket and laid it on the table. Porter swallowed his Adam's apple.

"No police," he said.

7

A Tree in the Forest

Archie's spare car was a Mercedes SL 600 coupe. It had more amenities than most third-world countries, and while sitting at a traffic light, Valentine played with the different buttons on the dashboard.

He hit the button for the CD player and was assaulted by a throbbing rap song. The lyrics were about abusing women and killing cops, and he ejected the offensive music. Archie was of his generation—big band, Sinatra, the other crooners. This crap wasn't him at all, and Valentine tossed the CD into the glove compartment.

His motel room had been cleaned, the tread marks fresh in the carpet. The red light on the bedside phone was blinking, and he dialed into voice mail. Two messages awaited him.

"Hey, Pop," his son said. "I just got a call from my bartender. Big Tony took over this morning and fired everybody. He's running my bookmaking operation and has some scary colored guys collecting bets for him. I've got to get him the money. Call me, will you?"

Valentine couldn't believe his son's nerve. The bar was *his*, and he wasn't going to pay for it a second time. He erased Gerry, then played the second message.

"Tony," Mabel said. "I need your help. Please call me."

He glanced at his watch. It was nearly eleven thirty. He had promised to call Mabel every morning at nine sharp and hadn't done so once. He dialed his house.

"Grift Sense," she answered.

"Hey, kiddo, how's it going?"

"There you are. You must start leaving your cell phone on. I've got another panicked customer on the line."

"Who?"

"Frank Beck."

"Never heard of him."

"He's the new head of security at Harrah's in Lake Tahoe. He's holding on the other line."

Harrah's was a good customer, and he sat on the edge of the bed and unbuttoned his jacket. "What's the problem?"

"Beck thinks he has a dice cheater in his casino. This player wins money *every* time he bets. Beck can't figure out what he's doing."

"Ask Beck if the guy is throwing the dice, or just a bettor."

Mabel put him on hold, then came back. "Beck says he's just betting."

"Ask him to describe the type of bets the guy is placing. This might get a little complicated, so you'd better write it down."

She was gone a little longer this time.

"This is so exciting," Mabel said when she returned. "The man is in the casino *right now*. Beck says he always puts $1,000 on the Field bet, $600 on Place bet on 10, $600 on Place bet on 9, $200 on 12 'On the Hop,' $200 on 11 'On the Hop,' and $600 on any 7. Whatever that all means!"

Valentine closed his eyes and ran over the bets in his head. Opening them, he said, "Tell Beck I'll call him right back."

Mabel put him on hold. When she returned, she said, "Do you have any idea what this man is doing?"

"Yes. He's part of a crew. They're laying sixes. It's one of the oldest dice scams in the world."

"Why didn't you have me tell him?" she asked, sounding a little miffed.

"Because I didn't want to embarrass him."

"Why would that embarrass him?"

"Because if Beck knew anything about craps, he would have made the scam. Only he doesn't, which means he's new."

"If Beck doesn't know anything, how did he get his job?"

"He must know somebody upstairs. That happens a lot in casinos. It's called having juice." Valentine glanced at his watch. A minute had passed, and he had Mabel give him Beck's phone number. Then he said, "You still liking the job?"

"It's very exciting," his neighbor said.

"Talk to you later."

He hung up, then punched in Beck's number. Beck answered from the floor of Harrah's casino. He was panicking and sounded a heartbeat away from a stroke. Valentine explained the scam to him. "You've got three crossroaders at your craps table. One member throws the dice, but palms one in his hand. Another member at the opposite end of the table places a late bet and leaves a duplicate die on the layout with the six up. A third member does the betting and always makes the bets you described to my office manager. The bettor wins money on every outcome except an eight. Which is an 84 percent winning percentage."

"Why am I not seeing this?" Beck said belligerently.

"You will if you tape it and watch it in slow motion," Valentine said.

"Arrest them," Beck told someone standing nearby. To Valentine he said, "Thanks for the save."

"Call me if you need me," Valentine said.

Hanging up, he went into the bathroom and splashed cold

water on his face. It had been a long day and it wasn't even noon. He was looking forward to getting some lunch, maybe taking a nap later. He heard the phone ring in the other room.

He waited a minute, then picked up the message. The caller was Liddy Flanagan, and she sounded more distressed than any woman who'd just lost her husband needed to be.

"Oh, Tony, I need your help," she said. "I found a notebook of Doyle's while I was cleaning. It's filled with the strangest entries. I think you should see it."

The message ended without her saying good-bye. He stared at the phone while listening to his stomach growl. Lunch would have to wait. Taking his coat off the bed, he headed out the door.

◆

The ten-minute drive to Doyle's house took twenty on the icy roads. The Mercedes was drawing a lot of stares from schmucks driving beaters, and Valentine was happy for the tinted windows. Himself, he drove a '90 Honda Accord, a good solid car with roll-down windows, the odometer stuck at 160 thousand miles.

Liddy met him at the front door. She wore faded jeans and a fluffy green sweater, her hair done up nice. Only her bloodshot eyes betrayed her true feelings.

"The boys are here," she said.

He followed her into the living room. Sean sat on the couch with a spiral notebook in his lap. He read aloud to Guy, who stood by the fireplace puffing nervously on a cigarette, his eyes fixed on the blue-orange flames.

"It's not like stealing from a friend, it's a goddamn casino. They expect it. Hell, they even budget for it." Sean flipped the page. "Here's some more. 'Nobody got hurt, so nothing really happened. I don't do this all the time, so I'm not really a thief.'"

Sean stopped, unable to make something out. Valentine sat on the couch beside him. Sean handed him the notebook.

"You try."

The page was covered with Doyle's infamous chicken scratch. Valentine deciphered the line at the top of the page.

"It's like a tree falling in a forest. If no one catches you, are you really breaking the law?" He looked up at Liddy. "Where did you find this?"

"I was changing the bed," she said. "It was stuck between the mattress and box spring. I didn't understand it at first, but the more I read, well, it seems like Doyle is denying something that he's done."

"He wasn't denying anything," Guy spouted angrily, his gaze still fixed on the roaring fire. "My father didn't steal anything from anyone in his life."

An uneasy silence filled the living room. Valentine glanced at Sean; Doyle's older son did not seem so sure. Neither did Liddy. Sensing his family's betrayal, Guy crossed the room and ripped the notebook from Valentine's hands. Flipping to the first page, he shoved it in front of Valentine's face.

"Look," he said.

On this page, Doyle had drawn a floor plan of The Bombay, with tiny X's for banks of slot machines, O's for blackjack tables, R's for roulette wheels, and so on. In the margins were mathematical calculations, the numbers blurry from repeated erasure. There was also a scribbled name: Detective Eddie Davis. And the detective's cell phone number.

"My father was talking to the police," Guy snapped. "He found something rotten at The Bombay, and he called Detective Davis. My father wasn't a criminal."

"Guy, sit down," Valentine said.

"You don't believe me!"

"Guy, I said sit down."

Guy angrily marched out the front door. Moments later they heard car wheels spin as he backed down the drive. Liddy sat on the couch next to her older son.

"Poor Guy," she whispered.

Valentine studied Doyle's map. Neither Frank nor Archie had mentioned that Doyle was talking to the police, which meant Doyle hadn't told them. He flipped the pages and reread the quotes. Had someone inside the casino told Doyle about something that was going on?

He stood up from the couch. He didn't know Davis, but there were a lot of new cops that he didn't know.

"I'm going to have to take this to the police," he said.

Liddy's head snapped. "You are?"

"Yes."

"But it makes Doyle look bad . . ."

"Liddy, it's evidence. Detective Davis should have a chance to examine it. He'll probably want to put the notebook through an Electrostatic Detection Apparatus, which picks up indented writing. If Doyle wrote something and later tore out the page, the ESDA will see it."

"But what if . . ."

"Doyle was doing something dirty? I don't believe that for a minute."

Liddy lay her head on Sean's shoulder. Valentine stood in the center of the living room, hoping she'd agree. Only she wasn't returning his gaze. He buttoned his overcoat, sensing it was time to go.

"Do what you must," Sean told him.

8

Davis

Valentine pulled into an empty space at the Atlantic City Metro Police headquarters lot and killed the Mercedes engine. He hated to admit it, but the car was growing on him. It was built like a tank and clung to the road like a piece of gum. He liked safe, always had, and the car was the epitome of that. He locked the Glock in the glove compartment, then took Doyle's notebook off the passenger seat.

Walking through the front door of police headquarters, he passed through a metal detector, then entered an L-shaped room with plastic benches screwed into the walls. Forlorn-looking people sat in groups, talking among themselves. A teenager with a crying baby, her mother, and grandmother; a family of Chinese; a blind man, his guide dog, and doting wife.

On the far side of the room, a familiar face sat behind bullet-proof glass. Alice Torkalowski held up a finger, then said good-bye to someone on the phone.

"That was a great story you told at the funeral," she said.

"Thanks." He hadn't seen Alice at the funeral, but she was only four-four and got missed a lot. "How you been?"

"Up for retirement next June. Don't know if I should take the plunge or not. You liking it?"

Valentine shook his head. "I'm working again."

"That bad?"

"I didn't count anymore," he said, knowing that of all the people in the station house, Alice would understand this statement, having lived in the shadows of others all her life. "I opened up a consulting business."

"Let me guess. You're making more money than before," she said, cracking her gum.

"That wouldn't be too hard. Is Detective Davis around?"

Alice punched a button on the console of her phone, then put the receiver to her ear. "Hey, Shaft, Mr. Tony Valentine in the lobby to see you. Shake a leg."

"Shaft?" Valentine said.

Alice smiled. "That's what I call him. He looks just like the actor who played Shaft. Real snappy dresser. Handsome, too."

"You mean Samuel L. Jackson?"

"No," she said, "the first Shaft. What's his name . . ."

Valentine couldn't remember the actor's name either. Alice's phone lit up. She started punching in buttons and answered the first line. *Take care,* she mouthed.

He sat on a bench and waited for Davis to come out. Alice had been around a long time. So long that she knew the score. So, when a stylishly dressed African-American appeared in the lobby a minute later, he tried to treat him like anyone else, knowing damn well that only a handful of blacks had ever risen to the rank of detective in Atlantic City.

"*The* Tony Valentine?" Davis asked.

Valentine smiled, instantly liking him. "That's me."

"Ed Davis. My friends call me Eddie. I'm guessing you're here about Doyle Flanagan."

"I am." He'd been carrying Doyle's notebook beneath his armpit and handed it over. "Doyle's wife found this. I thought you'd want to have a look."

Over coffee in the cafeteria, Davis browsed through Doyle's notes. Looking up, he said, "You read this, I suppose."

"No, I sealed it with Scotch tape and ran over here. Of course I read it."

Davis's eyebrows rose an inch. "Any idea what this stuff means?"

A cop Valentine knew passed by, and they shook hands. When he was gone, Valentine said, "I was hoping you'd tell me. Your cell number's on the first page."

Davis dropped the notebook on the linoleum table. "You conducting an investigation of your own?"

"Archie Tanner hired me."

Davis smiled. "Must be nice, working for yourself."

Valentine's consulting work paid well, only talking about it made him uncomfortable. He finished his coffee in silence. Davis drummed his fingertips on the table.

"Let me guess," the detective said. "Five hundred a day, plus expenses."

Valentine crumpled the Styro cup in his hand. "I was hoping we could share information. If you're not interested, I'll get out of your hair."

"A grand," Davis said. "You make a grand a day, don't you? Man, what a life."

Valentine found his attitude toward the detective changing. What he made was none of Davis's business. He stood up to leave. Davis rose as well.

"You mind my asking you a question?" the detective asked.

"What's that?"

"I heard a story that you once caught a blackjack dealer cheating, only you were standing with your back to him. That true?"

Valentine nodded that it was.

"You got eyes in the back of your head?"

"What do you think?"

Davis scratched his chin. "Then how could you see what he was
doing?"

"I didn't."

"Come again?"

"I didn't see anything," Valentine told him. "My eyes were
closed."

"Your eyes were closed?" Davis crossed his arms, clearly per-
plexed.

"I heard it," Valentine said.

"Heard what?"

"He was dealing a deuce."

"What's that?"

"He was dealing seconds."

"The second card from the top?"

Valentine nodded. "A second deal makes a tiny click when it
comes off the deck. Even the best card mechanic can't hide it.
Whenever I suspect a dealer of dealing seconds, I stand next to his
table, close my eyes, and listen."

Davis smiled. It had obviously been bugging him. He stuck his
hand out. Valentine shook it. It was a common trick in police
work to wait until the end of a conversation to ask a loaded question, and Valentine took a chance.

"So what was Doyle talking to you about, anyway?"

Davis nearly fell for it, then caught the words as they started to
come out of his mouth.

"None of your business," he replied.

◆

Valentine turned up his collar while walking through the
parking lot. Eighteen months in Florida and his blood had

already thinned out. Hearing footsteps, he turned to see a guy that bore a striking resemblance to Gerry walking behind him. The guy's clothes were old and dirty, and Valentine watched him walk out of the lot and down the street, hands shoved in his pockets.

Sitting behind the Mercedes' wheel, Valentine felt a wave of guilt sweep over him. Why was he trying to solve everyone else's problems while ignoring Gerry? He needed to help his son, no matter how angry his boy made him.

Then he had an idea.

AT&T had a great service that let him get a phone number from anywhere in the country for fifty cents. A minute later he was laying it on thick to a police sergeant at the police precinct near his son's bar in Brooklyn.

". . . and the next thing I know, some hood named Big Tony Mollo has taken over my bar and is running things."

"And this Big Tony is no relation, nor in your employment," the sergeant said skeptically.

"No, sir," Valentine replied.

"What is your son's relation to Big Tony?"

"The same as his father's."

"Your son doesn't know him?"

"No, sir," Valentine lied.

"Why do you think Big Tony took it upon himself to take over your bar?"

"Beats me."

"You said you were a retired cop?"

Valentine gave him his credentials. He heard the sergeant's fingers tapping away on a computer keyboard, checking him out.

"Here you are," the sergeant said. "Thirty years on the force. Two citations for bravery. I'm impressed."

"Just doing the good Lord's work," Valentine said.

The sergeant reeled off the name of every cop he'd ever known in Atlantic City. Finally he said a name Valentine knew.

They traded stories. Satisfied, the sergeant said, "Okay, Tony, so what would you like done with this unwanted visitor on your property."

"Get rid of him."

"You don't want us to press charges?"

"Only if he resists. I have no gripe with this guy."

"That's very decent of you, Tony," the sergeant said.

"I'm getting soft in my old age," Valentine confessed.

9

Honey

According to the scuttle at Doyle's funeral, the bomb that had killed him was pretty fancy. A quarter pound of cyclotrimethylene trinitramine, commonly called RDX, attached to a mercury switch. A trucker inside the McDonald's had likened the explosion to overheating a bag of popcorn in a microwave, with pieces of car flying in every direction.

Because Doyle's cell phone had briefly stayed on, Valentine had assumed it had landed behind a bush or beneath a car. He'd also assumed a cop on the scene would find the phone, and a check would have been run to see whom Doyle was talking to. That would have led to the police's contacting him and grilling him to find out what he and Doyle had been talking about.

Only none of this had happened.

Leaving Atlantic City Metro Police headquarters, he drove to the McDonald's where his partner had died, just to see if the police had forgotten to look someplace obvious.

He parked behind the restaurant. Hard as it was for him to spend money, he was starting to understand how people got attached to these cars. Smooth ride, great seats, an unreal sound system. He needed new wheels. Why not a Mercedes?

He took a walk around the property. It sat on a small parcel of land. There was a handful of trees, the rest of the landscape lunar. He decided he wanted to get on a higher elevation. Going inside, he found a pimply kid mopping floors and stuck a sawbuck in his hand. His name badge said *Harold.* Valentine whispered in Harold's ear what he wanted.

Harold met him behind the restaurant, ladder in hand. Propping the ladder against the wall, he pointed at his watch. "Sixty seconds. Just like we agreed."

"Right."

"The clock's ticking."

Valentine scampered up the ladder. He walked around the roof edge, and to his surprise, saw a cell phone sitting near an air vent. Picking it up, he rubbed its cold blue steel against his pant leg. The explosion had blown its cover off, but otherwise it appeared intact.

A flicker of silver caught his eye. Out of the snow he plucked a silver dollar–size coin. It looked real, only instead of Eisenhower's profile it was stamped with Archie Tanner's grinning mug. Funny Money.

"Hurry up," Harold called.

He climbed down the ladder. Reaching the bottom, he shoved the items he'd found on the roof into his pocket.

"What did you find?" Harold asked.

"None of your business."

"You're not going to split what you found?"

"Why should I?"

"I thought we were partners," the boy said with righteous indignation.

Valentine looked at him scornfully. Harold had carrot red hair and enough rings on his face to hang a shower curtain. A sullen-faced manager came around the corner.

"Harold? What the hell's going on?"

Harold spelled it out to him. Traitor. Walking over to the Mercedes, Valentine got in and drove away.

◆

When you threw in tax and the extra battery the cute sales-girl at the AT&T store talked him into buying, the charger for Doyle's cell phone set Valentine back fifty bucks. It was ridiculous: People were spending a small fortune to do something that only cost a quarter. It was like the four dollar coffee at Starbucks, and ten dollars to see a first-run movie. Someday, everyone would be a millionaire, and a burger would cost a grand.

Sitting in his motel room, he plugged the charger into the wall and Doyle's cell phone lit up in his hand. The salesgirl had thrown in an instruction manual, and he taught himself how to access the phone's memory bank and scrolled through it. It contained six names.

Guy. Sean. Home. Tom. Tony. Honey.

Valentine stared at the last name. Who was Honey? Doyle had never mentioned her. That wasn't like him. Then he had an unsettling thought. Was Doyle seeing someone on the side?

The idea seemed absurd. When it came to women, Doyle was like him: a square. They'd both married their high school sweethearts, both stayed loyal through thick and thin. Only the evidence was staring him in the face.

He pulled a Diet Coke out of a paper bag and popped it. Whoever this woman was, he needed to talk to her. Chances were, she knew something. That was the real reason guys had girlfriends. You could get sex just about anywhere these days. But finding someone to talk to, that was tough.

He retrieved Honey's number and hit Send. After three rings a woman's groggy voice said, "Yes?"

60

It was nearly two in the afternoon. What kind of woman slept this late? Then he had a bad thought. What if it was someone he knew? Putting his hand over the mouthpiece, he said, "Is this Honey?"

The woman caught her breath.

"I'm a friend of Doyle's," he said.

The phone went dead in his hand. He finished his Diet Coke, wondering how many more unpleasant items he was going to discover about his old pal.

Something in his bones told him Gerry was trying to call him. Taking out his own cell phone, he dialed into voice mail and found a lone message awaiting him.

"Pop, do you have any idea what you've done?" his son said. "The cops raided the bar and arrested Big Tony. They told him *you'd* sent them! *How could you do this to me?*

"Now Big Tony's brothers are looking for me! Goddamn it, Pop, I'm a dead man. Do you understand? *A dead man!* This is the last time I ever ask you for help. *The last time!*"

He erased the message. You try to help out, he thought, and look where it gets you. The door to his room banged open. A Mexican chambermaid pushing a vacuum came in. Plugging the vacuum into the wall, she started cleaning.

"Come back later!" he yelled over the vacuum's roar.

She smiled sweetly, not understanding a word.

"Later," he yelled, pointing at his watch.

She pointed at his cell phone. He looked down; it was all lit up. Crossing the room, he unplugged her.

"Later," he said. "Please."

He chained the door behind her, waited a minute, then dialed into voice mail. It was Frank Porter.

"Call me," Porter said.

Valentine called him.

"Guess who just waltzed into The Bombay," Porter said.

It sounded like the opening line of a joke.

"Jimmy Hoffa?"

"The European. He's already won five grand."

Valentine felt his heart start to race. The Bombay was on the north side of town, a good ten-minute drive from his motel.

"I'll be there in five."

"Meet you by the front door," Porter said.

10

The European

Valentine pulled up to The Bombay's valet stand five minutes later, having run every red light and broken every speed limit in the city. The stand was deserted, and he left the keys in the ignition and hurried in.

Porter was waiting just inside the front door. Pulling him aside, he handed Valentine a New York Yankees baseball cap.

"There's a transceiver with an inter-canal hearing aid taped in the rim," Porter explained. "I'll be able to talk to you from the surveillance room, but no one else will be able to hear me."

Valentine put the cap on and adjusted the strap. "Where's he sitting?"

"Table 42."

Because The Bombay was so large, Porter had written instructions to Table 42 on the back of a business card. Going over to a Funny Money cage, he took a bucket of the special coins and shoved them into Valentine's hands.

"Carry this. Makes you look like a tourist."

"What do I look like now?"

"An old cop."

Valentine dropped Porter's card into the bucket, reading it while he walked across the crowded casino. The European had picked an out-of-the-way table, close to an exit. By the time Valentine reached it, Porter was talking to him from his desk in the surveillance control room on the third floor.

"How's the sound?"

"Great."

"He's the third player at the table. See him?"

The European was not hard to spot; his piles of black hundred-dollar chips towered over everyone else's.

"Uh-huh."

"He doesn't see you."

Valentine circled Table 42 and sized the European up. He was thin, late thirties, and seemed in a sour mood, which was odd considering the amount of money he was winning. His clothes were nondescript: black pants, black turtleneck sweater, and a black sports coat. And then there was his haircut. It was a bowl job, the kind they used to give guys in prison.

Valentine sat in front of a Funny Money slot machine and watched the European play. The European won another five thousand dollars, yet did not tip the dealer once. That was odd: Most hustlers tipped the dealer heavily, just to keep them happy.

"Does this guy ever lose?" Valentine said into his hat.

"Not that I've seen," Porter said.

The other players at Table 42 were women. Valentine looked at each one, and spotted the dark-haired beauty from the video Doyle had sent him. She'd dyed her hair red, but the resemblance to Audrey Hepburn was unmistakable. Their eyes met.

Turning on his stool, Valentine took a handful of coins from his bucket, and started feeding them into the Funny Money slot machine.

"I think I've been spotted."

"He's not even looking at you," Porter said.

"The woman sitting to his immediate left."

"You think they're a team?"

"Yup."

"I think you're okay. Keep playing."

Soon Valentine was down to his last coin. He fed it into the machine and jerked the handle. Slot machines were for dummies, a chimpanzee having the same chance of winning, and he cringed as the reels fell his way and the GRAND PRIZE sign started flashing.

A big-bosomed hostess appeared lugging a bulky cappuccino maker. Panting, she dropped the box into his hands.

"Congratulations," she said.

"No thanks," Valentine replied.

The hostess snarled at him. "Take it," she insisted.

"I don't want it."

The hostess lowered her voice. "Listen, buster. It's my last cappuccino maker. They're heavy and my back is killing me. Make a girl happy, okay?"

Valentine glanced over his shoulder. The European and his accomplice were leaving. The cappuccino maker fell from his hands and hit the floor with a loud crunch.

"Sorry," he said.

"Bite me," the hostess replied.

♦

Clutching the Glock in his pocket, Valentine followed them across the casino floor. The European was making a beeline for the men's bathroom, while his red-haired companion was heading toward a side exit.

"You got someone following the girl?" he asked Porter.

"No."

"Why not?"

"I've got a brawl on the other side of the casino," Porter said. "There's no security in your zone."

"What do you want me to do?"

"Let her go."

Valentine followed the European. The door to the men's bathroom resembled the entrance to one of the great pyramids, with a pair of sword-wielding genie statues standing guard. The European slipped past them and disappeared inside.

"I'm going in."

"Let me get backup over there," Porter said.

"How long?"

"Two minutes, tops."

Two minutes was too long. What if the European put on a disguise, or wiggled out through a pipe? Stranger things had happened. "I can't risk losing him, Frank."

He heard Porter suck in his breath.

"Be careful, you hear me?"

Valentine touched the handle of the Glock. It felt cool and smooth in his hand. Then he touched one of the genies' swords for luck and went in.

The men's bathroom was massive. The stalls covered an entire wall, and he got low, looking at pant legs. The European's black pair was at the row's end. He entered a stall two away and latched the door.

He dropped the crown and had a seat. By lowering his head, he was able to see the European's shoes. They were scuffed and needed a good polish.

Moments later, a man wearing Nikes took the stall next to the European's. An exchange followed in a language Valentine did not understand. The European began passing handfuls of hundred dollar chips underneath the stall. Smart hustlers never cashed in their own winnings. Instead, they passed their chips on to a member of their crew, who split the chips up among other crew members, who turned them into cash. That way, the loss was less noticeable to the casino.

The transfer done, the man in sneakers left. Valentine counted to five, then unlatched the door. At the same time, his left hand removed the Glock from his pocket.

The European stood waiting on the other side. He was breathing hard, his pocked face pouring sweat. His hand clutched a .38, the barrel pointed at Valentine's heart.

"Give me your weapon."

Valentine handed him the Glock. Then said, "Don't shoot," knowing the words would make Porter jump out of his skin and trigger every alarm in the casino.

The European weighed the Glock in his hand, then slipped his own .38 into his pocket.

"Let me guess," Valentine said. "It's not loaded."

"Not a real gun," the European replied. "But yours is."

It was Valentine's turn to start sweating. Anyone who carried around a fake gun couldn't be trusted to handle a real one. The European pointed at the stall he'd just come out of.

"Sit," he said.

Valentine sat on the crown, then covered his head with his arms. One shot was all it was going to take. Did he have any regrets? Only one, he decided, and that was making Gerry his sole beneficiary.

"Look at me," the European said.

Valentine stared into the European's face. He was a sad-looking guy with lifeless eyes. He placed the barrel of the Glock against Valentine's nose. Valentine closed his eyes.

"Stop following us," the European said.

He heard the stall door close. The air slowly escaped from his lungs. He waited, then rose and stuck his head out. The European was gone.

Taking the baseball cap off, he started yelling into it.

♦

Five minutes later, Valentine was sitting in Porter's office in the surveillance control room on the third floor. There was no greater jolt to the nervous system than having a gun pointed at you, unless the gun happened to go off.

A cup of hot coffee brought him around. As his head cleared, he was struck by the realization of what an incredibly stupid thing he'd done. Not only had he allowed the European to escape, but he'd given him an illegal hand gun with *his* fingerprints on it.

"I'm sorry, Tony," Porter said. "I thought I told you the transceiver doesn't work in the bathroom. Something to do with the tiles."

"You might have, and I might have forgotten," Valentine said. "You nail him?"

"He flew by us."

"*What?*"

"He turned his coat inside out before he came out of the bathroom, stuck shades and a hat on. He walked right past two guards coming to help you. I didn't realize it was him until it was too late."

Valentine tossed his cup in the trash, wanting to yell at Porter, but knowing it wasn't his fault. He'd messed up by going in alone, and that was all there was to it.

Porter extracted a jelly doughnut from the Dunkin' Donuts box on his desk and took a healthy bite. Gooey red stuff dripped onto a picture frame on the desk. It was an eight-by-ten glossy of Frank with the comedian Rodney Dangerfield. The inscription read *To Frank, You stink! Rodney.*

"I opened for him once," Porter said glumly.

Valentine felt bad for him. Not only had Frank let the European get away, he'd also let him steal another ten grand. That would not sit well with his employer.

Valentine took the four decks of playing cards used on Table 42 off Porter's desk. Removing them from their boxes, he examined their backs. They were Bees, and made exclusively by the U.S. Playing Card Company.

"I already checked the cards," Porter said.

"And?"

"Clean as a whistle."

He held the cards up to the light. Marking playing cards was considered an art among hustlers. Paint, daub, shade, and a substance called juice were commonly used. Sometimes, the cards were nicked with a finely sharpened fingernail. All of these marks could be seen by a trained eye, and the cards from Table 42 appeared clean. Then he had an idea.

Taking a pencil off Porter's desk, he ran it down the face of the card and checked for warps, a sophisticated method of crimping that put a subtle bend in the card that was almost impossible to remove. Again, he found nothing.

"Damn," he said aloud. He'd told Doyle the dark-haired beauty was marking the cards. And he'd been wrong.

"You're stumped," Porter said. "That's a first."

Valentine snatched the last doughnut from the box and bit into it. The red stuff was artificially sweet and disgustingly good.

"Any suggestions?" the head of security asked.

Valentine finished the doughnut, thinking about it.

"Maybe I should be the one to tell Archie what happened."

Porter didn't get it. "Why?"

"I'll build the European up, tell Archie he's the greatest blackjack hustler I've ever seen."

"You think he'll buy it?"

"He should."

"Why's that?"

"Because he may be the greatest blackjack hustler I've ever seen."

Porter considered it. Then shook his head.

"He's still going to fire me."

"How can you be so sure?"

Porter let out a laugh. He'd once told Valentine that working in a casino required a sense of humor, because you never knew what was going to happen next.

"Because Archie fires *everybody*," he replied.

11

Debt

To reach Archie Tanner's penthouse office, Valentine had to take an elevator to the main floor, cross the casino, then talk to Archie's personal secretary through an intercom, who then sent a private elevator down.

As Valentine waited for the elevator to arrive, he saw a woman with streaked hair and fingernails painted in custom car colors win a jackpot on a slot machine. The woman started screaming like she was having twins. Soon management would come and pay her off. And comp her room, give her tickets to a show, the usual sweet grease. And she'd go home a few days later, broke. They always did.

"Can I give you some advice?" he asked.

The woman smiled coyly. "Well . . . that all depends."

"Run," he said.

◆

Archie's private elevator deposited him in a hallway facing an ostentatious wall of chrome and glass. A door without handles buzzed open and he went in.

"Mr. Tanner is on a conference call," the secretary said. "Please go in and make yourself comfortable."

Walking around the desk, he opened the mahogany door to Archie's office. The door had come from a sunken pirate's ship discovered off the Florida Keys. It wasn't pretty, the wood stained and gnarly, but that had never been the point.

Inside, he found Archie at his desk, screaming profanities at the intercom. His shirt was unbuttoned, exposing the jungle of blue-black tattoos adorning his chest. Valentine took a seat, pitying the poor saps on the receiving end of his tirade. He watched Archie take off one of his shoes and start beating the desk.

"Did you hear what I just fucking said? The Micanopy Indians can't do that! The law says they can't, the governor of Florida says they can't, and *I* say they can't! You get that useless fucking Florida Department of Law Enforcement to raid that fucking reservation and rip those machines out. And if you don't, I'll fly down there and kick your asses until your noses bleed!"

"Yes sir," several voices chorused meekly through the box.

"Good-bye!"

Hanging up, Archie slipped his shoe on. Then he came around the desk and fixed them drinks at the bar. Moments later they were sitting in a pair of cushy leather wing backs, enjoying the suite's spectacular view.

"Chief Running Bear of the Micanopy tribe is trying to fuck me," Archie explained. "The chief used to wrestle alligators in the Everglades. Now he's running a casino on his reservation and thinks he's a player. Florida law restricts the kind of games he can operate. So what does Running Bear do? He smuggles in a truck-load of video poker machines and offers to split the profits with the state. Over my dead body."

Video poker was the most popular game of the last ten years and generated enormous profits. *Any* casino benefited by having them, and Valentine said, "I thought the reservations were pro-tected by the U.S. Constitution."

Archie scratched his chest like a monkey. Outside it was snowing, The Bombay's multicolored neon sign painting each flake a different hue. "You think I'm going to let the Indians get the upper hand before I open my casinos? I've got the governor of Florida in my back pocket. Those were his aides I was just talking to."

Valentine watched Archie's face grow flushed as the drink took hold. Then he said, "I've got some bad news for you."

Archie stared at him, waiting.

"The European who killed Doyle showed up in your casino today."

"Did Porter jam him?"

"I made Frank back off."

Archie's face twisted in anger.

"He got away," Valentine added.

Archie shook his forefinger in Valentine's face. "What kind of little league horseshit is that? *He got away.* If we didn't go back so far, I'd run you out of town."

The casino owner cursed him out for another minute. When he was done, Valentine said, "There's more."

"You're a bad news buffet," Archie said.

"Your blackjack tables aren't safe. The European has come up with a new system. I'm as fooled as everyone else."

The Waterford tumbler left Archie's hand and flew across the room, shattering against a bookcase. "You're fooled? So what the hell are you suggesting I do?"

"Close down, dismantle the tables, give every employee a polygraph test. Otherwise, you're a lame duck."

Archie leaned over, breathing gin on Valentine's face. "I can't close down. To use an eighties expression, I'm leveraged up to my fucking eyeballs. The Bombay's cash flow is what's paying for my deal in Florida."

Valentine swirled the ice cubes in his drink. He wanted to ask Archie if he had enough money to pay *him*, but didn't want to go there just yet.

"You want my advice?"

"Yes," the casino owner said emphatically.

He put his soda on the antique coffee table. "Distribute flyers in the casino with the European's picture. Offer a reward for his arrest. It's not the best solution, but it will keep the European from playing, and that's all you can ask for."

"You're saying I should swallow my pride, and admit I got ripped off."

"Yes," Valentine said.

"We'll never catch the European then, will we?"

"Once the flyers appear, he'll leave town for sure."

Archie got up and went to the window. The snow was coming down heavily, making it hard to see. Valentine stared at Archie's reflection in the glass. The casino owner looked worried.

"I'll do it," he said. "but only if you agree to keep working for me."

Valentine joined him by the window. "Doing what?"

"Find the European."

There was real worry in Archie's voice. This scam had cut deep, and not just because six million had flown out the window. It had shown him how vulnerable he was, and Valentine had a feeling that Archie wasn't going to sleep well until the European was out of the picture.

And neither was Valentine.

12

Teacher

"So, what you're telling me is, I'm still gainfully employed," Porter said, eating an inch-thick roast beef sandwich with mayo oozing out of the sides.

"You sure are," Valentine said.

Porter beamed through a mouthful of red meat. The good news had lifted his spirits, and he swallowed and said, "You know what I was going to do if Archie fired me? Go back into show business. I've got this great new act I've been working on. It's called 'Why Men Aren't Secretaries.' "

"Sounds politically incorrect," Valentine said.

"It is. Here's my opening. This woman comes home, and on the refrigerator finds a note from her husband. It says, 'Honey, your doctor called, and said Pabst Beer is normal.' "

Porter slapped his desk, laughing hysterically.

"Keep your day job," Valentine told him.

◆

Driving away from The Bombay's valet stand, Valentine found Sinatra on the radio and jacked up the volume, remembering when there had always been Sinatra on the radio.

He headed south on Atlantic Avenue. He needed to find the European and guessed he had twenty-four hours before the flyers were distributed in the casino. Several ideas came to mind. But before he got started, he had to get a grip on a few things. The first was that he'd embarrassed himself at The Bombay. He'd spent the last eighteen months in the comfort of his living room, getting paid to watch casino surveillance tapes. His instincts had faded, and he hadn't realized it.

The second was that the European was smarter than him. Twice he'd gotten the best of him, and Valentine had a feeling that the next time they squared off, the European would beat him again.

Which was why he drove straight to Madison and parked in front of Master Yun's School of Judo & Self Defense. If anyone could help him get his head screwed on straight, it was his teacher. Entering the unheated stairwell, he went up.

On the second-floor landing he halted, seeing no light beneath the door. A piece of paper was thumbtacked to the door. *Master Yun ill. Classes canceled until further notice.*

He trudged downstairs. He'd come here three times a week for the better part of twenty years and couldn't remember Yun ever pulling a sick day. Which meant something was *really* wrong. They'd always gotten along, and he wondered if his teacher would mind if he showed up at his house unannounced.

He supposed there was only one way to find out.

◆

He'd been to Master Yun's house only once, and that was the night he'd won the New Jersey heavyweight judo championships for a fifth time, and Yun had wanted to show him off to his relatives, a pair of toothless old hens with cackling laughs. The place looked the same—manicured yard, rock garden, shaded windows—and he pushed the doorbell and waited.

Lin Lin, Yun's agelessly beautiful wife, cracked the front door. Her eyes were puffy, and he guessed she'd been napping.

"What do you want?"

"Mrs. Yun, I don't know if you remember me. I was here many years ago . . ."

A look of recognition spread across her face. "Of course I remember you. Tony Valentine. One of my husband's favorite students. Come in."

He entered and Lin Lin took his coat. She wore a green bathrobe and pink slippers. On the couch a toy poodle cracked an eye, decided he was harmless, and fell back asleep.

"Yun told me you retired, moved to Florida," she said.

"That's right."

"You like it there?"

"Can't beat the weather." He drifted across the living room. On the mantle over the fireplace he spied a curled snapshot of him and Yun at the state championships, the big moment. "I went to the dojo and saw the sign. I figured it must be serious, so I came over."

"They have judo in Florida?"

He nodded and put the photo back in its place. "Not a dojo like Yun's, but I get a good workout, and that's all I care about." He turned to face her. "How bad is he?"

Lin Lin flopped down on the couch. "I don't know what I'm going to do. It gets worse each day." She pointed at a rocking chair across from where she sat. "Please."

"I know it's none of my business," he said, the rocker moaning as he sat in it, "but what's wrong with him?"

She sighed heavily. "He stays in bed all day, only gets up to eat, use the bathroom. I tell him, it's no big deal, what this girl has

done to you, but he doesn't see it that way. He *helped* this girl, you
know? And she disgraces him. Damn bitch."

"A student?"

"Yes. One he took off the street, single woman with a kid. Got
fired from her casino job. They accused her of cheating. Of course,
she said it wasn't so. And she had an abusive boyfriend. Real sob
story."

"Cheating how?"

"Something with the tray."

"Dumping the tray?"

"I think so."

Dumping the tray had turned more than one casino into a
garage. A dealer would overpay a player, or secretly pass chips to
him. If caught, the dealer would pretend it was an honest mistake.
It went on constantly.

"Which casino?"

"The Bombay."

He realized he was getting off track, and said, "So Yun took her
under his wing and trained her, huh?"

She nodded. "One day, Yun invites her over. Over dinner, she
tells me, 'Your husband saved my life.' I think, wow, Yun has
helped many people, but no one ever says this. It makes me
happy all over. Yun too."

Lin Lin pushed herself off the couch. "I'm being rude. How
about a cup of coffee?"

"That would be great."

"Cream and sugar?"

"Black, please."

She glided past, her feet making no sound. He listened to her
grind the beans, then let his eyes drift down the hallway leading
to the back of the house. His eyes snapped open.

At the hallway's end stood Yun in his skivvies, his gaze cold and unfriendly. He'd lost weight and looked like a bantam rooster, all skin and bone.

"Hey," Valentine said.

Yun stared right through him.

"It's me, Tony."

"I know who you are," his teacher growled.

Valentine started to get up from the rocker.

"Don't," Yun told him.

"I was in town, thought I'd drop by, see how—"

"Not interested," his teacher said.

"I need your help."

"Doing what?"

"Catching a killer."

That got his teacher's attention. The scowl momentarily left his face and his voice softened. "I thought you retire."

"I unretired."

His teacher considered it. "I let you know."

Yun went into the bedroom and shut the door. Valentine felt a mug of hot coffee being put into his hands. Sitting on the couch, Lin Lin petted the sleeping poodle, then continued her story.

"Couple weeks ago, Yun hears this woman is really a pro wrestler. He goes to the armory, and she is on the show. Judo Queen. Yun tells me she fights in the uniform he gave her, with the sacred crane stitched to her bosom."

"You're kidding me."

"No. *Damn bitch.*"

Yun had come to the United States with the shirt on his back and his family's traditions buried deep in his soul. The sacred crane, a symbol of grace and hidden strength, had been in his family for centuries. Only in competition had Valentine worn it on his uniform, and only with Yun's permission.

"Did he talk to her? Ask her to take it off?"

"She told Yun to get lost. 'Girl's got to make a living,' she says."

The coffee was scalding hot, just the way he liked it. "You want me to talk to her? I used to be a cop, you know."

A smile appeared on Lin Lin's face, and Valentine realized it was exactly what she wanted. Finding a pen, she wrote on a notepad, then tore off the paper and handed it to him.

"This is where she practices her judo now."

He stared at the address. Body Slam School of Professional Wrestling, 1234 Winston. It was a bad part of town, filled with rowdy bars and guys on Harleys who didn't sell stock during the day. "This woman got a name?"

"Kat."

"I'll make sure I bring a whip and chair."

They finished their coffee. Then Lin Lin got his coat and walked him to the door. As she opened it, the toy poodle darted through Valentine's legs and disappeared into the bushes.

"Tell Yun I'll be back," he said.

♦

He was a block away from Yun's house when a Chevy Caprice appeared in his mirror. The Atlantic City Police Department had been buying Chevies for as long as he could remember, and people on the wrong side of the law usually knew when a plainclothes detective was crawling up their behind.

He pulled off the road and parked. The Chevy parked behind him. Valentine hit the button that unlocked the passenger door and watched Detective Davis climb in.

"You're something else," Davis said.

"I am?"

"You come by the station with Doyle's notebook, I figure you're a friend. Next thing I hear, you're at the McDonald's poking your nose where it doesn't belong. That's an Italian thing, isn't it? Kiss 'em before you fuck them."

"The manager file a complaint?"

"Sure did. Said you had no right going on his roof."

"His employee supplied the ladder. Did the manager tell you that?"

Davis glared at him. Angry, he looked almost brutal, his eyes fixed in a vicious gaze.

"Doyle was my best friend," Valentine explained. "I wanted to see where he died, okay? You don't like that, take a hike."

"The kid at the McDonald's saw you put something in your pocket. Give it to me, or I'll arrest you."

Valentine tapped the steering wheel with his fingertips. How long had Davis been a detective? A few years? You never let a suspect empty their own pockets. You cleaned out their pockets yourself. He extracted the Funny Money coin, while leaving Doyle's cell phone. He handed the coin to Davis.

"Huh," Davis said. "You found this on the roof?"

"That's right," Valentine said.

"You think it was in Doyle's car?"

"I think Doyle was holding it when he got killed."

"How can you be sure?"

"Doyle was always playing with money, sort of a nervous tic."

The detective rolled the coin across his knuckles, showing some skill. He was calming down, and Valentine sensed he was going to let him off the hook. Alice was right; he did look like Shaft from the first version.

"You know the skinny about these coins?" Davis asked him.

Valentine said that he didn't.

"Funny Money has been turning up in cash registers around town. Pizza joints, dry cleaners, bars. The police have been all over Archie Tanner about it. FBI, too."

"What did Archie say?"

"Archie says if the cashiers are stupid enough to take them, what's he supposed to do?"

Over the years, Valentine had known a lot of people who ran cash businesses. As a rule, they were meticulous about checking the money that went into their tills.

"That doesn't make sense," he told the detective.

"Tell me about it." Davis flung open his door and started to get out. Then glanced backward at Valentine. "Keep your nose clean, will you?"

"Sure. Can I give you some advice?"

The detective eyed him warily. "What's that?"

"Lose the Chevy. It's a dead giveaway."

Davis walked away muttering under his breath.

13

Judo Queen

"Richard Roundtree," Valentine said aloud, remembering the name of the actor who'd played Shaft as he drove away. A good-looking guy and a sharp dresser, at least in the movies. Davis looked a lot like him, although he wasn't nearly as sharp.

The roads had iced up, and he drove cautiously to the Body Slam School of Professional Wrestling, the daylight doing a slow fade in his mirror.

He parked in front of the building and got out. A knot of middle-aged bikers stood around the storefront window. From inside he could hear bodies slamming the canvas, the concussive sound making the glass vibrate. The burly boys in leather shook their heads.

"I'd like to do her," a ponytailed biker said.

"Do her?" another mocked. "Hell, she'd do you."

Valentine shouldered his way to the front. The wrestler getting all the attention was a knockout in a black leotard, her braided hair hanging halfway down her sweaty back. She was beautiful in an overwhelming sort of way. Big all over, and proud of it. The ponytailed biker tapped Valentine's shoulder.

"Hey," he said.

Valentine glanced at him. "Hey yourself."

"You're blocking the view, old man."

"Is that Judo Queen?"

"Sure is."

Through the window, Valentine saw a muscular guy in sweats climb through the ropes. Judo Queen charged across the ring and took him down with a perfectly executed dropkick. The pony-tailed biker tapped Valentine's shoulder again.

"Like what you see, old man?"

"She's something else," Valentine admitted.

The bikers erupted, making barnyard sounds. They were pushing fifty, big-gutted, their lives running out of road. Valentine opened the front door and went in.

The school's interior was sweaty hot. Up in the ring, Judo Queen had her opponent in a hammerlock, a classic submission hold. Wrestling and judo had a lot in common, with cleverness playing as great a role as technique. Laying his overcoat over a metal folding chair, he took a seat.

For the next twenty minutes, he watched Judo Queen practice the gimmicky moves of her trade. He could see why Yun had taken a liking to her. Hard worker, no nonsense, eye-of-the-tiger intensity. Mixed in was a nasty attitude—it was there every time she took her opponent down—and right away he could imagine her hurting someone.

At the session's end, her opponent clapped his hands and said *"Go!"* Judo Queen ran across the ring, hit the ropes, then sprinted back and rebounded off the other side like a human slingshot. It gave new meaning to conditioning, and after five minutes she staggered to a corner and fell into the ropes.

"See you Monday," her opponent said.

"Right," she gasped.

Her opponent climbed through the ropes. Rising, Valentine went to the ring apron. Judo Queen lifted her head.

"Would you believe I pay that guy two hundred bucks a week to go through this?"

84   "It's sure paying off."

"Thanks. Those mutts with you?"

Valentine glanced over his shoulder. The bikers were still there, their collective breath fogging the glass.

"No," he said.

Judo Queen grimaced and stood erect. "I've got a knot in the middle of my back. Know anything about massage?"

"A little."

"Please. It's killing me."

He climbed into the ring and got behind her. With his thumbs, he worked the troubled muscle up and down. Normally, he didn't go around touching strange women, but he had an audience and she'd asked. Seize the moment, seize the day.

"Thanks," she said. Turning, she stuck out her hand. "Kat Berman."

"Tony Valentine."

Her handshake was firm. The Mercedes was visible from the ring, and Valentine had a sneaking suspicion she'd seen him arrive and decided he was someone important.

"So, what can I do for you, Tony?"

"I need to speak to you."

Kat smiled. "Let me guess. WCW. No, WWF."

He had to think. Those were the wrestling federations. Kat thought he was a promoter, here to make her dreams come true.

"AARP," he confessed.

She giggled like a little kid. She didn't seem so nasty anymore, so he let the bomb drop.

"I'm a friend of Yun's."

Her face turned to stone. "Did he send you?"

"His wife."

"I've got no argument with the Yuns," she said, jabbing his arm to make her point. "I offered to pay him for those lessons. Did Lin Lin tell you that?"

"That's not the issue."

Another jab. "I've got a kid to support. A little girl."

"Did you have to wear the crane on your uniform?"

"I couldn't afford another one, Mr. Mercedes Benz. When I'm famous, he'll be flattered I've got that stupid bird on my tit."

"I doubt it."

Her hand came up to slap his face. Valentine intercepted it, squeezing her wrist and holding it firmly. Outside, the bikers were jumping up and down. One waved a Budweiser can.

"I've taken a thousand body slams and a dozen fat lips to get where I am," she hissed through clenched teeth. "Nobody is going to stop me from succeeding. *Understand?*"

And with that, Kat pulled her arm free, grabbed his wrist, and turned sideways, getting her weight centered to throw him. She was standing in a corner, which meant she planned to hurl him over the ropes, and into a row of folding chairs.

That got Valentine mad. Didn't she see the gray hair? For all she knew, he was wearing a pacemaker. Grabbing her braid with his free hand, he yanked it hard.

Kat yelped and stood up straight, a beginner's mistake. With his right leg, he swept her feet out from under her. She hit the canvas hard.

She lay on her side, stunned. A drop of blood appeared beneath her left nostril. She covered her face with her hands.

"Go away! Leave me alone!"

Valentine turned around. Glancing at the bikers, he saw a guy who had not been there before. Tall, thin, with a widow's peak and a murderous gleam in his eyes. Was this the abusive boyfriend Lin Lin had warned him about?

The boyfriend pointed at him. Then drew his forefinger across his throat.

"Go away!" Kat screamed.

Valentine went away.

◆

Outside, the bikers were sharing a twelve-pack. The boyfriend was gone. At the end of the block, a black Mustang pulled away from the curb with a squeal of tires.

"You know that guy?"

The bikers' faces were solemn, the fun gone.

"You're a real jerk," the ponytail said.

"Why'd you have to hurt her," another biker said.

Valentine heard the threat in their voices. Was it the beer, or the fact that they outnumbered him? He removed his hands from his pockets.

"I didn't see any of you rushing in to defend her. But that would have taken guts, and courage. Something you poor slobs drank away years ago." He waited for one of them to start something. There were no takers, so he finished his discourse. "I've spent most of my life dealing with losers like you, so let me give you some advice. Get a haircut, get a job, and get a life. Oh, and one more thing. Get out of my way."

They obliged him. Driving away, he glanced in his mirror. The ponytailed biker was holding his beer can as if to throw it. He hit the brakes hard.

The biker lowered his arm, then sauntered away. The others followed like a pack of sheep. Valentine punched the accelerator and watched them disappear in his mirror.

14

Ann

Valentine lay on his motel bed and stared at the cheap popcorn ceiling. He'd had crummy days before, but none like this. He'd brained his son, let a crook slip through his fingers, and knocked down a crazy broad. It had to be some kind of record.

He closed his eyes and tried to nap. It didn't work. Something was weighing on his mind. Then he realized what it was. He still needed to change motels.

He didn't go far. Two blocks south was the Blue Dolphin, and the manager rented him a room behind the swimming pool for fifty bucks a night. He unpacked, then took out his cell phone and punched in Mabel's number.

"I moved," he informed her.

She wrote down the new number and filled him in on the day's events. Then she said, "I decided you were right. I need a dog for protection. Everyone says that mutts are the best. What do you think?"

"Beats me. I never owned a dog."

"I'm going to check the pound. If one licks my hand, I'll bring it home with me."

"You were always a sucker for a warm tongue."

"Stop that."

"I need you to research something on your computer," he said. "It's called RDX."

"Sounds intriguing. Should I use Whoopee?"

For Christmas, he'd given Mabel a subscription to an Internet service called Road Runner. He'd never been a fan of cyberspace, but seeing the joy it gave his neighbor, he'd decided it wasn't such a bad thing after all.

"Yahoo," he said.

"I know what it's called. I like Whoopee better. Now, is RDX a vegetable, animal, or mineral?"

"It's a powerful explosive. That's all I know about it."

"Is this what killed your friend?"

A stiff wind banged his motel room door, and Valentine jumped an inch off the bed. Like a ghost in an Edgar Allan Poe story, he imagined Doyle's spirit hanging outside, keeping tabs on him.

"Sorry," his neighbor said.

◆

He got dinner from the Burger King down the street and ate while watching *Hogan's Heroes* on the mute TV. A station out of Newark liked to show the old stuff. It was such garbage, you didn't need the volume to figure out what was going on.

He stared at the set while thinking about the European. A bad haircut, a fake gun, and a blackjack system that let him always win. That was the part that bugged him. Every blackjack system that didn't rely on outright cheating was based on card counting, and card counting wasn't infallible.

He remembered a crew of card counters he'd encountered years ago. They'd had five members. Four were expert counters. The fifth was a businessman who played the role of the BP, or Big Player, and carried a huge bankroll.

The counters sat at different blackjack tables and did their thing. Card counting was based upon the fact that a deck rich in high cards—the tens, jacks, queens, and kings—gave the players an edge. When the deck became rich, the counter would signal the BP, and the BP would come over and play.

Only on the night he'd seen this crew play, the BP had lost all his money. And all because of a statistical principle called standard deviation. Standard deviation was the average number of misses that might occur in a game of chance and often produced a large swing in the odds. In blackjack, it could wipe out a card counter's edge.

Somehow, the European had gotten around this, which was like saying he'd learned how to walk on water.

The show ended, and he killed the power with the remote. Tomorrow was going to be a better day; he was just sure of it. Turning off the lights, he buried himself in the sheets.

◆

The phone on the night table interrupted his dreams. He cracked an eye. Almost eleven. Mabel was a night owl, and he answered the phone with, "So what did you find?"

"Is this Tony Valentine," a woman with a thick accent said.

He turned on the lamp on the night table. He'd heard that accent earlier today in the bathroom at The Bombay.

"That's me."

"Do you know who this is?"

He hesitated. "I think so."

"There is a bar on Atlantic Avenue. The Chatterbox Lounge. Do you know it?"

Since before you were born, he nearly said. "Yes."

"Go there and take a booth in the back. Come alone, or I won't."

"Wait—"

"You have twenty minutes."

The line went dead. Slipping out of bed, he took his wallet off the night table and removed Davis's card. He punched in the detective's cell number. Five rings later, a woman with a dreamy voice said, "Yes?"

"I need to speak to Eddie."

"He's not available."

"You sure about that?"

Her voice turned sharp. *"Who is this?"*

"Tony Valentine. Get him, will you?"

The woman went away. Valentine glanced at his watch, its face glowing in the room's dim light. A minute slipped away, then another. Davis's lady friend came back on the line.

"Eddie wants to know if it's urgent," she said.

"It sure is," he said.

Then he hung up on her.

◆

The Chatterbox was a longtime hangout of Atlantic City's underbelly. Valentine parked under the busted neon sign and went in. In the smoky room he made out a few vague forms shooting pool. Otherwise, it was dead.

The bar was in the shape of a horseshoe and surrounded by a dozen stools. For drug deals and illicit rendezvous there were booths on the far wall, each lit by a single candle. He caught the bartender's eye and ordered a Diet Coke.

A few stools away sat a woman of negotiable affections. Her skirt was hiked up to her crotch, exposing red satin underwear. Without looking his way, she said, "See something you like?"

"Not in here."

She spun on her stool, facing him. "You sure?"

She sounded desperate. In her face he saw a hard life hidden behind the paint. She smiled, thinking he was warming up to her.

"Scram," he said.

"What are you, pops, a cop?"

"How bad do you want to find out?"

She flung her purse over her shoulder and bolted. The bartender placed his soda on the bar. "*Are* you a cop?"

"Ex."

"You look familiar. Soda's on the house."

The bartender was a guy his age, lots of character in his face. Sometimes Valentine regretted that he didn't drink. Some of the finest people he'd ever met served booze for a living.

He slipped into a booth and sat with his back to the wall. He looked at his watch. Eleven-eighteen.

Two minutes later, the European's accomplice entered the bar, her wool cap flecked with snow. She stopped and ordered a draft beer, then came to the booth and slid onto the other seat.

"Hello," she said.

Close up, she was even prettier than he'd expected. But what struck him was her smell. She smelled of cigarettes, or more precisely, a few thousand cigarettes, her teeth stained from years of abuse. She removed her cap and shook it out on the floor.

Valentine kept looking at the two exits, waiting for one of her partners to come in.

"I'm alone," she informed him.

"You got a name?"

"Ann."

"What do you want, Ann?"

"Are you always so . . . direct?"

Only with thieves, he nearly said. "Yes."

Ann pulled a square of paper from her pocket, unfolded it, and slid it across the table. His eyes scanned the page.

Wanted!!!

For the murder of Doyle Flanagan and stealing money from The Bombay. If you see either of these individuals inside the casino, alert a pit boss or security immediately. These people are armed and extremely dangerous.

Do Not Attempt To Apprehend These Individuals!!!!!!

Beneath the screaming type was Ann's picture, lifted off a surveillance tape, another of her partner. Not good shots, but she was so pretty, it would be easy to spot her. He slid the flyer back.

"Let me guess," he said. "You didn't do it."

She took a long swallow of beer. It left a wet mustache on her face that she did not seem to notice.

"New Jersey has the death penalty, you know."

"We are not murderers," she said. "Your friend was involved in something else."

"You think so?"

"It is the only logical explanation. We are being turned into—what is the expression?"

"Fall guys," he said.

"Yes," she said. "Fall guys."

"But you *are* ripping off The Bombay."

"Ripping off?"

"Stealing."

"Yes, yes, we are doing that. But we did not kill your friend. We would never do such a thing. You must believe me when I say this."

Valentine drank his soda. He got the feeling Ann was being sincere, which could only mean one thing. Her partners had planted the bomb in Doyle's car without telling her.

"Why should I?" he said.

She took another swallow of beer. "The Bombay hired you to investigate Doyle Flanagan's murder, yes?"

"That's right."

"And you are an ex-policeman."

"Right again."

"You have an open mind, yes?"

Valentine shook his head. She didn't understand, so he spelled it out for her. "Doyle Flanagan was my partner *and* my best friend. Did your sources tell you that?"

Ann leaned over the table. *"The night your partner was murdered, we were playing blackjack at The Bombay."*

"Prove it."

She killed the beer and her cheeks grew flushed. "As you are probably aware, we play at tables which are not being monitored by surveillance cameras."

"So there's no film," Valentine said.

"No. But a member of our team did cash in our winnings—"

"—and since the cage is always being filmed," Valentine finished, "your partner would be on tape."

She slapped her hands on the table. "Exactly!"

"Honey, all that tells me is that *one of you* was in The Bombay that night."

The Chatterbox's front door banged open. A dozen uniformed men stormed in, bringing an arctic wave of cold air with them. They ripped off their fireman's jackets and bellied up to the bar, loudly ordering pitchers of beer.

Ann's eyes went wide. Seconds later she was out of the booth and beating a path toward the back door. Wearing his soda, Valentine ran after her.

"Try to keep it civil," the bartender called out.

Ann hit the back door like a truck. The door swung open, and Valentine saw her run into the parking lot, then suddenly stop, looking in both directions. Had her ride gone and left her?

Being old definitely had its advantages. For one, people were always underestimating his physical prowess, and Ann let out a scream when he grabbed her by the shoulders and spun her like a top. He started to shake her.

"Tell me where your partners are," he said.

"Do not . . . be stupid."

That got Valentine mad. She was the stupid one. Any other hustler would have left town. He started to reply, then felt something hard tap the back of his skull.

♦

He awoke on an icy metal floor, his wrists handcuffed to an exposed hot water pipe. Voices danced around him; three men and a woman. The cold floor was doing a number on his bowels, and he fought the urge to soil himself.

He tried to make out the conversation but couldn't place the language. Not Turkish or Greek or Albanian but similar, from that part of the world. He cracked an eye open, and got a look at the other two males who made up the gang. Late thirties, gaunt, with sallow complexions, their faces without humor.

The room they had brought him to was filled with litter. Mostly beer cans but also shattered crack pipes, and he guessed he was in an abandoned warehouse on the west side of town.

Ann stood in the room's center. She'd changed into sweats and wore a Walkman around her neck. She came over and knelt beside him. Coming out of the earphones was Vivaldi's *The Four Seasons.* Her hand touched his brow.

Valentine opened his eyes. "Hi."

The gang circled him. Taking out a penlight, the European shined the tiny beam into Valentine eyes. Then he said something reassuringly to Ann.

"Good," she said in English.

Valentine rattled his handcuffs against the water pipe. "Would you mind undoing these? I'm not going anywhere."

"Only if you'll tell me something," the European said.

"What's that?"

"I want to know how you spotted me in the casino." Then he added, "No one else has."

"These first," Valentine said.

The European took out the keys and opened the cuffs. Pushing himself into a sitting position, Valentine leaned against the wall and watched the room spin.

"Out with it," the European said.

"You cut your own hair, don't you?"

The European nodded. "We take turns."

"Well, it shows."

"You're saying my hair gave me away?"

"Afraid so."

"Your country is filled with strange-looking people. And so are your casinos. Why would I stand out?"

Valentine tried to think of a delicate way to explain it. Some of the worst-dressed human beings could be found in American casinos. Only these people did not play at the five thousand dollar blackjack tables. They played keno and the quarter slot machines. The gamblers at the five-thousand-dollar tables wore Rolex watches and had hundred dollar haircuts. They had dough, and they flaunted it.

Valentine said, "Well, it's like this. You look . . ."

They were all staring at him.

"Poor," he said.

The European winced. Valentine had hit a nerve.

"You haven't been in this country long, have you?"

The European put his hand on Valentine's shoulder. "You are a clever man, and if we keep letting you talk, I'm sure you'll find out plenty about us. So, shut up."

"You bet," Valentine said.

♦

They huddled on the other side of the room. Valentine used the break to take deep breaths and try and get his heart to slow down. An old martial arts trick that he'd never been any good at. He saw Ann break away from the group. She came over and knelt down beside him.

"Will you please listen to me," she said.

"I'm listening."

"We have played blackjack all over the world. Eventually, the casino figures out they cannot beat us, and we are eighty-fived–"

"Eighty-sixed."

"Thank you. So we go elsewhere. Monte Carlo, Nassau, San Juan. A month here, a month there. It is always the same."

"I'm not reading you," he said.

"Eventually, we are barred," she explained. "The casinos figure out they cannot win and throw us out."

"Okay."

"The Bombay was different. We played and won and kept playing. Each night we wondered, 'When will it end? When will the house make us leave?' It was too good to be true."

"You're saying The Bombay *let* you cheat them?"

"Yes."

Valentine had heard a lot of ridiculous alibis over the years, but this took the cake.

"Wow," was all he could think to say.

She stormed out of the room. The other three came over, and the European knelt down. From his leather jacket he removed a familiar-looking Glock and stuck the barrel against Valentine's cheek. Valentine pressed his knees together. He was seconds away from peeing on himself.

"I would kill you, only Ann would never speak to me again," the European said. "So go back to wherever you live and enjoy your golden years. Understand?"

"Yes," Valentine said.

The European tossed the Glock over his shoulder. One of his partners caught it. Then he handcuffed Valentine back to the water pipe, and the three men left the room.

15

RDX

They left him with a long piece of string with a handcuff key tied to the other end. Valentine took his time pulling the string in and freeing himself, not inclined to run after them. Getting KO'd was no fun, especially at his age. He'd feel the effect for days, maybe longer.

The cold had seeped into his bones. Rising, he took a piss in the corner, then walked around the room. Stopping at a window, he stared at a white van sitting at a traffic light a block away. It was the same van he'd seen outside the IHOP, a real junker. It didn't make sense. They'd stolen six million bucks, why not get a decent set of wheels?

He found the stairwell and descended cautiously, clutching the railing for dear life. A rat ran past, brushing his ankle. Kicking down a splintered door, he stepped into a backyard strewn with bottles and cast-off tire rims. The building next door looked familiar and he peered over the fence. Two blocks away, he saw the Chatterbox's neon sign. He hopscotched his way to the sidewalk, then started walking.

The temperature had dropped, his breath as white as freshly fallen snow. At the corner, a woman stepped out of the shadows. It was the hooker from the Chatterbox. She parted her jacket and he saw that she'd stripped down to the red underwear she'd so kindly shown him earlier.

"Scram," he said.

The Chatterbox was closed. He banged on the front door anyway. The bartender came to his rescue, microwaving him a cup of coffee and giving him an ice pack. Fifteen minutes later he climbed into the Mercedes. He had the key in the ignition when he heard a voice inside his head.

Never let your guard down.

Yun had said that to him a hundred times the year he'd gone undefeated. He got out, dug a newspaper out of a trash bin, and spread it on the macadam. Then he looked under the car.

"Jesus Christ," he said.

◆

Davis arrived with the Atlantic City bomb squad.

He'd taken Valentine's advice and ditched the Chevy for an immaculate '74 Thunderbird. Driving it, he didn't look like a cop anymore, a fact he seemed to appreciate as much as anyone.

"She's my baby," he said. "Bought her secondhand when I got out of high school. Put a new engine in, refurbished the interior. The whole nine yards."

He'd brought two cups of police house coffee. Valentine found himself liking the detective again. Sitting in the Thunderbird, they watched the bomb squad defuse the explosive device taped to Valentine's starter and drop it in a bucket of water. The captain of the bomb squad waved to Davis. Davis replied by flashing his brights.

"How long were you on the force?" Davis asked.

"Thirty years."

"Was Doyle your partner the whole time?"

"Just about."

"Like being married, huh?"

"Worse," Valentine told him.

"How was it worse?"

"No sex."

The detective spit coffee through his nose.

"You're brutal," he said.

Valentine wasn't going to argue with him there. The bomb squad van drove away. Davis leaned against his door, staring at him in the semidarkness. "You realize I'm going to have to investigate this."

"Of course."

"Anything you want to tell me?"

Valentine shrugged. "I was in the bar, I came out, found a bomb under my car. What else is there to tell?"

"How about that bump on your head?"

"I slipped on the stoop."

"Alice Torkalowski told me you were New Jersey state judo champ five years running."

"That's right."

"Then you didn't fall down coming out of some bar."

Valentine sipped his coffee. "Sorry."

"So here's the deal, my friend. Don't leave town. In fact, don't leave your motel. I'll call tomorrow, and you'll come down to headquarters and talk to a bunch of detectives and try to get this straightened out. Dig?"

"Yes, sir."

"Because if not, I'll haul you in and toss your ass in jail. Understand?"

"*Yes, sir,*" he said.

◆

Valentine drove around town looking for the European's white van because that was what his instincts told him to do. Looked in every alley and obscure side street and came up with air.

Slowly the night turned into day. He stopped and bought Advil and a bottled water from a crazy-looking soul sitting behind bullet-proof glass. Taking four, he drove back to the Blue Dolphin and soon was fast asleep.

His dreams were tortured, the events of the last three days mixed up in the bouillabaisse of his subconscious. Mercifully, the chambermaid knocked on his door at 10:30 A.M., and he dragged himself out of bed.

He took the usual shit, shower, shave, then lay on the bed and waited for his head to clear. He was beginning to wonder what the hell he was doing. He'd nearly bought the farm twice in the past two days, and still was no closer to avenging Doyle's death. Maybe there was something to be said for staying put in Florida and growing old with his neighbors.

His cell phone rang. He waited a minute, then dialed into voice mail. It was Mabel. He called her back.

"I was worrying about you," his neighbor said.

"I'm okay," he said.

"You don't sound okay."

"Nothing that a fifth of bourbon won't cure."

"But you don't drink."

"There you go. Any luck on Yahoo?"

"Come to mention it, I've had a very productive morning. You wouldn't believe how much information there is on the Internet about bomb making. Pipe bombs, Molotov cocktails, fertilizer bombs. You name it, it's out there. There wasn't a lot about RDX, or should I say, what is out there is classified information. So I called the Pentagon."

The ceiling had stared to spin. Valentine closed his eyes and said, "You didn't."

"I'm a taxpayer. Anyway, this nice young lady did a search on her computer. She said that RDX is used by the army and not available on the open market. It has many of the same components as nitroglycerin, only it's ten times more powerful. She said that only really experienced bomb makers use it, because of the danger."

"Where is it manufactured?"

"In the good old U.S. of A. Oh, hold on. There's a call on the other line."

Valentine put a pillow over his head. Then he tried to make sense of what Mabel had just said. The European was using an explosive that wasn't available on the open market. So how had he gotten his hands on it?

"It's that slimeball Nick Nicocropolis," his neighbor said, coming back on.

"Who's ripping him off now?"

"Some guy at blackjack. Nick taped him scratching his arm, and says you can see him sticking his hand up his sleeve. Nick thinks he's switching cards. He had the player detained, but he wasn't wearing a holdout, whatever that is."

A *holdout* was a generic term for any device that allowed a crossroader to keep a playing card hidden on his body. Some holdouts were intricate pieces of equipment that cost thousands of dollars, like the Kepplinger body harness, while others were simple devices, such as a bulldog clip attached to a piece of elastic.

"So the guy was clean," Valentine said.

"Nick said all he found was some trash around the player's chair."

"What kind of trash?"

"I'll ask him." She put him on hold, then returned. "Gum

wrappers, a broken rubber band, some cigarette butts, and an eight-by-ten index card."

"There's his evidence."

"Where?"

The pillow wasn't doing any good, and he tossed it on the floor. "The rubber band and the index card. The crossroader wears the rubber band around his biceps with the index card tucked beneath the elastic. That's what holds the cards. When he smells trouble, he sticks his hand up his sleeve and breaks the rubber band. The evidence falls to the floor."

"Can Nick prosecute with that?"

Valentine smiled into the receiver. Mabel was starting to sound like a cop. She really wanted this gig to work, and he found himself wanting it to work as well.

"No, but the crossroader is still screwed."

"How so?"

"Nick has his face on film. He'll make his security team memorize it. He'll also send a picture to the Griffin Detective Agency, and they'll put it in a book that they sell to the other casinos. The crossroader won't be able to get a game of jacks."

She giggled. "That's wonderful. One more question."

"Shoot."

"When are you coming home?"

He heard a knock on his door. Sliding off the bed, he stuck his eye to the peephole in the door. It was Detective Davis, and the look on his face was not friendly.

"Soon," he told his neighbor.

16

Betrayal

The windowless interrogation room in the basement of the Atlantic City police department reeked of butts and body odor. Valentine had grilled many suspects here but had never realized how revolting the air truly smelled.

Davis turned on the tape recorder sitting on the desk. "Let's start from the beginning."

It was not easy playing stupid, but Valentine did his best, and ended up saying nothing the detective didn't already know. Disgusted, Davis shut off the tape recorder.

A ham-faced guy in an off-the-rack suit entered the room. Late forties, fat, with stringy blond hair and a chipped front tooth. Davis introduced him as Detective Coleman. Coleman's beat was working security at The Bombay.

"How'd you like to get fucked?" Coleman said, popping a piece of bubble gum in his mouth.

Valentine thought he already was fucked. A bead of sweat ran down his spine. He'd made a lot of suspects sweat over the years and always found it comical. Now it didn't seem funny at all.

"Not really."

Coleman eyed him, chewing away. "My partner and I have

been investigating The Bombay. It's bad enough they got swin-
dled and didn't tell the law; it's worse they went and hired you.
It's called obstructing justice. You with me so far?"

Valentine nodded.

"We don't know what Archie Tanner's trying to pull, but he's
about to get himself royally screwed. Still with me?"

"Yes."

"My partner and I had a chat with Frank Porter this morning,"
Coleman said, his fingers tapping the silent tape recorder. "I told
him about the bomb in your car, asked him who might want you
dead. Frank told us what happened between you and a European
blackjack cheat in The Bombay yesterday."

"Oh," Valentine said.

Coleman leaned forward, getting in his face. "Frank said that
you're carrying an illegal Glock. That true?"

The words hit Valentine like a kick in the stomach. He didn't
know what bothered him more, the detectives knowing about the
gun, or Porter's betrayal.

"Yes," he said.

"Still have it?"

"No."

"Mind telling me where it is?"

"The European took it away from me."

Coleman's eyes went wide. Davis muttered under his breath. A
third man entered the room, a detective's badge pinned to the
lapel of his jacket. Valentine swallowed hard. It was the guy with
the widow's peak he'd seen standing outside the Body Slam
School of Wrestling. Kat's abusive boyfriend.

"This is Detective Marconi, my partner," Coleman said.

Marconi got up close to Valentine's chair. He was tall and skinny, with piercing eyes that didn't blink. Leaning forward, he said,
"Feel my face."

"Excuse me?"

"You heard me. Feel my face."

Valentine gently touched Marconi's chin.

"Feels soft, doesn't it? I got mauled by a Doberman as a kid. The plastic surgeon grafted skin from my ass onto my face. Pretty good job, don't you think?"

Valentine took his hand away. "Could have fooled me."

"It fooled *everybody*. Only my brother told everyone in town. Kids called me Ass Face. And you know what?"

"What?"

"I've had a shitty attitude ever since."

"I bet."

"You're a hair away from going to jail, mister."

"I know."

"Want to prevent that?"

"Yes."

"Stay out of this investigation, or the next time we catch you meddling where you don't belong, it's a bust."

"I will," Valentine promised. Then added, "Scout's honor."

He hadn't meant the remark to sound flippant, but it came out that way. Marconi made a fist and reared back as if to hit him. Coleman intervened and grabbed his partner's arm.

"He's not worth getting suspended over, Vic."

The two detectives marched out of the interrogation room. Davis shook his head wearily.

"Get out of here," he said.

◆

Valentine got into the Mercedes and stared at the dashboard. He was too old for this kind of nonsense. And the idea of going to jail, even for just a few days, worried him more than getting hurt.

He started the engine. He was ready to fold his tents, but before he did, he needed to have a talk with Frank. They'd known each other a long time, so long that he considered him more than just a friend. Which was why he had to find out why Frank had betrayed him.

The Bombay's valet stand was quiet when he pulled in fifteen minutes later. Throwing the kid on duty the keys, he walked inside the casino. And waited.

The Bombay had over a thousand pan/tilt/zoom cameras, commonly called PTZs. And a dozen were aimed at the front doors. The people in the surveillance control room constantly watched the doors to make sure no known crossroaders came in. Next to the cage, where the money was kept, it was the most heavily watched area in the casino.

Soon a security guard appeared, and led him over to a house phone. Valentine picked up the receiver and put it to his ear.

"God, Tony, I'm sorry," Porter said.

"You sold me down the river."

Valentine heard a crunching sound. Porter was at his desk, eating something. He started to hang up the phone.

"Tony, wait . . ."

Valentine put the phone back to his ear.

"Those pricks Coleman and Marconi leaned on me," Porter said. "I had to give them something."

"You gave them *me*."

"I'd just gotten off my shift; I was tired and wasn't thinking. When they asked me if you were carrying, I slipped and told them about the hot gun."

Valentine gripped the receiver, feeling the cold plastic seep into his palm. He'd shown Frank the gun in Sinbad's. But he was positive he hadn't told him it was hot.

"I've got a great joke," Porter said. "Want to hear it?"

"No."

"I saw this enormous woman with a sweatshirt with GUESS on it. So I said, 'Thyroid problem?' "

"You're not funny," Valentine said.

Then he walked out of The Bombay.

17

Sparky

Valentine parked the Mercedes in the narrow alley beside Sparky Rhodes's house, then stood on his porch and rapped three times on Sparky's front door. Moments later he was standing inside the darkened foyer, looking down at the paralyzed cop in his wheelchair.

"I lost the Glock," he explained.

Sparky scratched the day-old stubble on his chin. He wore a flannel bathrobe and had bread crumbs on his chest. Tucked into the belt of his robe was his trusty .38. Valentine could not remember ever seeing him without it.

"You want another gun?"

"Yes."

"This one's gonna cost you," Sparky informed him.

"I brought cash."

"Good." Sparky turned the wheelchair around and headed toward the kitchen. "Because I don't take credit cards anymore."

His hoarse laughter filled the dreary house. He wheeled himself down the hall, zigzagging to avoid a pile of trash in his way. His wife had split after he'd been shot, and Valentine didn't think he'd had the place cleaned since.

They went into the kitchen. On the table sat the remains of lunch: a half-eaten baloney sandwich, a bag of potato chips, and a long-necked bottle of Budweiser. Stopping at the table, Sparky took the sandwich and shoved it into his mouth, chewed a few times, then washed it down with beer.

"What did you have in mind?"

"I was thinking of a .38," Valentine said. "Something dependable. Like the gun you carry."

Sparky drew the .38 from his robe and kissed the barrel. "Smith and Wesson makes a lot of guns, but none finer than this baby." He then proceeded to tell Valentine about the time he'd shot a fourteen-year-old black kid breaking into his house. The district attorney had wanted to prosecute but eventually dropped charges. Because it was a black kid that had shot *him,* Sparky had seen the act as vindication.

"You understand what I'm saying?" Sparky said.

Valentine didn't. But he didn't say so.

"Can I see it?"

Sparky handed him the .38. Valentine examined it, then put the gun on the counter, out of Sparky's reach.

Sparky stared at him. "What the fuck you doing?"

"I have a question to ask you."

The paralyzed ex-cop pursed his lips.

"Why'd you tell Frank Porter that you gave me a hot gun."

"I didn't tell Porter nothing."

"That's a lie," Valentine said.

"Fuck it is."

"Frank got grilled by two detectives this morning, and he coughed up that I was carrying an illegal piece. I didn't tell Frank, so it must have been you."

Sparky started to say something, then clamped his mouth shut. Valentine leaned against the counter and waited him out. Behind Sparky's cow-brown eyes he could see the gears shifting. Sparky picked up his beer and polished it off.

"Well," the paralyzed cop said, "it's like this."

And then he threw the bottle at Valentine's head.

Valentine had just enough time to duck, the bottle hitting the cabinet behind him and shattering. Sparky spun around in his wheelchair and bolted for the hall. Stopping at the door leading to the basement, he jerked the door open and shot down the ramp. Valentine grabbed the .38 and ran after him.

111

He heard a cat scream, followed by Sparky letting out a scream of his own. Then a loud crash. Reaching the stairwell, he flipped on the basement light.

Sparky lay on his back, his neck twisted at an unnatural angle. His wheelchair lay beside him, both wheels spinning. Clinging to his bathrobe was a terrified black cat.

Valentine ran down the stairs. The cat cowered in a corner, hissing.

"Sparky? You okay?"

He put his ear next to Sparky's mouth. The paralyzed cop's breathing was shallow. "I . . ."

"What?"

"I'm . . . sorry."

"About what?"

"You know . . ."

"Tell me."

"Doyle . . ."

Sparky's breathing grew faint and his eyes closed, and then he wasn't breathing at all.

"Oh, Jesus," Valentine whispered.

◆

Valentine tried to think.

The smart move was to run. That was what crooks did in tight situations. *Run.* That was his best option. Only he'd left his fingerprints all over the house.

Going back upstairs, he laid his overcoat and scarf on the kitchen table, got a dishrag from the sink, and went around the house rubbing down anything he might have touched. Then he did the same in the basement. Climbing up the ramp, he turned out the light and left the door ajar.

Finding the cat's bowl, he filled it with dry cat food, then filled another bowl with water and put it on the floor. Tomorrow, he would make an anonymous phone call to the police and ask them to let the cat out.

He started to open the front door as mail came through the slot. He went to the living room window and saw the mailman walk down the path. A woman in curlers was standing on the sidewalk. They started to chat. He took a seat by the door.

Then he played back what had happened.

And got nowhere.

It didn't make sense. He'd known Sparky a long time. All he'd wanted was a straight answer.

He kicked Sparky's mail with his foot. It scattered across the floor. Bills, flyers, and something from the IRS. He picked up the IRS letter by its corners and peered through the plastic window. The words *Final Notice* popped out.

The letter struck him as odd. Sparky was broke. So why was the IRS breathing down his neck?

He boiled water on the kitchen stove and steamed the envelope open, then used a fork to remove the letter. His eyes ran down the page. Sparky had made two ten-thousand-dollar deposits into his account, which his bank had reported to the IRS, as it was required by law to do. The IRS was now holding the money, and demanding an explanation of its origin.

Valentine put the letter down. Where the hell had Sparky gotten twenty grand?

He found a pair of rubber gloves beneath the sink, put them

on, and searched the house. Sparky's bedroom was behind the kitchen, and he checked all the places the paralyzed cop could reach. On the bottom of the dirty clothes hamper he hit pay dirt and removed a shoe box wrapped in rubber bands.

The box was heavy. Opening the lid, he stared at the stacks of brand new hundred-dollar bills. He dumped them onto the bed. He used to be good at counting money at a glance and guessed the box contained thirty grand. He counted it just to be sure.

Thirty grand on the nose.

He sat down on the bed, his head spinning. Had Sparky made the money selling hot guns? It was the only logical answer he could think of. The phone on the night table rang and he nearly jumped out of his skin. On the fourth ring the answering machine picked up.

"I'm not here," Sparky's recorded voice said gruffly. "Friends can leave a message. Everyone else, go to hell."

"Sarge," a woman's voice rang out. "You there? Pick up. I need to talk to you."

The woman hung up. Valentine stared at the phone. Who the hell was Sarge?

He searched the other drawers in Sparky's dresser, and in the bottom one found a framed photograph taken during Desert Storm. Sparky stood in the back row with his regiment, looking sharp in his army uniform. Valentine stared at the other faces; half were men, the others women. There was too much sunlight to make anyone out. He took the photograph out of its frame and stared at the back, hoping to find the regiment's name or call numbers. It was blank.

He went to the front of the house and looked out the living room window. The mailman and next door neighbor were gone.

He got out of the house as fast as he could.

18

Honey

Sitting behind the wheel of the Mercedes, he peeled off the rubber gloves. Then he backed out of the alley next to Sparky's house. There were times when being in a flashy car wasn't good, and this was certainly one of them.

He drove for several miles, then parked next to a Wendy's and sat in the parking lot for several minutes, trying to gather his thoughts. Sparky's dying words were already starting to haunt him. *You know . . . Doyle . . .*

He stuck his hand in his pocket and took out Sparky's trusted .38. He'd told Sparky he needed another gun, and now he had one.

He stuck the gun back in his pocket. Then he tried to make sense of what had happened. Fifty grand was a lot of dough. Selling hot guns couldn't be that lucrative. Even if it was, it didn't explain why Sparky had thrown the bottle at him. Nor the fear in Sparky's eyes. That was bothering him the most.

Going inside the restaurant, he bought coffee, then sat in his car and drank it. Soon his head was buzzing like a cheap TV. During his last checkup, his doctor had ordered him to cut out caffeine after 4 P.M. He'd said sure and gone right on drinking coffee and diet Cokes, caffeine the one addiction he planned to take with him to his grave.

Doyle had been a caffeine junkie as well. And an ex-smoker. They'd been alike in a lot of ways. So much so that Valentine had known his partner inside out. And if Doyle had one flaw, it was his inability to keep a secret. If Sparky was talking to Doyle, and had told Doyle *anything* worth repeating, Doyle would have told someone. It was simply his nature.

He fished Doyle's cell phone out of his pocket. Powering it up, he retrieved Honey's number. He needed to talk to this woman, just to see what she knew.

He hit the Send button. On the third ring, a woman's sleepy voice answered.

"Is this Honey?"

The woman let out a gasp.

"Look, you don't know me, but my name is Tony Valentine, and I–"

"Tony?" the woman said.

"Yes?"

"Oh my God, is that you?"

◆

Liddy Flanagan met him at the front door of her house. She'd been lying in bed when he'd called–"No reason to get up," she'd explained–and had thrown on jeans and a threadbare sweater and brushed out her hair. She looked like a ghost, her skin creamy white and translucent, showing every hidden vein. They went into the kitchen and she poured herself a cup of that morning's coffee and stuck it in the microwave.

"Honey was Doyle's nickname for me," she said, sitting in the nook. "It came from his favorite song, Van Morrison's 'Tupelo Honey.' When you called the other day and used that name, I cried for hours."

"I'm sorry."

"It's not your fault."

He watched her drink the steaming brew. Even the smell of coffee put his brain in high gear, and he reached across the nook and touched her arm. "Liddy, why did you lie to me the other day?"

The question jolted her out of her lethargy.

"I didn't lie to you."

He lowered his voice to a conspiratorial whisper. "Yes, you did. You said you found Doyle's notebook hidden under the bed. That wasn't true, was it?"

Liddy did not reply.

"You found it in the safe," he went on, "where Doyle kept all his important documents, like his life insurance and his savings bonds."

"Who told you about the safe?"

"I helped him install it, for Christ's sake."

"Oh, God, how stupid of me." Liddy ran her hands through her hair. A number of expressions battled for a place on her face. A smile won out. "I never should have thought I could pull a fast one on you."

They shared a long silence. Then he said, "You gave me that notebook hoping I'd unravel this thing. Well, every time I turn a rock over, I discover another snake. Doyle must have told you something."

"I'll tell you what Doyle told me," she said, lowering her voice. "But please keep me and the boys out of it."

He promised her he would.

"While Doyle was doing his investigation, he heard a story about another scam, one that involved a gang of employees. At first, he didn't believe it. Doyle had so many friends at The Bombay. But then he got a call from a phone operator who worked there. He told Doyle the scam was real."

"Do you remember this phone operator's name?"

"Sparky Rhodes. He's in a wheelchair. He'd been in Desert Storm with several Bombay employees. He told Doyle the Desert Storm gang had decided to rip Archie Tanner off."

"Why did Sparky call Doyle?"

"He told Doyle he was afraid they'd be caught, and he'd end up in prison. He said gimps don't last long behind bars."

"What happened then?"

"Doyle went to Sparky's house. Sparky had secretly taped a meeting the employees had, and he played it for Doyle. The employees were angry because Archie Tanner had spent their pension money buying hotels in Florida. They talked about ripping off The Bombay."

"How?"

"Slots."

"And that's where the quotes in Doyle's notebook came from."

"Yes."

"What did Doyle do with the information?"

"He called the Division of Gaming Enforcement and the Casino Control Commission and spoke to the auditors. They checked into it and told Doyle The Bombay's slot take was normal. Doyle asked them to check the take again, and got the same answer. Then he contacted Detective Davis."

"Why Davis?"

"Davis was handling the Funny Money investigation. You know, all the fake coins showing up around town."

"So Doyle thought the cases were connected."

"I guess."

"What happened then?"

Liddy stared into the depths of her coffee cup. "Doyle was supposed to meet with Davis the night he got killed."

"Did Doyle tell you anything else?"

"He said he wished he'd never taken the job."

She went to the sink to wash her hands. She was moving in

slow motion, the permanence of Doyle's death finally catching up with her. Valentine came up from behind, and put his hand gently on her shoulder.

"One more question."

"What's that . . ."

"Was Frank Porter involved?"

He saw the corners of her mouth turn down. Then remembered that Frank was Sean's godfather.

"I don't know," she said.

"Please don't lie to me, Liddy."

Her shoulders tensed. "How do you know I'm lying?"

For as long as he could remember, Valentine had known when people were lying to him. It was a gift, yet also a curse.

"I just do."

A tear did a slow crawl down her face. "Yes. Frank knew."

He handed her a paper napkin from a basket on the counter and watched Liddy dab at her eyes. He struggled for something insightful to say to lessen her pain.

Nothing good came to mind.

19

Money Plays

Going back to his motel, Valentine flopped down on the bed with his clothes on and pulled out his cell phone. From memory he punched in Joe Cortez's number at the Immigration and Naturalization Service.

There were days that would always stay in his memory. His first great Christmas. Kissing Lois for the first time. Seeing Gerry take his first real step. Special days that would remain fresh, no matter when he thought of them.

For Valentine, one of those special days had occurred because of Joe.

It had happened like this. In 1982 he'd been assigned to work the high rollers room at the old Resorts International casino. A Japanese billionaire named Toki Mizo had been playing blackjack, and asked the house to raise the stakes to a half-million dollars a hand. The dealer, an imported French guy in a pointy-collar tux, had objected.

"But, sir, it is unheard of," the dealer said.

Mizo slapped the table angrily. He was down four million bucks and hadn't broken a sweat. A handful of casino employees hovered around him, tending to his every whim. Mizo glanced across the room at Valentine, who was leaning against the wall.

Mizo knew he was a cop—high rollers always drew heat—and motioned him over to the table.

"Hey, Mr. Policeman, what do you think?"

Valentine shrugged his shoulders. "None of my business."

"Come on," he said. "You been around."

That Valentine had. And seen a lot of blackjack played. Playing one-on-one against the dealer like Mizo was doing was a dangerous proposition. A player could go broke in the time it took to smoke a cigarette.

"Well," Valentine said, "you know what they say."

"What's that?"

"Money plays."

Mizo had to think about it. Then he smiled. "And that's what makes the world go round, my money."

"It sure as hell isn't *my* money making the world go round," Valentine said.

Mizo burst out laughing. So did everyone else in the room. Even the dealer let out a snort. The casino's general manager slipped under the red rope that separated the Worthy Few from the Unwashed Mob, and whispered in the dealer's ear.

"A half-million dollars it is," the dealer announced.

Valentine went back to leaning against the wall. A cocktail waitress appeared, testing her strength with a tray of drinks. She'd served him a Coke.

Valentine sipped the drink. By the time the glass was empty, Mizo was down twenty-six million dollars.

It would go down as the single biggest loss in casino history. Out in Las Vegas, where Mizo had been lured from, it had pissed off everybody. And, it had made Valentine's reputation, the expression *money plays* becoming a slogan in one of the city's advertising campaigns.

"I remember that little bastard," Special Agent Joe Cortez of the INS said. "That was a fine piece of police work you did tracking him down."

"Couldn't have done it without you," Valentine said.

"No," Cortez said, "you couldn't have."

Where the story had gotten interesting was when Mizo had tried to blow town and not pay off his marker. On a hunch, Valentine had called Joe and found out which airports had direct flights to Japan. The earliest was out of Philadelphia on JAL, and he'd driven there and convinced the local cops to let him board. He'd found Mizo hiding in a john.

"I need your help," Valentine said now.

Cortez worked in Newark on the third floor of a brick building with old-fashioned fire escapes and an American flag hanging out front. He said, "For you, anything."

"I'm trying to track down a gang of European blackjack cheats. My guess is, they're here on some type of special visas. I was hoping you could help me finger them."

"Tony, two hundred thousand foreigners visit New Jersey each year," Cortez said. "That's a tall order."

Valentine told Joe what he knew: three guys, one woman, well educated, late thirties. He'd thought a lot about their accents and said, "My guess is they're from Yugoslavia, that part of the world."

"I don't think Yugoslavia is a country anymore."

"Shows you where I've been."

"Well, that winnows it down. You said they were blackjack cheats?"

"That's right."

"Well educated?"

"Very. One of them listens to Vivaldi."

"Anything else I should know?"

"The woman is beautiful. Like a young Audrey Hepburn."

"How are they cheating?"

"I honestly don't know. They've got a system, and I'm beginning to think it's mathematical."

"They must be good if they've got you stumped. Think they
might be here on teaching visas?"

"There's a thought."

He listened to Cortez's stubby fingers pry information from
the INS's super-computer located in the basement of his office.
Joe cleared his throat and Valentine sensed he'd found something.

"I looked through all the foreigners in New York and New
Jersey staying here on teaching visas," he said. "There's 647
names. I looked to see if any were in groups, and narrowed the list
down to 360. Now I need to sort through them."

"How much time do you think it will take?"

"That's hard to say. I may have to work on it at home tonight."

"I really appreciate this, Joe."

"What are pals for," Joe said.

◆

Valentine's eyes snapped open to the sound of the telephone
ringing.

He'd fallen asleep fully dressed. It had grown dark outside his
motel room. He heard his stomach growl. Had he eaten today?
He honestly didn't remember. He looked at his watch. Three
hours had passed since he'd spoken to Joe. He picked up the
phone.

"There you are," Mabel said by way of greeting. "You *must* start
leaving your cell phone on."

"Why should I do that?"

"Because people are looking for you."

"That's no reason to leave it on."

"Stop being obtuse," his neighbor said.

He sat up too quickly and the room started to spin. He touched the bump on the back of his head and saw stars.

"Who's looking for me?"

"Your son. He called this morning. He said the Mollo brothers are chasing him all over New York. He begged me to ask you to reconsider lending him fifty grand."

Valentine laughed into the phone. He was feeling better already. "So how's your day going?"

"The afternoon was quiet. I started reading one of the books on cheating I found in your library. I have a question."

"Shoot."

"What's a monkey's paw?"

"It's the furry thing at the end of a monkey's leg. They use it to peel bananas."

"Very funny. I mean in casino cheating."

"It's a mechanical device that cheaters stick up the coin tray of a slot machine," he explained. "It has a light on the end which activates the slot machine into paying out even when the reels aren't lined up correctly."

"The book said casinos lose millions to monkey's paws."

"At least," he said.

"Speaking of paws," Mabel said. "I went to the pound and saw a wonderful dog, very affectionate, only it has a black tongue. I don't know why, but it gave me the willies. The lady in charge said the dog was half Chow, half who-knows-what. You know anything about the breed?"

As far as Valentine was concerned, dogs were dogs. Until they started walking on their hind legs and talking, he didn't care who their parents were. "No."

"I looked it up on the Internet. Bred to protect the royal family in Japan. I've got two days to make a decision. Either he comes home with me, or off to doggie heaven."

He sensed that Mabel had made up her mind and just wanted some reassurance. And since it had been his idea, he figured he

124 ought to be giving it to her. But part of him wanted to see the dog first, feel its vibes. They were animals, capable of equal amounts of good and evil, and he didn't want one in Mabel's house until he felt sure it wouldn't turn on her.

"Why don't you wait until I get home," he said.

"Is your job done?"

"No, but I'm leaving tomorrow anyway."

For a moment he thought he'd been disconnected.

"You're leaving in the middle of a job?" she asked.

He took the bottle of Advil off the night table and unscrewed it. Once Joe fingered the European, he planned on turning the information over to Detective Davis and getting out of Atlantic City. Seeing Sparky Rhodes die had convinced him that it was time to pull up stakes.

"That's right," he said.

There was another pause. He popped four Advil into his mouth and swallowed them dry.

"Do you know what that Greek slimeball Nick Nicocropolis said about you?" his neighbor asked.

"No."

"He said you were the world's champion grifter catcher."

"I'm touched," Valentine said.

"Tony."

"Yes, Mabel."

"World champions don't quit."

He found himself too stunned to reply.

"There's the other line," his neighbor said. "Ta ta."

20

The Mollo Brothers

Valentine decided he was hungry.

Going outside, he spied Davis's Thunderbird parked in front of the motel. Then he saw Davis in the motel office. He was talking to the manager and looked pissed off. Valentine got into the Mercedes and turned the engine on. On the Big Band station Jerry Vale, the poor man's Sinatra, was singing "Why Do Fools Fall in Love?" *That was easy,* Valentine thought. *Because they were fools.*

Davis came out, saw him, and pointed an accusing finger. He was dressed in jeans and a black gunslinger's jacket and looked cool. Valentine envied anyone who could look cool on thirty-eight grand a year. Moments later, the detective was sitting beside him.

"There's a warrant out for your arrest," Davis said.

Valentine swallowed hard. Sparky's .38 was in his pocket. If Davis arrested him, he'd do a search, and Valentine would do jail time. He could not imagine any worse nightmare.

"I regularly look through each day's arrest warrants," the detective said. "Lady named Kat Berman says you knocked her down last night. Says she has witnesses. This ringing any bells?"

Valentine nodded.

"I'd suggest you go talk to her and get things straightened out. Okay?"

Valentine felt the air trapped in his lungs escape. The detective was letting him go. He didn't think he had a better friend in Atlantic City.

"I'll get right on it," he said.

◆

He drove to the Body Slam School of Professional Wrestling and parked by the front door. There were no groupies tonight, and he stood before the storefront window and watched a pair of well-proportioned men working on their choreography. *What a sorry way to make a buck,* he thought.

In the back, Kat was chatting with another lady wrestler. She'd brushed her hair out, and he was surprised by the effect it had on him. He put his hand on the door handle, then stopped. What, exactly, was he going to tell her? *Sorry about last night, would you mind dropping charges?* Or maybe he should be a little less direct. *How's the schnoz? Hope I didn't break it!*

He backed away from the door. Apologies had never been his strong suit. He was going to have to write something down and memorize it. Otherwise, she'd see right through him.

He drove up Atlantic Avenue and parked in front of his favorite pizzeria. When it came to being creative, he'd always worked better on a full stomach. Mario was closing as he went in, but was not above sticking two slices with anchovies and mushrooms in the oven and pouring him a Mister PiBB.

"I remember you," the pizza maker said. "You retired, went down to Florida."

"That's right. Paying the bills without me?"

"I can't complain."

"You had two boys, right? How they doing?"

"Both in college," he said proudly.

Valentine flipped through Mario's family album while the pizza maker took the slices from the oven and sprinkled both with oregano. Mario had borrowed from a loan shark to open his business, then paid off the debt at 50 percent interest, which said a lot about his pies.

"Your wife used to call in the orders," Mario said. "Louise, right?"

"Lois."

"How she doing?"

He bit into a slice. "My wife died a year and a half ago."

"I'm sorry for you," Mario said.

"Thanks," Valentine said. It was strange: After Lois had died, he'd dropped twenty pounds. Now he was talking about it with a mouth full of food.

"How's the pizza?"

"You still make the best sauce. You have a piece of paper and a pen I can borrow? I need to compose something."

Mario handed him a napkin and a pen. "You writing to a lady?"

"Yeah. An apology."

"You say something nasty to her?"

"I bloodied her nose. Now she's pressing charges. What do you think I should say?"

Mario scratched the iron stubble on his chin. "That's a tough one. Wait. I got it. You like this. 'Roses are red, violets are blue, I'm-a so sad, I smacked you.'"

He went back to closing his store, Valentine to his apology. He had a few lines written down when he felt an icy chill on his neck. Another customer had come in, and he glanced at the back counter mirror. A figure was standing behind him, glaring. Valentine slowly turned around.

It was his teacher.

♦

"You something else, Tony boy."

Valentine sat in the bucket seat of Yun's ancient Toyota Corolla, trying to figure out what he'd done to make Yun so mad. His teacher spun the wheel and he was thrown against his door.

"One of my students calls, says you beat Kat up," Yun said. "That doesn't sound like you. I think maybe something else going on. So I park down the street from the Body Slam School. Then I see you pull up. You got a date with her, huh?"

"I wanted to talk to her."

"You saw her tits, huh? Pretty nice, huh?"

"This has nothing to do with her tits."

"Watch out. Next, you making babies."

"Oh, for the love of Christ," Valentine swore.

Yun drove around for a while. Once, after a tournament in which he'd lost to an inferior opponent, Yun had driven around until the monotony had nearly sent him over the edge.

"You want my opinion?" his teacher said.

"Do I have a choice?"

"You really horny. Stay away from her, if you know what's good for you."

"Thanks for the advice."

There were only so many roads in Atlantic City, and soon they were driving past motel row. The Drake, Valentine's first motel, came into view. A black 531 BMW was parked in front. It looked like Gerry's car. A guy that was not his son was standing with his foot on the rear bumper. A big guy, his weight making the car sag.

"Pull over," Valentine said.

Yun turned down a side street and parked. At the street's end was the beach; beyond it, the churning ocean. Valentine started to get out.

"You going to explain?" Yun said.

"That's my son's car. The guy standing on the bumper is hood Big Tony Mollo. My son owes him fifty thousand bucks. Big Tony has come to collect."

"This is some son you got."

"He's the *only* son I've got," Valentine said.

"Maybe we should talk to this hood together," Yun suggested.

"You up to it?"

"I manage."

Hands in pockets, Valentine strolled up motel row. He wondered why Big Tony had come to the Drake, then remembered that he hadn't told Gerry he'd switched motels. He stopped a few feet from his son's car. Big Tony stared right through him. *Grow old*, Valentine thought, *and you grow invisible.*

Big Tony pushed himself off the bumper. About six-four and three hundred pounds, a body nurtured on garlic meatballs and lasagna and lots of grappa.

"You Gerry's old man?"

"No," Valentine said, "we just look alike."

"Very funny."

Big Tony slapped the roof of the BMW. Two guys hopped out. They appeared to be your typical Italian miscreants. One tall and very skinny, the other smaller and slightly retarded, his hair in a fifties pompadour. The family resemblance was scary.

"These are my brothers," Big Tony said. "Joey, and Little Tony. This is Gerry's old man. Guys, show Mr. Valentine what his son's been doing for the past few hours."

Joey produced a key ring and popped the trunk. Lying in back were his son and a woman Valentine assumed was Yolanda. Their mouths were covered with duct tape. Joey slammed the trunk hard.

"You're lucky I didn't kill them," Big Tony said.

"Over a marker?" Valentine said.

"I got arrested because of you," Big Tony said.

"You never been arrested before?"

"You know what happened to me in that fucking jail?"

Valentine gave it some thought. "You got buggered."

"*What?*"

"Raped, sodomized, made to give up your manhood. Am I getting warm?"

"I'm going to mutilate you," Big Tony said.

Yun had appeared by Valentine's side. His teacher had removed his overcoat and wore a baggy sweater and loose-fitting trousers. His forehead was glistening, and Valentine realized he'd been doing his warm-up. Yun walked up to Big Tony. It wasn't going to be fair, but who ever said life was?

"See if you can hit me," his teacher said.

Big Tony eyed him. "Say what?"

Yun jabbed him in the stomach. Big Tony winced.

"Come on, fat boy. Hit me."

Big Tony obliged him and threw a haymaker that started by his knee. Blocking the punch, Yun grabbed Big Tony's arm and flipped him onto the icy ground. He twisted Big Tony's arm until the big man yelped *Uncle.*

Valentine had been watching Joey, who appeared to be the more dangerous of the two brothers. Seeing Joey slip his hand into his leather jacket, Valentine stepped forward and popped him on the nose. As Joey crumpled, a strange-looking weapon clattered to the ground. Valentine picked it up. It was an old-fashioned zip gun, the barrel taped to a wood handle. He pointed the weapon at Little Tony.

"Uncle, uncle," Little Tony chorused.

Valentine walked over to where Big Tony lay on the ground.

"Promise you'll leave my son alone?"

"Okay."

"Say it."

"I promise to leave Gerry alone."

Yun let him go. Big Tony sat up and rubbed his arm. Valentine went over to where Joey lay and removed the BMW's keys from his pocket.

And though it was a cold, miserable night and Valentine's head was throbbing, seeing Gerry climb out of the trunk safe and sound made it all worthwhile. Yolanda was okay, too, a happy ending if there ever was one.

Eating dinner in a restaurant a short while later, Gerry thanked his father as only he knew how.

"For the love of Christ," his son said belligerently. *"What took you so long?"*

21

The Devil's Playthings

Valentine woke up the next morning feeling better than he had in weeks. Saving his son's neck had something to do with it, but also the realization that Mabel was right. He couldn't start quitting jobs because he got cold feet.

He did his morning exercises, then called Joe Cortez at a few minutes before eight. People who were good at what they did usually got to work early, and he found Joe at his desk.

"I think I found your blackjack cheaters," Joe said.

Valentine grinned. He loved days that started out like this.

"I was sifting through the names when I had an idea," the INS agent said. "If these cheaters were staying in New York, they'd be playing blackjack at Foxwoods or the Mohegan Sun in Connecticut. So I concentrated on foreigners with teaching visas just in Jersey. Then I looked for three males and one female traveling together, and *bingo*, there they were."

"How can you be sure it's them?"

"The girl," Cortez said. "I pulled up her passport photo on my computer. You nailed her perfectly: She looks like Audrey Hepburn. Name's Anna Ravic. Born in Belgrade, thirty-five years young."

"What's their background?"

"Bunch of Croatian eggheads with Ph.D.s in numbers. They came over in late October from Zagreb, wherever that is. They're guests of the Institute for Advanced Study at Princeton University."

133

Cortez named the other members of the gang. Juraj Havelka, Alex Havelka, who was Juraj's brother, and Rolf Pujin. Cortez had called Interpol, just to see if they were wanted or had criminal records. He'd come up empty.

"I really appreciate this," Valentine said when Joe told him he had to run.

"What are friends for," Cortez said.

Valentine had rented the room adjacent to his for Gerry and Yolanda. He tapped lightly on the door.

It was Yolanda who greeted him, wearing one of his son's long-sleeve white shirts and nothing else. She was one of those remarkable women that looked great without any makeup and her hair a screaming mess.

"You sleep any?"

She stifled a yawn. "A little."

"Hungry?"

She rubbed her eyes and grunted in the affirmative. He took out his wallet and extracted a hundred-dollar bill.

"I'm going to Princeton for a few hours," he said. "Try to stay around the motel, okay? Just in case the Mollo brothers change their minds."

She stared at the money he'd given her. Valentine didn't know much about her, except she was studying to be a doctor and was head-over-heels in love with his son. Somehow, those two facts didn't mesh, and he found himself regarding her as a dumb broad for getting mixed up with his son. She sensed this, and shot him a scornful look.

"I'm not some floozy, or whatever it is you think I am."

"Did I say that?"

"It's written all over your face."

"What?"

"Your thoughts."

"Gerry didn't tell me you were psychic. You do parties?"

"You're a jerk," she said.

"And?"

"Get lost."

She slammed the door in his face and threw the dead bolt. Valentine laughed all the way to the car. Was she insinuating that she didn't want him to come back? That was typical of her generation; they opened their mouths without thinking about the consequences.

He checked beneath the hood for explosives, then climbed in and fired up the engine. If he didn't come back, who the hell did she think was going to pay for the room?

Yolanda opened the door and stuck her head out. "He's gone. You can come out."

Gerry appeared beside her. He'd asked Yolanda to answer the door, hoping his old man would take a liking to her. Only the opposite seemed to have happened. Yolanda was livid and gave him a mean stare.

"Your old man's a prick."

"He can be nice," he said defensively.

"So what do we do now?"

That was a good question. Gerry knew what *he* wanted to do.

Have a roll in the sheets, take a hot shower, get some chow. Only Yolanda's question was more big picture. So he scratched his belly and pretended to think.

"Where's the hundred my old man gave you?"

She pulled it from her shirt pocket. Gerry tried to take it, and she steadfastly held on to a corner.

"What's the plan, Stan?" she said.

"Do you feel lucky?" he asked.

"What have you got in mind?"

"Let's go gamble," he said.

◆

Princeton was a two-hour drive made shorter by Valentine's heavy foot. The turnpike was clear, and the Mercedes' twelve-cylinder engine took a deep breath at ninety miles per hour. He was a law-abiding citizen except when it came to being on an empty highway. There he drove like a lunatic and suffered the consequences if a cop happened to be around. His late wife had scolded him for it endlessly, and he'd never listened.

He found jazz on the local public station, Dave Brubeck on a Concord summer night. When it came to the airwaves, New Jersey had the Sunshine State beat by a country mile. Back home, he could never find jazz or big band or Sinatra, the stations held hostage by shock jocks and every bad Led Zeppelin tune ever recorded. Except for ball games, he rarely tuned in.

On the hour the news came on. The lead story was from Florida. The Micanopy Indian reservation was under siege.

"Earlier today," the announcer said, "Florida's governor ordered fifty shotgun-toting agents from the Florida Department of Law Enforcement onto the Micanopy Indian Reservation in Broward County. 'Video poker must go,' the governor told a group of reporters from his mansion in Tallahassee. But the Indians are fighting back. The tribe's leader, Chief Running Bear, released dozens of alligators into the casino. According to reports, the FDLE agents have fled.

"Reaction from Indian tribes across the nation has been negative. Legally, federal agents are forbidden from entering Indian reservations. Many tribal chieftains are calling upon Washington to intervene."

The rest of the news was blather, and he tuned it out. So Archie had gotten his wish. He felt bad for the Micanopys. He'd met Running Bear at a cheating seminar he'd done in Las Vegas and had learned a little bit about the tribe's history. They'd been treated like doormats for centuries, and he sensed they were about to get the short end of the stick once again.

A road sign said PRINCETON, 60 MILES. His foot challenged the accelerator, and he watched the speedometer creep past a hundred miles per hour.

◆

Princeton University is in the center of New Jersey, the hilly landscape thick with hundred-year-old oaks and a history of higher education. The university's campus is as big as a large town, and he had to stop twice to ask for directions.

He pulled into a spot in front of the Institute for Advanced Studies and killed the engine. The mathematics department, for which the university was world renowned, resided here, and he watched a group of students walk by. He'd never made it to college and had always regretted it. Not that being a cop hadn't been an education, but all of its lessons had come the hard way.

He went inside. A bulletin board in the foyer announced the

day's seminars. In Lecture Hall 1, physics of oscillatory integrals. In Hall 2, vorticity in the Ginzburg-Landau model of superconductivity. Hall 3, geometric analysis of Chow-Mumford. You needed a degree just to understand the language. Walking into an office, he found a receptionist sitting behind a desk, filling out a form on an old-fashioned typewriter. Looking up, she said, "Can I help you?"

"I'm looking for a visiting professor named Juraj Havelka. He's here as a guest of the mathematics department."

She thumbed through a log of visiting professors. Valentine leaned over the desk, reading the upside down page she stopped at. One line caught his eyes. Juraj's sponsor was a teacher named Peter Diamondis.

"Sorry," the receptionist said. "But he left last fall."

"Did he leave a forwarding address?

"I'm afraid not."

Back in the foyer, he consulted the teacher list tacked to the bulletin board. Dr. Peter Diamondis, head of the probability department, was in Fine Hall, Room 408. He asked a student for directions and was soon hiking across campus.

Fine Hall was what a college building was supposed to look like. Six-story, redbrick, with ivy-covered walls. Every student that passed through its doors was weighted down with books. Going inside, he took the stairs to the fourth floor.

The climb got his heart racing. Room 408 was at the end of a cavernous hallway. He tapped on the frosted glass door, then stuck his head in. "Dr. Diamondis?"

Diamondis sat hunched over a PC. He reminded Valentine of the absent-minded professors from the old Disney movies. A scholarly type in his late fifties with pince-nez glasses, his hair resembling cyclone fencing. Above his desk hung a photograph of Albert Einstein sticking his tongue out.

"Yes?"

"I was wondering if I could speak to you."

Valentine entered with his business card in his hand. The professor put the card under his nose and scrunched up his face. "Tony Valentine. Your company is called Grift Sense. What's that?"

"I'm a private consultant for the gaming industry."

"May I ask in what capacity?"

"I help catch crossroaders."

"Is that any relation to cross-dressing?"

"They're miles apart. May I sit down?"

"I have a class in twenty minutes."

"It shouldn't take that long."

"Be my guest."

Valentine took the chair across from the desk and unbuttoned his overcoat. "Crossroaders are thieves who specialize in ripping off casinos. It's a big business—about a hundred million a year in Las Vegas alone."

"And you catch these people?"

"Yes. I can sense when things aren't right on a casino floor and I just take it from there."

"Grift sense."

"That's what hustlers call it."

"You must be very good."

Valentine nodded that he was.

"And you've come to see me because of my work on cheating at blackjack?"

Valentine hesitated. He'd read just about everything written on hustling blackjack, and Diamondis's name didn't ring any bells. But sometimes it was better to keep your mouth shut and play along, so he nodded his head. He was rewarded when Diamondis removed a deck of playing cards from his desk.

◆

"Take out the cards and shuffle them," the professor said.

Valentine broke the seal on a fresh pack of Bees, the cards used at hundreds of casinos around the world. He gave them a cursory exam; no marks, crimps, or shaved ends.

"Do it this way," Diamondis instructed him. "Riffle-shuffle, then cut, then riffle-shuffle, cut again, then riffle-shuffle and cut again. As I'm sure you're aware, this is the same shuffling sequence used by most casinos in the country."

Valentine shuffled as instructed. He kept the cards tight to the table the way a dealer would, with none of the faces being exposed. Finished, he handed the deck to his host. Diamondis declined with a shake of the head.

"I don't want to touch them," he said. "You deal."

Valentine hesitated. Had he missed something?

"What are we playing?" Valentine asked.

"Blackjack."

"How many hands?"

"Four. The fourth will be yours, the others mine."

Diamondis cleared a space on the cluttered desk. Valentine dealt three blackjack hands to Diamondis, one for himself. The professor played his hands, busting on two, winning one.

"Now," Diamondis said, "would you say that everything is aboveboard, or to use the gambling lexicon, on the square?"

"I would."

"Good. On the next round, would you be suspicious if I decided to bet heavily on my hands? This is a hypothetical question, of course."

Valentine thought about it. He'd started with a new deck and handled the cards throughout. If Diamondis had rigged the game, he was at a loss to explain how.

"How heavily?" he asked.

"Say, five thousand dollars a hand."

"Yeah, I'd be suspicious."

"But you wouldn't know why, would you?"

"No."

"This time, deal five hands," his host said.

Valentine did so, sensing that he'd been led down the garden path. The professor turned his hands over. He had a twenty, a blackjack, a nineteen, and a sixteen, which he drew a card on, and busted. Valentine flipped his own hand over. He had a seventeen. Had they been in a casino, Diamondis would have won twelve thousand five hundred dollars.

Valentine stared at the professor's cards. Three of his hands contained aces. Juraj had drawn a lot of aces as well. In blackjack, aces were the magic cards, and gave a player a 500 percent better chance of beating the house.

The professor stuffed a pipe with tobacco and fired up the bowl, thoroughly enjoying himself.

"Do it again," Valentine said.

♦

Valentine got burned the second time as well, but on the third go around the proverbial lightbulb went off in his head. It was the shuffle. Diamondis was having him shuffle the deck the same way *every* time, just like casino dealers did. It was predictable, which had allowed the professor to devise a formula to track how cards descended in the deck.

The professor thumped his desk. "Very good! You know, I have several graduate students who spent weeks trying to figure it out. I don't suppose you have a degree in mathematics?"

"Atlantic City High, class of '56."

"I'll be sure to tell my students that."

"I'm confused about one thing," Valentine said.

"And what is that?"

"No dealer shuffles the same. How do you know when the cards you want will come up?"

"I cheat," Diamondis said, puffing away.

"How do you do that?"

The professor grinned. He obviously enjoyed putting one over on a pro. "I have two methods. If the deck is new, the cards are in perfect order. I simply look for the cards which come before the aces. For example: The king of spades proceeds the ace of diamonds in a new deck. So, when the king of spades appears, I know the ace of diamonds is right around the corner.

"Now, if the cards are mixed, my job is tougher. The deck has to be played, and I must memorize the cards which come before the aces. These cards act as my cues."

"But you don't know *exactly* when the aces will come out," Valentine said. "You're still having to guess."

"I offset any miscalculations by playing multiple hands," the professor said. "By playing four hands, I ensure the aces will come to me. And since aces often produce blackjacks, I often get a better payout." The professor glanced at his watch. "I need to run."

"Did you ever try this out? I mean, in a casino?"

"Of course."

"How much did you win?"

"A few hundred dollars. I'm not much of a gambler."

A bell rang and a hundred pairs of shoes clattered noisily past the office. Shoving papers into a battered leather satchel, Diamondis headed for the door. Valentine grabbed his overcoat off the back of his chair and followed him.

They joined the throng of students in the stairwell and descended to the first floor. The professor entered an oval-shaped lecture hall that was quickly filling with students. Climbing onto the stage, he put his satchel down beside the podium. Valentine was right behind him. "One more question. Your system is limited to dealers who break the cards dead center and riffle evenly."

"A colleague posed the same problem to me," Diamondis replied, checking the podium's microphone. "So I devised a schematic for all known blackjack shuffles. It requires some mental gymnastics, but it works."

Was his name Juraj Havelka? Valentine nearly asked, but thought he knew the answer.

"I published my findings last year," the professor said. "Would you like a copy?"

"I'd be honored."

Diamondis removed a stapled manuscript from his satchel and handed it to him. *The Devil's Playthings. A Mathematical Examination of Riffle Shuffles, their Cycles and Descents.* Several students had approached the podium, trying to get his attention. Valentine slipped the manuscript under his arm. "Thanks for being so generous with your time."

"Good luck catching whoever you're trying to catch," the professor said.

Valentine tried to hide his surprise. "Who said I was trying to catch someone?"

A smile flickered across the professor's otherwise serious countenance. "It's what you do for a living, isn't it?"

22

True Love

It had taken Gerry five minutes to squander his father's hundred bucks in The Bombay's casino.

Luckily, Yolanda hadn't seen him do it. She'd gone to play Funny Money, convinced that she'd duplicate her sister's good fortune and win a brand new car.

Gerry had lost his father's money playing keno. According to a tent card on the bar, keno was an ancient Chinese game, and had been used by the Chinese government to pay for the Great Wall. What the card didn't say was that it was a game for suckers, the house advantage an astonishing 35 percent.

Sitting at the bar, Gerry had bought a ticket, called a blank, from a cute runner in a miniskirt. Using a crayon, he picked ten numbers from the eighty on the blank, then gave the runner the blank and his money. Going to the keno lounge next door, the runner gave the blank to the keno writer who recorded the wager, then returned to the bar and handed Gerry the duplicate.

And stared at him.

Gerry squirmed. Taking fifty cents off the bar that another patron had left, he handed it to her.

"Good luck," she said icily.

He sat and waited. And dreamed of winning the jackpot.

A buzzer went off, signaling the winning numbers were being drawn. He stared at the electronic keno board above the bar. *Yes, yes, yes!* he thought, getting the first three right. Visions of Italian sports cars and Rolex watches filled his head. Then, *No, no, no!*, the last seventeen numbers betraying him like a jilted lover, his father's hundred gone in a blink of an eye. He tore up the worthless blank.

A man entered the bar and came toward him. His nose was zig-zagged by white adhesive tape, his eyes ringed black. Gerry got off his stool.

"Get lost."

"I want to show you something," Joey Mollo said.

Gerry followed him across the casino to the front doors. A veil of snow had dusted the cars in the parking lot. A black Lincoln blinked its lights. Gerry stared. Big Tony and Little Tony sat in the two front seats. Sandwiched between them was Yolanda. Her eyes were filled with fear.

My old man is gonna kill me, he thought.

◆

Valentine drove back to Atlantic City in an hour and a half, the New Jersey highway patrol cruisers conveniently parked on the other side of the turnpike. He sang with the radio most of the way, a hot wire igniting his blood.

Rarely did cheaters come up with new ways to beat the house. In twenty years he'd seen it only a handful of times. Yet Juraj Havelka—with Peter Diamondis's aid—had done just that. And he'd added a clever twist. Juraj was never at the blackjack table very long, which meant Anna was tracking the aces. When the deck was primed, she signaled for Juraj to come over. That way, Juraj drew no heat. A perfectly orchestrated scam.

No wonder no one had caught on.

♦

Archie Tanner was hurling things off his desk at the giant screen TV in his office when Valentine walked in a short while later. Cowering behind him were Gigi, Monique, and Brandi. Today's color was blue, and the three women wore matching Chanel outfits. They appeared ready to flee at any moment.

Valentine glanced at the screen. CNN was showing highlights of Indian uprisings taking place around the country. In a rare showing of unity, tribes from Connecticut to California had vowed to expel U.S. government officials from their land if the Micanopys were not given their casino back. The governor of Florida had issued a terse statement, vowing to remain firm.

"Fucking redskin tribal leaders haven't spoken to each other in two hundred fucking years," Archie roared. "Now, they're rallying around the totem pole because Chief Running Bear is defying whitey!"

Valentine fielded a paperclip holder as it flew past. "We need to talk," he told the irate casino owner.

Archie nearly came over the desk at him. "For Christ's sake, can't you see I'm busy?" Doing a one-eighty in his chair, he faced the three woman standing behind him. "I want you to call the TV stations and threaten to pull my ads if they don't stop running this Chief Running Bear horseshit."

The women looked stunned. It was Brandi who found the courage to answer him. "You mean the New Jersey stations?"

"I mean the national stations. NBC, CBS, ABC, CNN, Fox."

"But Archie, we *can't* do that."

"Don't *ever* use that word around me."

Her face darkened. "We *shouldn't*."

"Why the hell not?"

"Because we'll create a *worse* public relations nightmare."

"You think so?"

Brandi nodded. The casino owner shifted his gaze to Gigi and

Monique to see what they were thinking. Both women nodded their heads in agreement.

"You want to wait tables at Sinbad's? Or deal blackjack? Or do one of the hundred other crummy fucking jobs that pay minimum wage in this casino?"

The question was aimed at all three of them. Wisely, Brandi shook her head no, as did Gigi and Monique.

"Then make the fucking call."

Eyes downcast, the women walked out of the room. Stopping at the door, Brandi glanced over her shoulder. "Are you sure about this?"

"You'd look good in one of those little keno runner skirts," Archie told her.

The pirate's door rattled on its hinges. Picking up the remote on the desk, Archie jacked up the TV's volume. CNN's Wolf Blitzer was interviewing Chief Running Bear from his hideaway in the Florida Everglades. Running Bear wore camouflage fatigues and appeared ready for a long haul.

Valentine stood with his jacket in his hand, waiting. Finally Archie looked up at him.

"Can't this wait?" the casino owner asked.

"Not really."

"Tell one of the girls about it," he said, staring at the TV.

◆

Valentine nearly told Archie to go to hell. Only this was a job, and he intended to finish it, just like any other job. He walked into the reception area and saw Brandi waiting for the elevator. He touched her sleeve.

"Archie said I should talk to you," he said.

"Okay," she said.

They went downstairs to Sinbad's and found an empty booth
in the back.

"It's real simple," Valentine explained after they'd been served. "Your blackjack dealers need to shuffle the cards more. Five times should do the trick. The cards will be closer to a random order, and your tables will be safe from anyone tracking the cards during the shuffle."

"Is this a new method of cheating?"

"It sure is," he said.

Brandi smiled, clearly impressed. She'd ordered a cup of herbal tea and now spooned in a teaspoon of honey. "I'm sure Archie would have appreciated hearing this, if he wasn't so pre-occupied."

"I'm sure he would have," he said.

"This will cost the casino money, though."

"How's that?"

"The extra shuffles. Anything that slows a game down costs the casino money. That's how Archie sees it, anyway."

"Look at it as insurance," Valentine said.

She blew the steam off her drink and Valentine found himself staring at her. She was beautiful, but it was a beauty that struck him as unique. High cheekbones, flawless skin, perfect teeth. She was almost regal. Had he known her a little better, he would have asked where she was from and tried to figure out the bloodlines.

"Why do you put up with him?" he asked.

She put her drink down. "Do you always say what's on your mind?"

"Usually."

"Well, it's a long story."

"Those are my favorite kind."

"Why do you care?"

"You seem like a nice kid."

"And Archie's a prick, right? Okay, well here it is in a nutshell. I worked the front desk for three years, then graduated up to accounting. I came into contact with Archie a lot. We hit it off."

"You're kidding," he said without thinking.

The remark didn't faze her. "Archie's a powerful man, charming when he wants to be. I come from mixed parents, so the idea of having a relationship with him didn't bother me."

"Oh," he said.

"One night, Archie called me up to the penthouse, said he needed to see a report. I brought it, and he asked me out to dinner. That's how it started."

"It must be serious," he said.

"That's a very old-fashioned expression."

"I'm an old-fashioned guy."

Undoing the top button on her blouse, Brandi tugged on a gold chain hanging around her neck. Valentine stared at the diamond engagement ring hanging from it, the stone bigger than most of his teeth.

"Archie promised to marry me after the deal in Florida is done."

"Congratulations," he said.

She slipped the chain back into her blouse. "You've known Archie a long time, haven't you?"

Too long, he nearly said. "Yes."

"Could you see it? Him and me?"

Sure, he thought. Thugs like Archie Tanner married smart, attractive younger women like Brandi all the time. It was called the halo effect. It made them look good to the public.

"I sure can," he replied.

Her face melted into a beautiful smile.

"Thank you, Mr. Valentine."

"You're welcome."

He removed his overcoat from the back of his chair and got up from the table. "Tell Archie I'll send him my bill."

"I know he appreciates everything you've done," she said.

"I'm sure he does," he replied.

23

Shaft, The First Version

Valentine couldn't believe it: Gerry and Yolanda were gone. He knocked on the door to his son's hotel room again, just to be sure. Then saw the hand-written note lying on the ground. Kneeling, he picked it up.

Went to catch a dream. Back by 6.

"You dope," Valentine said. He heard the phone ringing in his room as he unlocked the door. There was only one person he felt like talking to right now, and that was Mabel. Taking a chance, he answered the phone and was rewarded by the sound of her cheerful voice.

"You're going to be so proud of me," she said.

"What did you do?"

"I solved my first case."

He made the bed sag and unbuttoned his coat.

"Tell me."

"Well, you got a FedEx package this morning marked URGENT, so I figured I better open it. Inside was a letter from a joint in Laughlin, Nevada, called Lucky Lill's, and a check for two hundred dollars. Lill wrote the letter herself. She sounded desperate."

Valentine couldn't help but smile. Mabel had called the place a joint. Casinos with names like Lucky Lill's *were* joints. His neighbor was learning the business fast.

"I know two hundred dollars is below your minimum fee, but you know how I am about money. So I figured maybe I could help her. Lill's husband died a few months ago and left the casino to her. Lill doesn't know much about gambling. She sent a surveillance tape of three Asian men who beat her for five thousand dollars at blackjack. I watched the tape for hours and figured out they were card counting."

"You sure?"

"I'm positive."

"How?"

"One of the books in your library said that the best way to spot card counters is by bet fluctuation, so I wrote down how the Asians bet. Any time they quadrupled their bets, I got suspicious. I wrote down the time showing on the surveillance tape, then rewound it and played the tape back. Then I wrote down which cards came out of the shoe. They were all high-valued. Which meant they were counting."

There were easier ways to spot counters, but Mabel's method would do in a pinch. She was right: He was proud of her.

"You tell Lill this?"

"I most certainly did. She was most appreciative."

"Congratulations," he said.

"I assume you've decided to stay in Atlantic City and finish your job."

"I have. Thanks for the pep talk yesterday."

"You're welcome. One last thing. Detective Davis called about an hour ago. He said if you didn't call him by three o'clock, he was going to track you down and have you arrested. I assume he's joking."

"Of course he's joking." He glanced at his watch. It was a quarter till three. What had he done wrong now? He started to sign off, then said, "You did good, kid."

"You think I have a future?"

"I sure do," he said.

◆

He called Davis on his cell phone and caught the detective driving in his car. Davis did not sound happy. They agreed to meet at the IHOP.

Ten minutes later Valentine pulled into the vacant lot and parked. Locking the .38 in the glove compartment, he went inside.

Dottie, his least favorite waitress, was manning the register, an impossibly long ash dangling from her cigarette. He'd never come back for his change, and he stopped at the counter.

"Remember me?"

"Nope."

"I was in the other day with my son. I gave you a hundred-dollar bill for breakfast; you said you didn't have any change. Told me to come back later."

"Wasn't me," Dottie said.

"Sure it was."

"Look mister . . ."

"I want my change," he said irritably. "The meal was nine bucks. Add a buck tip, and you owe me ninety dollars."

"I'm telling you, it wasn't me."

Valentine could tell where this was going. He should have come back immediately and not let Dottie write him off. In the back counter mirror he saw Davis's Thunderbird pull in. The detective came through the front door with a stern look on his face, his designer shades vanishing into his breast pocket. He was wearing hip-hugger jeans and a black leather jacket and looked just like he'd stepped off a movie set. Valentine motioned him over.

"Dottie, this is my friend Eddie."

"Hi," she said stiffly.

"Hello, Dottie," the detective said.

"Dottie and I have a little disagreement," Valentine said, "which you could settle by showing her your credentials."

"Excuse me?"

"Your badge."

Davis flipped open his wallet and stuck his silver detective's badge in the mean-spirited woman's face. Dottie changed colors, her waxy cheeks glowing red. Davis kept the badge out, and Valentine sensed that he was enjoying himself. Maybe he'd come in for coffee once and Dottie had been slow serving him. Or hadn't bothered serving him at all. That kind of crap went on every day in America.

"So what do you think?" Valentine asked her.

The NO SALE flag appeared on the register. Dottie counted ninety dollars into his waiting palm. Valentine handed her two dollars back. "Two coffees, when you get a chance."

"I hope she's not in the back pissing in our cups," Davis said as they slid into the farthest booth from the counter. "I've seen that one before."

"Why don't you ask her?" Valentine suggested.

"You're just filled with good ideas, you know that?"

Their coffee came, Dottie bringing giant mugs and pouring from a fresh pot, treating them like normal customers. Davis spooned cream and sugar into his mug, then said, "I thought you told me yesterday you were going to apologize to Kat Berman."

So that was what this was about. Feeling relieved, Valentine said, "I got sidetracked."

"Well, she called the station this morning. The call got transferred to me. I told her we'd spoken, and how sorry you were. I *promised* her I'd find you and get you to apologize."

Davis was starting to grow on him. He said, "Did she give you a number where I can reach her?"

"You're not getting off that easy," Davis said.

"What do you mean?"

"I called her ten minutes ago and told her I was meeting you here. She'll be by soon. You can apologize to her in person."

Valentine's cheeks grew warm. He felt like he was six years old and his mother had just scolded him. "I really appreciate this, Eddie."

"I bet you do. So here's what I want in return." Taking a piece of paper from his leather jacket, he unfolded it, and slid it across the table. "The lab boys put Doyle's notebook through an ESDA machine yesterday. The machine detected an impression of a page that had been torn out. It was a note Doyle had written to his brother, Tom. Take a look."

Valentine slipped his bifocals on. The ESDA machine made a copy that looked like a bad Xerox, and he had to squint.

Tom,

Sorry for the blow-up yesterday at lunch,
but this Bombay investigation has made me
a nervous wreck. So many of my friends seem
to be involved. I still don't know what to do.
Thanks for lending a sympathetic ear.

Doyle

Davis leaned forward and lowered his voice. "If I'm reading this note right, it seems that Doyle discovered another scam at The Bombay, one where employees were involved. Normally, I'd go and lean on Tom Flanagan and find out what Doyle told him. However, since you were tight with Doyle, I figure you might be able to get him to open up."

Valentine put his bifocals away, then slid the note back to the detective. "The scam Doyle is referring to involved slots. A lot of employees were in on it, probably a whole shift. But it never came off."

Davis sat up very straight. "Say what?"

"I spoke to Liddy Flanagan about it. She said Doyle spoke to the auditors at the Division of Gaming Enforcement, and the Casino Control Commission. They monitor the take on The Bombay's slot machines every week. And the auditors said the take was normal."

"So what happened?"

Valentine chose his words carefully. He hated guessing, but in this case, he had no choice. "My gut says Doyle stumbled onto the scam right as it was about to happen. The employees got scared and backed off."

"You don't think the employees killed Doyle to keep him quiet, do you?"

Valentine shook his head. "Doyle had a lot of friends at The Bombay. But I'll tell you this: Every one of them probably pissed in their pants when Doyle got killed."

"Thinking they'd get blamed," Davis said.

"Exactly."

The detective grew silent. Then said, "We're talking about what, a hundred employees who must have known about this."

"At least."

"People in the cage, security people, chip people, dealers. A lot of lives ruined if I decide to keep digging."

"A lot of lives."

Davis finished his coffee. Conspiracy to defraud a casino was a serious crime in New Jersey. But Valentine had a feeling the people involved had learned a lesson. Like Doyle, he had a lot of friends at The Bombay, and he did not want to see them go to jail for a crime that had never come off.

"Let it go, Eddie," he told the detective.

♦

Their check came. Davis was taking his wallet out when his eyes flew out the window. He whistled through his teeth. "As I live and breathe. What do we have here?"

Valentine followed his wolfish gaze. A navy Saturn had parked in the IHOP lot, and a knockout of a woman was getting out. He slipped his bifocals back on. It was Kat Berman.

"That's her," Valentine said.

"That's the woman you knocked down?"

Davis's eyes were dancing, the juices flowing to places they hadn't been flowing before. They both stood up as Kat entered the restaurant and approached their table. She was wearing makeup and had brushed out her mane of hair, the effect strong enough to make Valentine catch his breath.

"So let's hear it," she said, looking straight at Valentine.

"I want to apologize," he mumbled.

"So do it!" she snapped.

"I'm sorry about the other night. I was out of line."

She crossed her arms. "That's pretty lame."

"I'm *really* sorry," he said, feeling like an idiot.

"That's a little better."

"From the bottom of my heart."

"Much better." She glanced at Davis. "Hello."

The detective was grinning like a kid at his first school dance. "How you doing," he said cleverly.

She looked at Valentine. "Would you mind?"

"Mind what?"

"Introducing us."

Valentine was not used to having his tongue tied in knots. This woman was having a strange effect on him. He said, "Kat Berman, I'd like you to meet Richard Roundtree."

"Nice to meet you, Richard."

Davis stared at Valentine like he'd lost his mind.

"Who?"

"What did I say?"

"Richard Roundtree . . ."

Kat was laughing. "You know, you look just like him."

"Who?" the detective said.

"Richard Roundtree," they both said.

Davis was fuming, any potential for magic reduced to a shambles. He shot a murderous glance at Valentine, who busied himself staring at the floor.

"I need to run," the detective said. "It was nice meeting you, Kat."

"Nice meeting you, Richard," she giggled.

Valentine walked Davis to his Thunderbird. He put his hand on the younger man's arm and got the cold shoulder. "Hey look, I'm really sorry. I think it has something to do with growing old. Not all the neurons connecting."

Davis murmured something unpleasant under his breath, then got into the car. A moment later the window rolled down, his profile a study in constraint.

"You are one cagey old man," he said.

And before Valentine could ask him what he meant, the detective gunned the ancient engine and drove away.

24

Deal

Valentine slid into the booth, his seat still warm. Kat had slipped out of her leather jacket and was wearing a clingy black turtleneck that accented every vivacious curve. Dottie appeared with menus and a smug look on her face.

"Nice trade," she said.

When she was gone, Kat said, "She a friend of yours?"

"She tried to steal some money from me."

"You say the strangest things, you know that?"

He shrugged. "You mind my asking you a question?" When she didn't object, he said, "How did you get into the wrestling racket?"

It took Kat ten minutes to tell him her story. What it boiled down to was pretty simple: After she'd gotten canned from The Bombay, she'd gone looking for work and found that no other casino in town would touch her. The only other jobs she'd found were demeaning—stripping off her clothes, giving horny guys massages, or being a cocktail waitress and flirting for tips. So she'd taken up wrestling.

"One day, I saw an ad in the paper," she said. " 'Learn to wrestle, earn good money.' So I went and enrolled. And I was good. None of the other girls could touch me. It was my trainer's idea to wear the judo uniform. He thought I needed a gimmick, only I couldn't afford a costume. I had my uniform, so Judo Queen was born. Everyone tells me it sounds Japanese. You think I could pass as Japanese?"

Valentine had not taken his eyes off her. She wanted some-thing—women this beautiful did not talk to old guys with hair in their ears unless they wanted something—so he threw her a curve ball, just to see how she reacted.

"I guess there are a couple of women in Japan who have a body like yours."

She laughed out loud, then reached across the table and squeezed his arm. He remembered the electricity he'd felt the day before when she'd poked him, and he felt it again now.

"Do you say whatever's on your mind?"

"I think it's called being retired."

"If you don't mind my asking, how old are you?"

"Sixty-two."

"You're in some shape for sixty-two."

"You're sweet," he said.

Kat put her hand over her mouth, the laughter seeping out anyway. Dottie appeared, and they both said no to more coffee. Then they sat for a while, saying nothing. He saw Kat gaze dream-ily out the window and realized she was staring at the Mercedes.

"Want to go for a spin?"

"I thought you'd never ask."

◆

The Mercedes impressed her, but what impressed her more was that it belonged to Archie Tanner. Valentine wanted to tell her that he'd known Archie since he'd sold bootleg cigarettes out of the trunk of his car, but he didn't think it would win him any points. Archie was a local boy made good, and Jersey folks were passionate about loving their own. He found Sinatra on the dial doing a duet with Julio Iglesias. Kat hummed along, in heaven.

"I asked around about you," she said when they were sitting at a light. "Yun's prized pupil. I also heard you're an ex-cop, and wired in the casino business."

Valentine didn't know how wired he was, but decided to play along, just to see where she was going. "That's right."

"I need your help," she said.

The light changed and he gently tapped the accelerator.

"I've got a cop who's stalking me," she went on. "Name's Vic Marconi. Last summer, while I was working at The Bombay, I heard about a scam some employees were hatching. The ringleaders were over in Saudi Arabia during Desert Storm. Real gung-ho types. I was dating Vic at the time, so I told him. Vic and his partner found out who the employees were and put the muscle on them."

"Marconi told you that?"

Kat nodded. "He's in love with me."

"Oh," he said.

"Not long after that, I got canned. It took me a while to put the two together, but I guess the Desert Storm gang decided I was a threat. Vic told me not to worry about it. He said he and Coleman had joined the gang, and he was going to make enough money to take care of me for the rest of my life. I told him I didn't want any part of it and broke the relationship off."

The island of Atlantic City was only thirteen miles long, and Valentine had reached the northern tip and parked in a lot for Captain Starn's Pier. The slips were empty, the sleek yachts and cabin cruisers having migrated south for the winter. "And that's when Vic started stalking you."

"Yes."

"Have you filed a complaint?"

"With the police? No. Vic's a scary dude."

"How so?"

"Remember all those drug dealers that got robbed and killed a few years back? Vic told me he and Coleman did it."

Valentine tapped his fingers on the wheel. It sounded like the kind of boast a dumb cop might make. Because the casinos provided so much revenue to the state of New Jersey, Atlantic City cops were expected to be model citizens. With a few well placed phone calls, Valentine was certain he could either have Marconi demoted or out on the street looking for work.

"I'll make you a deal," he said. "I'll get Marconi to leave you alone, but I want something in return."

Kat shifted uncomfortably in her seat. Then she looked around the car, like seeing if there was someplace she could run to, if she didn't like what Valentine was offering.

"I'm listening," she said.

"Take the sacred crane off your uniform," he said.

It took a moment for the words to sink in.

"Is that all you want?" she asked.

"That's all I ever wanted," Valentine said.

◆

"Yun was the father I never had," he explained, driving down Pacific Avenue as he took Kat back to her car. "He took me under his wing, taught me a lot besides just judo. Seeing him down in the dumps the other day, it made me realize how much I owed him."

"I understand," Kat said.

He drove past motel row. The Blue Dolphin came into view, the sidewalks ankle-deep in snow. Gerry's black BMW was parked in front, just like he'd told his knuckleheaded son not to do. He swore under his breath.

162

"What's wrong?"

"My son. I need to stop for a second, if that's okay."

"Sure."

He pulled onto a side street and parked in front of the manager's office. "This will just take a second," he said.

Kat stayed in the car. Valentine walked down the path to his son's room. The motel was deserted, and he was about to knock on Gerry's door when he saw a plastic cigarette wrapper lying in the snow. His son didn't smoke and neither did his girlfriend. An alarm went off in his head.

"What's up?" the manager asked, turning down the portable TV on his desk as Valentine came into the office.

Valentine made a sawbuck appear. "I'd like you to call my son's room, tell him there's a package for him out front."

Pocketing the money, the manager made the call.

"Now call the police," Valentine said.

The manager scowled. "I don't want no trouble."

"Then make the call."

Valentine hid in the snow-covered bushes beside the path. Moments later, a bandaged Joey Mollo strolled past, heading for the manager's office. Stepping onto the path, Valentine kicked Joey's legs out from under him. Joey hit the ground hard. Valentine offered his hand, and as Joey took it, punched him in the face.

He marched down the path. The door to Gerry's room was ajar and he stuck his head in. His son and girlfriend sat in the room's center, roped to a pair of chairs. The Mollos had taped their mouths shut and tied bricks to their feet, like they planned to drown them.

Valentine heard a rustling behind him, then a woman's muffled cry. He turned to see Big Tony holding Kat in a headlock. In his other hand was a bag from Burger King.

"This must be my lucky day," Big Tony said. "I go to get some lunch, and I find this lovely lady sitting in your car."

"You need help?" he asked Kat.

"No," she said through clenched teeth.

She stomped on Big Tony's instep, then slipped free of his headlock. Grabbing the big man's wrist, she give it a twist, and he let out a yelp.

"Hey, lady," he whined, twisting in agony. "I didn't mean nothing, honest."

"Really?" she asked.

"Yeah," he said.

Kat kicked him in the balls. He doubled over, and she brought her knee into his face. Big Tony's eyes rolled up into his head, and he fell onto the frozen lawn with a deadening *Whumph!*

Valentine entered his son's room, and Little Tony jumped out from his hiding place behind the door. There was something clutched in his hand—a small knife or a blackjack—and as Valentine socked him in the jaw and sent him flying into the bathroom, the weapon fell from his fingers. Valentine picked it up. It was a blue Pez dispenser.

Valentine untied his son and fiancée. Yolanda let out a pitiful sob as the duct tape was pulled from her mouth. Valentine knelt down beside her.

"He *touched* me," she whispered.

Valentine stared at her chest. Her blouse was ripped open, her left breast hanging out. The skin looked scratched and raw. "Who did this?" he asked.

She started to cry. Gerry put his arm around her shoulder, and told her everything was going to be all right.

"Who did this?" Valentine demanded.

His son looked at him. He'd been slapped around pretty good, his cheeks puffy and discolored. "It was Big Tony. He fondled her right in front of me."

164

Valentine made Gerry open his mouth. His teeth were all there. He and Lois had nearly gone broke having braces put on them. Then he marched outside.

Big Tony was on the lawn on all fours, trying to reconnect with gravity. Kat hovered over him.

"Hey, stupid," Valentine said.

Big Tony lifted his head and gave him a blank stare, like he couldn't remember who Valentine was. A glimmer of recognition spread across his bovine features.

"What . . ?" he mumbled.

"Why'd you do it?"

"Do what?"

"Mess with the girl."

Big Tony spit contemptuously on the ground.

"Because she's a whore," he said.

Valentine stepped on his hand.

25

Call Me Dad

There were a lot of drawbacks to having a criminal record. In most states, you couldn't get a liquor license or vote in an election. If your crime was serious, you couldn't drive a car or work as a civil servant or sit on a jury or run for office. You became persona non grata, at least to the government.

Another drawback was that you couldn't have a serious conversation with a cop. Having a record meant you were criminal—even if you'd paid your debt to society and had been a model citizen ever since—and that made you an enemy in the eyes of the law.

Which was why his son didn't press charges when the police showed up a short time later. Although Gerry's rap sheet was nothing serious—an arrest for bookmaking, and a bust for marijuana when he was a dopey teenager—it was enough to paint a picture to a streetwise cop that he was no choirboy. Which meant the Mollos would get a chance to present their side of the story, namely that Gerry owed them fifty big ones. And, since New Jersey didn't have a problem with people collecting debts—the casinos went out of state to collect markers all the time—his son might find himself in court.

Standing on the curb to Atlantic Avenue, Valentine watched the Mollos drive away in a black Lincoln, its rear slung low to the ground. Their first stop, he guessed, would be a hospital emergency room. Then back on the prowl. Guys like this didn't learn their lesson; they kept coming back until you did something drastic to

stop them.

He stepped into the manager's office. The manager was working on a bottle of Johnny Walker, his eyes riveted to the portable TV on his desk.

"We're at war," he announced.

Valentine came around the desk. The TV was filled with shotgun-toting FDLE agents inside the Micanopy Indian Reservation Casino. Dead alligators were strewn about, some flopped on felt gaming tables, others belly-up on the roulette wheel, all shot in the head, oozing blood.

"Gators are an endangered species," the manager said. "Government broke its own damn laws."

"Did they nab Running Bear?"

"He's still hiding in the swamps."

Valentine dropped a twenty on the counter. "If those thugs show up again, call my room, will you?"

The manager pocketed the money. "I'll keep an eye out for them. I like the way that girl of yours handles herself."

Valentine was taken aback. *That girl of his?* What did the manager think, that Kat was his daughter?

"Me, too," he replied.

◆

Gerry was pacing his motel room like a caged animal.

"They'll be back," his son said. "You know that, don't you?"

Valentine sat down on the bed beside Yolanda. She seemed to be doing better, her toughness coming through once the initial shock of being molested had worn off. He took her hand with both of his. "I'm really sorry I was such a flaring jerk this morning."

She smiled faintly. "You made up for it this afternoon."

"You going to be okay?"

"I'll live."

He saw Kat glance at her watch, then make a face and grab her jacket off a chair. "I've got to go pick up my daughter from school. It's been nice meeting you folks."

Valentine walked her out to the sidewalk in front of the motel. The wind was blowing off the ocean mean and cold, and he draped his overcoat over her shoulders.

"Thanks," she murmured.

"Hey," he said, "thanks for helping out."

"You ever been to a wrestling show before?" she asked.

He had, as a kid, and hated every minute of it. The sight of big flabby guys in tights with monikers like Pretty Boy Williams and Mr. Wonderful was so repulsive to his childhood sensibilities that he'd asked his old man to take him home.

"Years ago," he said.

"Like it?"

"I had a great time."

"I'm wrestling at the Armory tomorrow night. Show starts at eight. I go on at nine-thirty."

"I'll be there," he heard himself say.

A checkered cab turned onto Pacific and he waved it down. Kat handed him his overcoat and got in. She lowered her window, and he knelt down so their faces were inches apart.

"I like the way you fight," she told him.

She closed her eyes, and Valentine realized she wanted to be kissed. Smooching the same woman for forty-five years had taken some of the thrill out of it, and he let his lips linger longer than he should have. She didn't seem to mind. Standing, he watched the vehicle head north until it had been swallowed up by the city, then headed back to Gerry and Yolanda's room.

◆

His son was putting a hole in the carpet. Valentine shut the
door and dead-bolted it, then said, "Something wrong?"

"You're not funny," Gerry said belligerently. "I asked you to
help me, and look what happened. Those bastards are going to
kill us. It's just a matter of time."

"They haven't killed you yet," Valentine said.

"Aw, for the love of Christ," his son said, throwing his arms
into the air. "I wish I'd never come to you with my problems. You
get pleasure seeing me suffer, don't you?"

"No," his father lied.

Gerry sat down on the bed beside Yolanda. "You could have
fooled me," his son moaned.

"Someday you'll have kids, and you'll understand."

Gerry looked at Yolanda and both of their faces seemed to melt
at the same time.

"No," Valentine said.

Gerry kissed the top of Yolanda's forehead.

"Yes," she whispered.

"Really?" Valentine said.

They both nodded that it was so.

"How far along?"

"Twelve weeks," his son said.

"Oh, boy," Valentine said.

In their faces he saw a pair of lovesick pups, happy about the
mistake they'd made. He put his hands on their shoulders and
drew them close to him, kissing Yolanda's forehead, then his
son's. Gerry looked at his father, smiling.

"Oh, boy," Valentine said again.

◆

"You've sure been good for business," Dottie said, refilling their coffee cups.

"It's the service," Valentine told her.

She cackled like a mother hen and walked away. Gerry resumed telling his father how he'd taken Yolanda for a stroll on the Brooklyn Bridge the previous week. It had started raining cats and dogs, so he'd taken his jacket off and held it over their heads, then popped the big question.

"It was so beautiful," his fiancée cooed.

Valentine was so damn happy he didn't know what to say. She was a smart, lovely girl with morals and a solid work ethic. What more could he ask for?

"We want to get married soon," Gerry told him.

"I'll cover it," his father replied. To Yolanda he said, "You want a big wedding?"

Yolanda wrapped her hand into his son's. "We should talk about this later, when things calm down."

"Okay," Valentine said. "Whatever you'd like."

Out on the street, a low-slung car drove past the restaurant and Valentine watched it pass. He didn't think the Mollos had gone far, and turned to his son. "Not to spoil the party, but would you mind telling me how those guys found you so fast?"

"I screwed up," Gerry said uncharacteristically.

"No, *I* screwed up," Yolanda said. "I told Gerry I wanted to go to The Bombay and play Funny Money. My sister won a car, so I figured maybe lightning will strike twice."

"The Mollos were there and spotted us," Gerry explained. "It was all my fault."

"No, mine," she said.

They were already sounding like a married couple. Their dinners came. His son had ordered pancakes and sausages. Down south, they came wrapped and were called pigs in blankets. A strange concept to northerners, but one that Valentine found oddly appealing. He watched his son smother his pancakes with maple syrup. He was going to be as big as a house one day if he didn't start watching what he ate. When he had a dripping forkful inches from his mouth, Valentine said, "I know it's been a rough couple of days, but how would you and Yolanda like to do a little detective work for me tomorrow?"

His son put his fork down. "You're kidding, right?"

"Not at all," Valentine said.

"After what we've just been through?"

"I'm just talking a couple of hours," he said.

"That's not the point."

Yolanda put her fork down, and placed her hand on Gerry's arm and gave it a gentle squeeze. His son looked at her. Yolanda whispered something under her breath. Gerry grimaced, trapped.

"Sure," his son said.

Valentine sipped his coffee, enjoying himself probably more than he should have. Since the day he'd started talking, Gerry had been defying him. With Yolanda in the picture, that was all going to change.

"We'd love to, Mr. Valentine," Yolanda added.

"Call me Dad," he told her.

26

Single's Day at Waldbaum's

The next day was Saturday, and Valentine got up at seven-fifteen, did his exercises, then walked down the block to Burger King and bought coffee and juice and biscuits. Back in the precasino days, there had been a dozen good breakfast spots in this part of town, but now there were only fast-food franchises that pretended to serve breakfast.

He stopped by the manager's office and talked him into lending out the yellow pages, then went to his son's room and tapped on the door. Gerry answered, his eyes half shut, his face puffed up from yesterday's encounter with the Mollo brothers.

"You're serious about this, aren't you?" his son said.

"Yes," Valentine replied.

"We'll be ready in ten minutes," Yolanda called from the bathroom.

"She's a wonderful girl," he told his son.

They ate breakfast while sitting on the bed in Valentine's room. "There's a group of hustlers I'm looking for," he explained to his son and Yolanda. "I think they've been wiring their winnings out of the country to a crime boss. I want to visit all the Western Union offices in town and see if anyone can identify them."

"And you want us along for company," Gerry said sarcastically.

Valentine found the ad for Western Union in the yellow pages and jotted down the addresses of all six branches in Atlantic City. Finished, he looked his son square in the eye. "All my life, people have been pegging me for a cop. Sometimes it helps with investigations, sometimes it doesn't."

"I still don't understand where we fit in," Gerry said.

"Your father wants us to help him with the people that it doesn't," Yolanda explained.

"Boy, she's smart," Valentine told his son.

◆

With his windshield wipers beating back the snow, Gerry pulled his BMW in front of the Western Union office on the seven hundred block of Indiana and killed the engine. Through the storefront window they could see an ornery-looking woman sitting behind the bullet-proof glass. Gerry said, "I'm not dealing with that one."

"She looks hostile," Yolanda said.

"Okay, okay," Valentine said from the backseat.

Three people were in line inside the store. Valentine waited for them to clear out, then went in. He'd once known a cop who went into bars, struck up a conversation with strange women, and after five minutes of chitchat, asked if they'd like to sleep with him. The direct approach. Which he now tried.

"I was hoping you could help me."

The woman behind the glass snorted contemptuously.

"I'm looking for a Croatian guy named Juraj Havelka. He told me to meet him at the Western Union office, but he didn't say which one. Has he been in?"

She eyed him suspiciously. "Who? What's this about?"

"His name is Juraj."

"I'm not good on names," she replied. "Describe him."

"About my height, blue eyes, blond hair. Not bad-looking."

"I wish," the woman said.

The next Western Union was on Pacific near Bally's Grand Casino. Gerry parked by the door and his father peered inside. Two frumpy women sat behind the glass, both in their mid-thirties.

"They look right up your alley," Valentine told his son.

"Spare me the compliments," Gerry patted down his hair and got out. Stopping at the door, he glanced back at the car. Yolanda blew him a kiss.

His son went in, and the two women behind the glass looked up and smiled.

"So how you ladies doing?" Gerry asked.

"Great," they chorused.

"I was wondering if you could help me out."

"Sure," the pair said.

Gerry worked off the script his father had given him. Unfortunately, neither woman had ever heard of Juraj Havelka. They both frowned when he said good-bye.

"Still the charmer," his father said as they drove away.

The third Western Union office was on the south side of town, a crime-riddled area filled with transients. Gerry parked in front and Valentine stared at the dark-haired Hispanic kid with a pencil-thin mustache behind the glass.

"If you don't mind," he said to Yolanda.

"This should be fun," she said.

"Don't let him get fresh with you," Gerry said.

Yolanda was laughing as she walked into the store. Gerry had never acted jealous until she'd broken the news that she was pregnant. The Hispanic kid behind the glass gave her a smile.

"You Puerto Rican?" he asked.

She nodded. As a rule, Puerto Ricans were pretty good about

sticking together, and without any coaxing the kid looked through a batch of receipts and pulled up Juraj's name.

"He was in yesterday. You're a friend of his?"

Yolanda could hear it in the kid's voice: He wanted to tell her something about Juraj. She nodded, then said, "He's my *best* friend. I really need to find him."

"I see him or his girlfriend at the supermarket most weekends. They're nuts about fresh vegetables and fruit. I think it's a European thing."

"Which supermarket?"

"The Waldbaums on Crescent and Hines."

Yolanda wanted to give the kid a hug, only the bullet-proof glass prevented it. Climbing back into the BMW, she shared her good news and immediately sensed that her fiancé and his father had been at each other's throats.

This has to stop, she thought.

◆

Waldbaums was a brightly lit, forty-thousand-square-foot box of steel and tinted glass. Connected to it was a strip shopping center, at its end a mom-and-pop Italian eatery called Gino's. Gerry edged the BMW into an empty space in the parking lot and they all got out.

"Why don't you two hang out in Gino's while I look around next door," Valentine said. Taking out his wallet, he handed Gerry two twenties, then started to walk away. He heard Yolanda whisper to his son.

"You want me with you?" Gerry asked.

Valentine turned around, not understanding.

"You know, as backup."

There was real concern in his son's voice.

"I'll be fine," he reassured him.

Waldbaums was jammed with shoppers. Stepping through the sliding glass doors, he was approached by a smiling female wearing a turquoise jumpsuit.

"Married or single?" she inquired.

He nearly told her it was none of her goddamned business, but she was wearing a store badge. "Single."

"Oh. Fresh blood. Your name?"

"Tony. And yours?"

"Louise, thanks for asking."

"Louise, thanks for asking. That's a nice name."

She giggled. "You're a cutie."

"Babies are cute," he said.

"And what are you?"

"Sixty-two."

She giggled again. "All right. You're a teddy bear."

She scribbled his name on a label and slapped it against his chest. "There you go, Tony the teddy bear. Welcome to Single's Saturday at Waldbaums."

He got a cart and started walking the aisles, getting hit on by women of every shape and size and age group. Women that he'd never have imagined in a thousand years would be interested in him. He hung around the produce department until the female onslaught became too much, and then fled to the liquor store that was part of the supermarket. Not surprisingly, no swinging singles were gathered there.

To kill time, he read the labels on vodka and gin bottles, remembering all the nights his old man had rolled home drunk and terrorized the family, only to wake up the next day remembering nothing. Whoever said booze didn't have therapeutic powers had never seen his father the morning after a bender.

After thirty minutes he'd worked himself into a real funk.

Thinking about his old man did that to him. He was ready to leave when he saw Anna stroll into the produce section next door.

He pressed his face against the glass wall that separated liquor from produce. Anna was squeezing the tomatoes, and several hot-blooded males pounced on her. She fended them off, then made her way to the checkout.

He walked to the front of the liquor store. From a cooler he pulled a Diet Coke. Paying for it, he went to the front and stood by the window. Anna strolled out carrying a bag of groceries. Clutching his drink, he went outside.

It had started to snow. Anna was a hundred yards ahead, walking toward a neighborhood that was a borderline slum. He followed her.

A minute later, she entered a run-down apartment house. Stopping at the corner, Valentine reached into his pocket and grasped the .38 resting there. Then thought long and hard about a promise he'd made to Doyle Flanagan in a hospital room twenty years before.

He walked down the apartment house's front path. A flickering light caught his eye. Up at a third-floor window he saw Anna standing at a sink, washing her vegetables. He jerked open the front door.

The apartment foyer was a pigsty, the frayed carpet piss-soaked by drunks. The elevator was out and he took the stairs, kicking beer cans all the way. Another part of police work he did not miss.

He walked the hall and checked the names on the doors. The apartment at the end of the hall had none. He visualized the window Anna had been standing at, and determined he had the right door. He knocked loudly, then stepped to one side, drawing the .38. He heard movement on the other side of the door.

"Yes?" a woman's voice said suspiciously.

"It's Peter Diamondis," he said, doing a bad job imitating the professor's scholarly tone. "I need to talk to Juraj."

"Peter?" The door swung in, and Anna practically danced into the hall. "How did you—"

Valentine slapped his hand over her mouth and stuck the .38 in her face. Anna's eyes went wide. Pushing her into the apartment, he kicked the door shut.

It was a one-bedroom efficiency with sleeping bags on the floor. In the alcove that served as the kitchen, soup cans and milk cartons filled the sink. He pushed over to the bathroom and kicked open the door. Empty.

"Know what happens if you scream?"

She nodded fearfully.

He lowered his hand. "Where are the others?"

"They left a half-hour ago."

"When will they be back?"

"I don't know." Then she added, "They went to the morgue."

He realized she'd been crying. He pointed at the room's only chair. She sat in it, crushing an empty pizza box.

"Who died?"

"Rolf. Juraj and Alex went to claim his body. How did you know about Peter?"

Valentine pulled a stool out of the alcove and sat down beside her. "I'm asking the questions. What happened to Rolf?"

Anna pulled a nasty-looking hanky from her pocket and blew her nose. "When Rolf didn't come home from work yesterday, Juraj got worried and called the police. Rolf was in the morgue. Someone had shot him."

"Where did Rolf work?"

"At The Bombay, washing dishes."

Extracting the pizza box from beneath her, she flung it across the room, hitting the picture on the wall and shattering its glass frame. It was just too much, and she started crying like there was no tomorrow. Valentine got a beer from the refrigerator and made her take a long pull.

"Why do you live like this," he said.

She gave him a cold stare. "Like what?"

"Like pigs."

Anna slapped his face. "How dare you call us that!"

Valentine grabbed her arm. "Don't do that again, hear me?"

She did not seem to care that he was holding a gun on her. "We are not rich like you, driving around in a fancy car, wearing nice clothes."

"At least you could be staying in a decent place."

"You don't understand," she said, "do you?"

"No," he said. "Why don't you explain it to me."

♦

Anna marched into the bedroom. Standing in the doorway, he watched her pull a knapsack from a closet and drag it past him into the living room. Clearing off the table they ate their meals on, she dumped out the knapsacks' contents.

Dozens of pink slips of paper hit the table. Valentine picked up several and stared at them. They were wire transfer receipts from Western Union. Anna gathered them, and started to arrange them in chronological order.

"Juraj always follows the same routine," she said. "Once we win money at the casino, he wires it home. It is always that way. He says it saves us from being tempted."

When she was finished, she handed him the stack. Valentine counted the receipts while noting the sums. They ranged between ten and twelve thousand dollars. Juraj's signature was on the bottom of each. And the recipient was always the same: M. Putja, Zagreb, Croatia.

Anna stood beside him, a defiant look in her eyes. "All the money goes home. We live this way because there is none left."

Valentine finished counting. There were ninety receipts in all. He quickly did the math in his head. They'd stolen less than a million dollars from The Bombay.

He counted the receipts again, just to be sure.

♦

The apartment was suddenly very warm. He slipped the snub-nosed .38 into his pocket, gathered up the slips, and stuffed them into the backpack. Then he went to the kitchen window and stared down at the snow-covered street.

"How long did Rolf work at The Bombay?"

"Do you believe me now?"

"Answer the question."

"Three months," she said.

"And he was feeding you information."

"Yes. He was our mule."

"Mole."

"Yes. We have all known each other since college." She folded her arms over her chest and started to cry. "I'm so . . . afraid."

"Of what?"

"The people who killed Rolf will find us."

"So move," he said.

"We have no money."

"None?"

"I have two hundred dollars in my shoe."

"There's some cheap motels on the beach."

"Will we . . . be safe?"

No, he thought, *but I'll sure know how to find you.* He went to the front door and opened it.

180   "Good-bye, Anna," he said.

◆

It was eleven-forty-five when Valentine walked into Gino's restaurant. His son had an appetite that wouldn't quit, and he was sharing a plate of fried calamari with his fiancée. Putting a gob of tentacles into his mouth, he said, "You want some?"

Valentine said no and pulled up a chair. The table was covered with empty plates and glasses. Hanging out in the supermarket had made him hungry, but now all he felt was numb.

"Something to drink? Coffee?"

Valentine said no. He felt Yolanda's hand on his wrist. He'd already learned she was good at reading thoughts. Their eyes met, and she said, "You okay . . . Dad?"

Valentine wasn't sure. He'd just discovered that everything didn't add up, and that was never okay.

The waitress brought the check. Gerry handed her the twenties his father had given him, then said, "Pop, do you mind helping out, here? I'm a little short."

Leave it to his son to spend more than he had. Valentine took out his wallet and settled the bill.

27

What Is Sin?

Valentine did not say a word during the drive back to the Blue Dolphin. He walked Gerry and Yolanda to their room, then took the precaution of doing a once-over around the motel. He didn't think the Mollo brothers were stupid enough to come calling in broad daylight, but he'd learned that it was never wise to second-guess Neanderthals.

"I need to go out for a few hours," he said upon returning to their room. "Promise me you won't do anything stupid, like sneak off to The Bombay to play Funny Money."

"It was my idea," Yolanda said.

"And it wasn't stupid," Gerry cut in. "Yolanda's sister won a brand new Suburban."

"You know what the odds are of winning a car playing a slot machine?" Valentine asked him. "The same as being struck by lightning . . . twice."

"It happens, Pop," his son said indignantly.

Nothing made Valentine angrier than idiot's logic, especially when it came to gambling. Going to the dresser, he opened the top drawer, removed the Gideon's Bible, and presented it to his son.

"Promise me on this Bible that you won't go out."

Gerry stared at him like he was crazy.

"Do it," his father said.

◆

It was twenty minutes after one when Valentine pulled the Mercedes into the empty parking lot at St. Mary's Cathedral and killed the engine.

Sitting in the car, he tried to remember the last time he'd stepped foot inside a church. He'd been raised a strict Catholic, going to Mass every Sunday, sometimes twice if his mother thought he needed to say a few more Hail Marys, but as he'd gotten older he'd abandoned the practice and eventually the church itself. He still believed in God and tried to live his life accordingly, but the faith he'd been raised in no longer worked for him. To be a good Catholic, you had to be a penitent or a supplicant, and he was neither. It was that simple.

Slipping into the confessional, he was surprised at how the cold little box had the ability to dredge up a ton of guilt, and he lowered his head in shame. Moments later the tiny window slid open.

"Forgive me, father, for I have sinned."

"And how have you sinned, my son?" Father Tom asked.

Valentine took a deep breath. He'd decided not to tell Tom about Sparky's dying, simply because he believed he'd done nothing wrong. But there were plenty of other things weighing heavily on his mind, and he proceeded to tell the priest how he'd knocked down Kat, lied through his teeth to Coleman and Marconi, taken Archie Tanner's money for a job he was already planning to do—something which hadn't seemed a sin when he'd done it but sure did now—and had gone to the Croatians' apartment intending to pump a few bullets into Juraj Havelka.

"You've been busy," the priest said.

Valentine stared at the confessional floor. "There's something else."

"What's that?"

"I stepped on a guy's hand."

Father Tom was a mouth breather, and his sharp intake of breath sounded like a small-caliber gun going off. "Please, explain."

Valentine did, spelling out the scene with Big Tony at the motel as best he could.

"Surely you've hurt people before," Father Tom said when he was done.

"I stepped over the line," Valentine said.

"And which line is that?"

He fell silent. The line between what was truly good and truly evil was invisible, yet he'd always known where it was drawn. And he'd stepped over it in a big way.

"The guy was defenseless," Valentine said.

"But he hurt your son and his fiancée."

"I stooped to his level. Maybe lower."

"Have you never done that before?"

He detected a hint of skepticism in Father Tom's voice. Like the sin he was describing was as common as the sun rising. Only Valentine didn't see it that way. He'd lived his life as purely as he could and hadn't inflicted pain unless it was justified.

"No."

"Then I'm sure God will forgive you this time," the priest said.

They stood on the front stoop, the wind whipping mercilessly at their faces. St. Mary's was located in a residential area off Route 9 in Swainton, the eighty-year-old church surrounded by apart-

ment houses with Murphys and O'Sullivans stamped on the mail-
boxes. Black smoke billowed out of nearly every chimney. Across
the way, two gangs of kids had joined forces to build a mammoth
snowman.

"I need to talk to you about Doyle," Valentine said.

"So the confession was just a way to get on my good side,"
Father Tom said, smiling thinly. "Doyle and I talked often, but
rarely about his work."

"But you spoke a lot."

"Yes."

"Mind if I ask about a particular conversation?"

Father Tom's face turned sour. He'd been handsome once,
with a ruddy Irish complexion and wavy blond hair, but with
age he'd turned gaunt and his hairline had receded. Seeing
something across the street he didn't approve of, he clapped his
hands and let out a shout. The misbehaving kids scattered in a
dozen directions.

"Sorry about that," the priest said. "Which conversation between Doyle and myself are you referring to?"

"It was a conversation where Doyle blew up. He later wrote you
a note and apologized about it."

Father Tom hesitated. He had come outside without a coat, yet
looked perfectly comfortable. All his life, Valentine had seen
priests walk around in the winter in street clothes, like God had
given them an extra layer of skin for joining up.

"Walk with me," the priest said.

♦

They took a stroll around the block. At an intersection they
found the same hellions Father Tom had disciplined a few minutes earlier hurling snowballs at passing cars. The priest ran into

the street and rounded them up while threatening to call their folks. It was fun to watch him work, and the troublemakers marched away with their heads lowered in shame.

Coming back, Father Tom said, "You seem to be enjoying yourself."

"If there were more people like you, there would be fewer people like me."

"Guilt is one of God's most powerful weapons," the priest said. "Humankind's capacity for sin is nearly unlimited. Without guilt, we'd all run amok, don't you think?"

"Sometimes I think we do run amok," Valentine said.

They were standing outside a bakery, the smell of pastries scenting the frigid air. The priest lowered his voice. "My brother was a good Catholic, loyal to his friends and family, subservient to his creator. Yet he was struggling with personal demons. I've never seen him so . . . apprehensive."

"What happened?"

Father Tom had to think about it. "One day at lunch Doyle got a call on his cell phone. The caller said something, and my brother said, *'What is sin?'* Then he got very angry. After he hung up, I said, 'Doyle, don't tell me you don't know what sin is?' And Doyle said, 'This is a different kind of sin, Tom.'

"I've thought about that conversation many times, but it never made sense. Perhaps you have an idea."

Valentine shook his head. All Catholics knew about sin. There was mortal, venial, spiritual, carnal, and capital sin. But a different type of sin? He had no idea.

"Was his caller a man or a woman?"

"A man."

"Did Doyle address him by name?"

Father Tom thought hard. "Bob? No, Barry. No, wait. Benny. It was Benny," he decided.

"You're sure?"

"Positive. Doyle addressed him several times."

186

The only Benny in town was Benny Roselli, a dumb-as-nails ex-cop who ran security at the Wild Wild West Casino. Why would Doyle be talking to Benny about religion?

They walked back to St. Mary's. A young couple stood by the church's front door, their faces flushed with excitement. Father Tom introduced them as the soon-to-be-married so-and-so. They looked so damn happy that Valentine found himself smiling.

"It's been good talking with you, Tony," the priest said. "Let me know if you find anything."

"I will," Valentine promised him.

"And Tony . . ."

"Yes, Father Tom."

"Try to stay out of trouble."

The priest's eyes were twinkling, as if knowing what he was asking was impossible.

"And if you can't, come back and see me," the priest said.

28

Benny

Country-and-western music had never been Valentine's idea of a good time, and the occasions he'd been forced to listen had bordered on cruelty. How the Wild Wild West, Atlantic City's only musically themed gambling establishment, could play such god-awful music and still make money was one of the great wonders of New Jersey. The costumes the blackjack dealers and croupiers had to wear were particularly offensive. White cowboy boots and fringed miniskirts for the ladies, ten-gallon hats and string ties for the gents. It was a regular hoedown.

He was serenaded by Dwight Yoakam's nasal baritone while riding an elevator to the second floor where the surveillance control room was headquartered. It was three-fifteen. He'd called Benny Roselli from the car, told him he needed to talk. Benny had agreed, saying things were pretty slow.

"Howdy, pardner," he said as Benny opened the surveillance control room's unmarked door.

"Up yours," Benny replied.

Benny locked the door behind him. The room's light was muted, and Valentine waited for his eyes to adjust. Sitting at a row of desks were two dozen surveillance personnel. For eight hours a day, they stared at a wall of video monitors, the screens flickering with black-and-white images of the action taking place in the casino below.

Benny crossed the room and stepped onto a podium, which housed the room's master console. The console was a recent technological marvel and contained a giant screen divided into a matrix of multiple camera angles. Like a king sitting on his throne, Benny could simultaneously monitor his crew and watch the action downstairs.

There was no chair for Valentine to sit on, nor was one offered, so he leaned against the console.

"Believe it or not, I'm glad you called," Benny said.

"Why's that?"

"Because we're getting ripped off, that's why."

Benny touched a joystick on the console, and a white arrow shot across the screen. Then a picture appeared. It was a live shot of a blackjack table, six players, and a chatty dealer.

"The suspect is playing third base," Benny said.

Third base was the last spot on the table. Surveillance cameras were not kind to hair pieces, and the suspect, a male in his early fifties, appeared to be wearing a skunk.

"I spotted him last week," Benny said. "He won five grand, came back a day later, won five more. I'm positive he's hustling us."

Valentine stared at the screen. Within a minute he'd made the scam, but he let several more pass before saying anything. Benny had lost his job as a New Jersey highway patrolman because he couldn't handle a radar gun. Benny knew he was stupid, but that didn't mean Valentine could rub his face in it.

"He's slipping the gitt," Valentine said.

"Great," Benny said. "Now tell me in fucking English."

"The guy wearing the rug is palming a dozen prearranged cards. It's called a slug. He's using sleight of hand to slip the slug to the dealer when the dealer picks up the discards. Watch him."

Benny stared intently at the screen. Then grimaced.

"So the dealer's involved?"

Valentine nodded. "Watch the dealer as he shuffles. He controls 189
the slug during the shuffle, then marks its position in the deck by
shuffling one card above it, and moving this card back a fraction
of an inch. It's called an injog."

"How's he do that?"

"Practice."

"Up yours."

They watched the dealer offer the cards to be cut. The guy wearing the rug cut at the injogged card, and brought the slug to the
top. The dealer dealt the round.

"Look," Valentine said, "The first, third, and sixth hands are
blackjacks. All the others are losers."

Benny's mouth dropped open. "You're telling me the dealer
and *three* other players are involved?"

Valentine nodded. "The slug is stacked for three winners and
three losers. This helps offset the money that's being stolen. Later,
the dealer palms the slug out."

"Let me ask you a question."

"Go ahead."

"What do you charge to be an expert witness?"

"A grand a day, plus expenses."

Benny leaned back in his chair. In order to prosecute, he needed to give the DA enough evidence to make the charges stick.
Since the scam was invisible to the cameras, an expert witness's
testimony would be crucial to his case.

"How about a little barter," he suggested.

"Such as?"

"Your testimony in return for whatever you want to ask me."

"Deal," Valentine said.

Benny picked up a house phone and called the floor. Twenty

seconds later, a swarm of security in blue blazers descended upon the table. Cheating was a felony in New Jersey, and the gang did not go quietly. Before it was over, several chairs were broken, and a guard was sporting a welt on his lip that looked like a blood sausage.

"I changed my mind," Valentine said as the hustlers were led away.

Benny shot him a murderous look. "That's not funny."

"Sorry."

"Your turn."

"What is sin?" Valentine asked him.

Benny scratched his chin. "It's when people do things that in the eyes of God aren't right. Is that what you came up here to ask me?"

"I think the expression has another meaning."

"Call the guys who run *Jeopardy!,*" Benny said. "Maybe they know."

"You don't know what I'm talking about?"

"Sorry."

Valentine lowered his voice. "Three, four weeks ago, you had a phone conversation with Doyle Flanagan. Doyle asked you *'What is sin?'* This ringing any bells?"

Benny's face got serious in a hurry.

"Is this about Doyle's murder?"

"It sure is."

The director of surveillance stood up, grabbing his overcoat off the chair. "Not in here," he told Valentine.

◆

They took a stairwell down to the first floor and went outside to a loading dock. The sun had burned away the clouds but it didn't feel any warmer. Delivery trucks came and went; food, linens, cutlery, liquor, all the basics to feed the monster. Beneath the bright sunlight Benny looked older than his years, his gray hair luminous, the lines in his face deep and hard. He fired up a butt and stood on the edge of the dock, looking down at a crew unloading a beer truck.

"You like Florida?"

"Can't beat the weather."

Benny made Valentine hold up his hand and compared his own against it. His skin was zombie-white, Valentine's tan and healthy.

"My wife wants to buy a condo in St. Pete. That's near you, isn't it?"

"Twenty minutes. Why don't you?"

"Because it costs money." Inhaling deeply on his cigarette, Benny struck a defiant pose, like the world owed him something. He was lucky he'd gotten as far as he had, but didn't see it that way.

"Why were you talking to Doyle?" Valentine asked.

"That's a good question." Benny glanced nervously at two deliverymen who'd walked up, then lowered his voice. "I know you and Doyle were buddies. Doyle and I weren't tight, but I owed him a huge favor, something I won't get into. Anyway, Doyle calls about a month ago, tells me he needs help. I say sure.

"He wanted to know if the Wild Wild West had been ripped off by a European at blackjack. I said, yeah, we had, and I told him the dates and so on. We lost fifty grand to that bastard and I lost my bonus *and* got reamed out. Doyle asked if any other casinos had gotten ripped off, and I said, 'Where you been, boy? Of course no one else got ripped off.' He didn't understand until I explained to him that every casino in Atlantic City is connected to a warning system to stop cheats. You familiar with this?"

"No."

"It started about a year ago."

"Must have been after I retired," Valentine said.

"Right," Benny said. "Time marches on, huh?"

"It sure does."

"Anyway, all the casinos are connected by the Internet. If a casino thinks its been cheated, it spreads the word about the suspect or situation at lightning speed, before the suspect can rip off another casino. The computers let us send pictures of suspects taken directly off the surveillance cameras, plus descriptions of what went down. It's called S.I.N."

"Sin?" Valentine said.

"No, no, that's what people on the outside call it. Casino people call it S.I.N., stands for Secure Internal Network."

"And Doyle didn't know about S.I.N."

"Not until I told him," Benny said. "When Doyle said, 'What is sin?' it told me he *really* didn't know what I was talking about."

Benny tossed his dying cigarette over the loading dock, nearly beaning a worker below. He took out a fresh pack of Marlboros and fired one up. "Want one?"

Valentine started to reach for the pack, his lungs begging for another rush of nicotine. Then found the willpower to stop himself. "No thanks. Is The Bombay part of S.I.N.?"

"It sure is."

"So they let the European play on purpose."

"*Someone* over there did," Benny replied.

"You're positive about this."

"Tony, look, I sent up a red flag. I even made the fucking van."

"What van?"

"The van the European was driving," Benny said. "I caught it on a surveillance camera that watches our parking lot. It was a real piece of junk. I sent that picture out along with pictures of him."

Valentine found himself wishing he'd taken Benny up on his offer of a cigarette. Benny glanced at his watch.

"Gotta get back to the salt mines. Been nice catching up."

They went back inside. Standing in the stairwell, Valentine took out a business card and handed it to him. Benny stared at the card, then him, not understanding.

"You want me to be an expert witness, right?"

"What if you're back in Florida?"

"Then I'll fly up."

"Whose nickel?"

"Mine."

"That's awful nice of you," Benny said, pocketing the card.

"I gave you my word," Valentine said, "didn't I?"

◆

He drove away from the Wild Wild West trying to sort out everything Benny had told him. The Bombay had known about Juraj, yet still let him play. He could pass that off to a lot of things, but the one that seemed most logical was revenge. Archie Tanner's employees were mad at him, and letting a known cheat play was a great way to screw the boss. But that didn't explain the missing money. Doyle had said six million bucks had been stolen, and Porter had confirmed it. If the Croatians had only stolen a million, where was the rest?

There were a lot of possibilities. Archie was one. Casino owners skimmed money off the top all the time. Another was that someone else had stolen it. And the third was, he just didn't know.

A fire truck came down the street, its siren wailing. An ambulance accompanied it, then a screaming police cruiser. All three vehicles were headed south on Atlantic Avenue, toward motel row. Punching the accelerator, he followed them.

29

Epiphany

The Mollo brothers had set Gerry's BMW on fire.

His knucklehead son had not bothered to move his car off Atlantic Avenue like his father had told him. So the Mollos had stuck a gas-soaked rag in the tank and lit a match. A fire truck was hosing the BMW down when Valentine got to the scene, the air thick with black smoke.

"No, I didn't actually see them," his son was telling the uniform writing up the report. "We were inside, watching TV."

"Did anyone see them?" the uniform wanted to know.

Gerry glanced at the Blue Dolphin's manager, who stood nearby, shivering without his coat. The manager looked at the ground, then off in the distance.

"No," his son said.

"I can't help you, then," the cop said. "Your insurance should cover this, if that's any consolation."

"I don't have insurance," Gerry replied.

Back inside their motel room, it was all Valentine could do to not strangle his son. Gerry was a gambler—horses, sports, cards—but when it came to intelligent gambling, like having insurance, he was out to lunch.

"They're gonna kill us," Gerry said, sitting on the bed. He looked up at his father. "Aren't they?"

Yolanda sat beside him, stroking his hair. "No, they're not."

Valentine sat on the bed and put his hand on Gerry's knee. "How would you two kids like to take a trip? Go away for a while, until this thing blows over?"

His son and fiancée looked up at him expectantly.

"You're serious?" his son said.

Valentine nodded. Yolanda squealed with delight and hugged his son. Gerry was not so sure, and kept looking at his father.

"On me," Valentine reassured him.

Outside, the last of the emergency vehicles peeled away, leaving an eerie silence. For a brief moment no one spoke.

"I hear Mexico's great this time of year," his son said.

"I had someplace else in mind," Valentine said.

"Where's that?"

"Croatia."

◆

If there was one thing that impressed Valentine about living in the modern world, it was what you could do over the telephone with a credit card. Just about any service could be arranged, any item bought, any mountain moved.

In less than ten minutes he'd reserved two business class tickets to Zagreb, Croatia, on TWA. Why this made him giddy, he had no earthly idea, and he went outside to share his good news. His son and Yolanda were standing by the covered pool, kissing. She was the greatest girl in the world, he'd decided.

"Here's the deal," he said when they came up for air. "Your flight's at eleven tonight out of Newark with a stopover in Paris. TWA has a special lounge for business class, so you can hang out there until the flight leaves, have a drink, or something to eat."

"You really want us to go to Croatia?" his son said.

"Just for a few days. I need you to check something out. Then you can go wherever you want: Italy, Spain—you name it." Valentine slapped his hand against his forehead. "For the love of Christ. It just occurred to me, you're both going to need passports to get out of the country."

"Got 'em," his son replied.

Valentine lifted an eyebrow.

"If you didn't help us out, Yolanda and I were planning to go to Mexico."

"Haven't I *always* helped you out?"

His son hemmed and hawed. "Yeah, I guess so."

And then Gerry surprised him. He put his arms around his father and hugged him like a son hugs his old man. Valentine hugged him back, his eyes tightly shut. His relationship with Gerry had been like a record stuck on skip for twenty years. Now, finally, the music was starting to play through.

"So what do you want us to do in Croatia?"

Digging into his pocket, Valentine removed the crumbled Western Union receipt he'd palmed out of Anna's backpack in front of her nose, and handed it to him.

"You'll be flying into a town called Zagreb. I want you to look up the name on that receipt without drawing attention to yourself. Find out who that person is. I have a feeling it's a local crime boss, so be *careful.*"

"So what do you want me to do once I find this guy?"

"Call me."

"That's it?"

"That's it."

"You gonna leave your cell phone on?"

"Yeah, I'll leave it on."

To his fiancée, Gerry said, "My father just stepped out of a cave, and you were there to see it happen."

"Wise ass," Valentine said.

◆

Valentine drove them to Newark Airport. He pulled into short-term parking and they got out and exchanged good-byes. Digging into the pocket of her jeans, Yolanda removed a silver coin and handed it to him. Valentine stared at the piece of Funny Money in his hand. "You want me to play this for you?"

"Please."

"Any particular machine?"

She thought about it, then shook her head. "You decide."

That wasn't going to be easy. The last time he'd walked through The Bombay's casino, he'd needed instructions to find his way around. "And if I win the Suburban?"

"I'll let you drive it on Sundays," she said.

God, he liked this girl. Extracting his ATM card from his wallet, he handed it to her and said, "The PIN number is 4273. The account has twenty grand in it. Take what you need."

"Number 4273," she repeated, putting the card in her purse. Then said, "What are you going to do for money?"

He showed her the wad of cash in his wallet. Gerry, who'd been standing idly by her side, could not hide his indignation.

"Why did you give the card to her?"

"Come on," Valentine said. "You think I was born yesterday?"

◆

The drive back to Atlantic City was long and boring, and he glued his eyes to the endless stretch of highway. Each year, thirty-seven million visitors made similar journeys, hoping to have a little fun, maybe catch a dream. Personally, he didn't see the attraction, but his perspective was different. He could remember when the Jersey shore hadn't needed the lure of false promises to pay its bills. He caught himself yawning and got off at the next exit.

Circle K had the best coffee for the money; ask any retired person. Paying with the change in his pocket, he got back into the car. Soon the coffee was gone and he was wide awake.

He took out his cell phone. He hadn't talked to Mabel all day. He started to punch in the numbers, then realized his phone wasn't turned on. Gerry was right about one thing. He did not embrace all the technological crap being shoved down peoples' throats. With the Internet came a flood of porn. With cell phones, more traffic wrecks. And laptop computers were great. Now, no one talked on airplanes. He turned the phone on, and a few moments later it began to ring. He had a feeling it was his son, and answered it.

"I changed my mind," Yolanda said.

"Which machine?"

"The one near the front entrance. That's where my sister won the car. Play that machine."

Valentine tried to envision where that particular machine was. And couldn't. He found himself remembering back two days ago, when he'd been standing in The Bombay with Porter directing him through his baseball cap.

"Give me a landmark," he said.

"There are only twelve Funny Money machines," Yolanda said. "It's by the front entrance. You can't miss it."

"Who told you there were only twelve?"

"The hostess. Gerry asked her if she knew which Funny Money machine had paid my sister's jackpot last month. And the hostess said, 'Well, there are only twelve, so it shouldn't be hard to find.'"

Valentine took a deep breath. All his life he'd been having epiphanies, and they always began with his asking himself a question. And the question he asked himself now was, *why weren't the* *Funny Money machines all situated together, with a big neon sign hanging over them?* That was how most promotions in casinos worked.

And the answer that came back was simple. So simple that it explained all the gnawing questions he'd been asking himself since counting the receipts in Anna's knapsack. The Funny Money machines weren't all together because it wouldn't have allowed the employees to rearrange the casino and secretly funnel money out. That was where the missing five million had gone.

"I'll make sure I put it in that machine," he said.

30

Hard Count, Soft Count

"I was wrong," he told Davis an hour later.

Valentine had looked everywhere for a restaurant besides the IHOP to meet Davis, and he'd come up short. It was the only decent place for miles that hadn't been closed down by the casinos' $5.99 all-you-can-eat buffets.

It was Davis's day off, and he'd arrived unshaven and out of sorts. Dottie served them Belgian waffles with sausages on the side. When she was gone, the detective said, "About what?"

Ignoring the advice of every doctor he'd seen in the past ten years, Valentine smothered the waffles in maple syrup and dug in. "The Croatians aren't the only people ripping off The Bombay. A group of employees are robbing Archie as well."

"You have proof?"

Dottie was lurking behind the counter with her antenna out. Valentine lowered his voice. "No."

"Then how can you be certain?"

"I just am."

"Is this your fabled grift sense?"

"Yes."

"So, what do you want from me?"

"I need you to help me make the scam," Valentine said.

Davis started to answer, then spotted Dottie. He leaned forward so their faces were less than a foot apart. "What are you talking about, *help you make the scam?*"

"I need you to create a diversion inside The Bombay."

Davis gave him a wild look. "What are you suggesting I do? Light a smoke bomb? Or fire my gun a few times? That should get them running, don't you think?"

"Nothing that drastic," Valentine said, trying to calm him down. "Just get a few security guards riled up."

"I'm a cop. This isn't the fucking movies. People know me."

"Put on a hat and glasses. It just has to last a couple of minutes. Maybe you can bring a few friends along."

"You mean, scary-looking friends."

"That's up to you."

Dottie came over to ask how their food was. Gossip was no doubt her great addiction, and it was a minute before she left. Davis devoured his food like he hadn't eaten in days. When he was done, he slid out of the booth and started to walk away. Then came back and tossed a five dollar bill on the table.

"Give me one good reason why I should help you," he said.

Valentine had to think about it.

"Because you're a swell guy," he said.

Valentine slipped into Frank Porter's office in The Bombay's surveillance control room an hour later and shut the door. The office walls were illuminated by grainy, black-and-white video monitors, the light so poor that for a moment he did not see Porter sitting at his desk, munching on a bagel.

"Hey," Porter said.

"Hey," he replied, pulling up a chair.

The room's temperature was a cool sixty-five degrees because of the delicate electronics, and Porter wore a baggy cardigan sweater beneath a blue blazer. Valentine knew the sweater well: He'd given it to Frank on his fiftieth birthday.

"I thought you weren't talking to me," Porter said.

"I'm leaving town. I wanted to say good-bye."

"You're not sore?"

"I'll get over it."

Porter's eyes briefly left the monitors. Like most people in casino security, he constantly played with angle and magnification with his joystick to avoid falling asleep.

"Thanks, Tony," he said. "Want to hear a joke?"

"You got any Diet Coke?" Valentine asked.

"Do I have any Diet Coke? You got me addicted to the stuff." He took a bottle from the mini-refrigerator behind his desk and filled two plastic cups, the carbonated bubbles overflowing onto the blotter. They clinked cups, and he said, "This woman dies and they have a funeral. As they're taking the casket out, it gets bumped against a wall. They hear a groan. The woman's still alive. She lives another ten years. Then she dies. They have another funeral. As they're taking the casket out, the husband says, 'Watch out for that fucking wall!' "

Valentine felt a bead of sweat run down his spine. He hadn't taken off his overcoat, the .38 resting in his jacket pocket with the safety off. He felt Frank staring at him.

"Ha, ha," he said.

"I'm going to close with that joke," Porter said.

"It's a good one."

"Thanks. When's your flight?"

"Couple of hours."

"Back to sunny Florida, huh?"

Valentine heard it in his voice: Porter wanted him to leave.

"Got to cash those Social Security checks," Valentine said.

The tension melted from Porter's face. The office door banged open. A member of Porter's surveillance crew stuck his head in. "We got a problem in the blackjack pit. Table 17."

Then the man slammed the door.

Porter tapped a series of commands on his keyboard. Table 17 came up on every video monitor in the room. Three sharply dressed African-American males were arguing with a female black-jack dealer. Fiddling with his joystick, Porter got in tight on the man doing most of the talking. It was Davis, wearing a black bowler and designer shades. Picking up the house phone, he called downstairs. "You got this under control?"

Porter did not like the answer he got. Fights were bad for business, and it was his job to diffuse any harmful situations before they got out of control. Standing, he grabbed a walkie-talkie off the desk. "I'll be right back."

At the door he stopped and gave Valentine a hard look. "Tony?"

Valentine turned in his seat. "What, Frank?"

"You are leaving town, aren't you?"

His cheery tone was gone. Valentine stared into his friend's face. "What kind of question is that?"

"Answer me."

"Delta Flight 1711."

The hard look vanished. "You want a ride to the airport?"

"That would be great," Valentine said.

◆

Porter left. Valentine went to the door and opened it an inch. Outside, Porter was talking to one of his crew, a bald-headed guy with a sinister Fu Manchu. The guy nodded, agreeing with whatever Porter was telling him. Valentine shut the door and tossed his cup into the trash. Then slipped his hand into his pocket and wrapped his fingers around the .38. Fu Manchu entered the office.

"How you doing?"

"Not too bad," Valentine said.

"Frank asked me to give you a tour of the casino."

"You don't say."

Fu Manchu smiled. "I do."

Valentine drew the .38 and pointed it at Fu Manchu's chest. With his other hand he pointed at the closet. "Let's start the tour in there."

Trembling, Fu Manchu entered the closet. Valentine shut the door behind him, then tilted a chair against the handle. Then he sat down in front of Porter's computer.

He tapped the Shift key and the screen came to life. On it was a matrix that contained different feeds from surveillance cameras around the casino, allowing Porter to simultaneously watch the action at the blackjack tables, roulette, Pai Gow, craps, and the slot and video poker machines. It also let him watch as the money was taken from the games, and counted in two special areas, called the Hard Count and Soft Count rooms.

Over the years, Valentine had investigated many employee casino scams, and one thing was always the same. The gangs had figured out clever ways to sneak money through the Hard and Soft Count rooms, then out of the casino. He did not believe The Bombay gang was any different.

Moving the cursor across the screen, he double-clicked the mouse, and the Soft Count Room filled the screen. Two middle-aged women were on duty. For eight hours a day, they counted bills. When their shift was over, they would be frisked by a Division of Gaming Enforcement agent. If the agent didn't like something, he might make them strip. Valentine used the joystick to look around the room. Everything appeared normal.

Returning to the matrix, he found the feed for the Hard Count room, and double-clicked the mouse. It was here that coins were weighed and wrapped. In the room's center sat a table that held a giant scale. Beside the scale was a coin-wrapping machine.

Everything in the Hard Count room looked normal, except for a second table propped against the wall. He fiddled with the joystick. On this table sat a smaller scale. He made the camera get close. What the hell was that for? Overflow?

He leaned back in Porter's chair. Was The Bombay gang taking buckets of coins taken from slot machines, dumping them onto the smaller scale, then spiriting the coins out of the casino?

He decided it wasn't possible. Every slot machine in The Bombay was video taped 24/7. These tapes were reviewed by teams of Division of Gaming Enforcement agents. The DGE counted how many buckets of coins were taken from each machine, and compared it to how many were dumped on the scale. If the numbers didn't match up, people got arrested.

Which meant he still had no idea what was going on.

He was getting disgusted with himself. He was better than this. Did losing his best friend and all the other nonsense in his life have something to do with his inability to think straight? Taking the bottle of Diet Coke from Porter's fridge, he unscrewed the top and swigged it.

"You still here?" Fu Manchu yelled from the closet.

Valentine tossed the bottle at the door. Then he tapped a command into the keyboard, and the matrix for the blackjack pit appeared on the screen. Porter was at Table 17, talking furiously to a dozen security guards. Davis and his pals were gone.

The guards dispersed. Using the joystick, Valentine followed them across the casino floor. Each guard appeared to be running toward an elevator, or one of the fire exits.

Valentine tapped in another command. Table 17 reappeared. Porter was still there. In his hand was a walkie-talkie. He raised the walkie-talkie to his mouth.

The phone on the desk started to ring.

Valentine hesitated, then picked it up.

"Tony?"

"Hey, Frank," he said.

"You fucking bastard," Porter screamed at him.

"What's wrong?"

Frank's face was twisted in fear. Which meant the secret to the missing five million was on his computer, and Valentine had failed to find it.

"You're a dead man," Porter said.

31

911

Hanging up on Porter, Valentine called Archie Tanner's office. He expected the conversation to be brief. He was going to tell Archie to call the cops. Archie could have any employee arrested for suspicion of stealing, regardless of whether he had evidence. The state gave him this power, along with every other casino owner in Atlantic City.

"I'm sorry," the receptionist said, "but Mr. Tanner is in Florida."

"Is Brandi there?"

"She's at home, sick."

"Who's in charge?"

"Frank Porter," the receptionist said.

He hung up. He guessed he had a minute before one of Porter's men reached the third floor and shot him. Picking up the phone, he dialed 911. "There's a fire at The Bombay," he told the operator.

He marched into the surveillance control room. The employees were gone. He opened the door to the hall and stuck his head out. Empty. He walked down the hall to a fire alarm and punched out the glass. A whooping alarm drowned out all sound.

He followed the red Exit signs to a stairwell. Stepping onto the landing, he heard someone coming up the stairs. Taking the .38 from his pocket, he aimed at the landing and pulled the trigger.

He heard the same pair of feet run down the stairs.

He fired two more times as he descended to the first floor. He wondered how he was going to feel if he shot an innocent person. Then it occurred to him that everyone who *wasn't* guilty was probably standing outside, waiting for the fire trucks.

The first floor landing was deserted. He opened the door and peered into the casino. Several pit bosses had remained at their stations. He thought of the fifty grand in Sparky's bank account and shoe box. Fifty into five million was a hundred employees. He couldn't trust anybody.

Soon, firefighters were streaming into the casino. He waited until one happened by. Opening the door, he shoved the .38 in the firefighter's face. "Get in here."

The firefighter obliged him. He was an Irish guy with freckles and flaming hair, and didn't seem terribly upset. Like he'd experienced worse than a .38 shoved in his face.

Valentine sent him up the stairs in his underwear. Then tried his uniform on over his own clothes. It fit. He saw the fireman standing at the top of the stairs, shaking his head.

The casino floor was pandemonium. Valentine passed several firefighters without drawing suspicion. He headed for the nearest exit, his heart racing out of control.

◆

He drove to an all-night grocery and parked between two delivery trucks. Inside, he bought cigarettes and fired one up once he was back in the car. Filling his lungs with smoke, he felt himself start to calm down.

Man, that tasted good.

So good, that he smoked two more before taking out his cell phone and dialing Davis's number. The detective answered on the first ring.

"An arrest warrant's been issued for you. You're considered armed and dangerous. Did you really stick a gun in the fireman's face and make him take off his clothes? What were you thinking?"

"Porter's men were trying to kill me," Valentine said.

"You made the scam?"

"No."

"Do you know any more than you did before?"

"No."

"I want you to turn yourself in," Davis said.

"*What?*"

"You're out of control."

"I am?"

"You're suffering from dementia, Tony. Running around town knocking women down and carrying a hot gun. Do you think that's normal behavior? For Christ's sake, you introduced me as Richard Roundtree yesterday."

Valentine watched two police cruisers pass by. When they were gone, he blew out a monster cloud of smoke. "I'm not nuts."

"It's your only defense," the detective said.

Davis was right. It was the one defense that would probably keep him out of prison. But if he pleaded insanity, there would be a price. He'd have to close his business and spend the rest of his days doing . . . nothing.

"Good-bye, Eddie," he said.

◆

His cell phone rang when there were three cigarettes left in his pack. He stared at the face. Caller Unknown. Answering it was a risk—cell companies could trace any phone in seconds—but he did so anyway, hoping it was Mabel or his son, wanting desperately to hear a friendly voice.

"Mr. Valentine?"

His prayers were answered. It was Brandi.

"I'm on the other line with Archie," she said. "He heard what you did at The Bombay tonight. He wants to know what happened."

Valentine put one of the last cigarettes in his mouth but didn't light it up. He chose his words carefully. "Tell Archie a gang of employees is ripping him off. Frank Porter is one of the ringleaders. I was trying to nail them. They got wise, and tried to kill me."

Brandi put him on hold, then came back. "Archie wants to know why you ran from the police."

"Because there are police involved."

"Do you have proof?"

"Yes," he lied.

She put him on hold again, then came back. "Archie said not to worry. He's taking his private jet home tonight. He wants you to come to my apartment and lay low until he arrives. He says he'll get everything straightened out."

Her tone was businesslike. He liked that. She gave him her address, and he realized he knew exactly where she lived.

"I'll be there in ten minutes," he said.

◆

Brandi lived in the Reserve, a pricy high-rise condominium overlooking the ocean. Ten years before, Valentine and his wife had looked at a one-bedroom and found they couldn't afford to pay the monthly maintenance fee, let alone the mortgage.

He drove to a movie theater several blocks away and parked

behind the brick building. He got out of the car and stripped out of the fireman's uniform.

He hiked up Arctic Avenue, the stiff ocean breeze fighting his every step. It felt ten degrees colder than the last time he'd been outside, and he wondered if his body was trying to tell him something.

A block before the condo, he ducked into an alley. At its end was a fire escape, which he climbed to the roof. Back when he was in uniform, he'd climbed this building many times while chasing suspects, the view the best around.

Standing on the roof brought back a flood of memories. He stared up and down the street. None of the original businesses were open anymore. Gone was the baker and the shoemaker and the pet shop. Not good businesses to run in a casino town.

The building he stood on had once housed a sausage factory. Two chimneys stuck out of the roof like buck teeth. Standing in their shadows, he stared across the street at Brandi's condo. Through the front doors he could see into the lobby. The night guard sat at a desk, reading the paper. There was no one else around.

The guard got up to stretch. He was in his thirties, square-faced with curly hair. Night guards were usually old geezers like him. The guy was too young for this kind of drudgery. Taking out his cell phone, he dialed 911 and made his second false report of the night.

Having nothing better to do, he timed the fire trucks. They reached the condo in six minutes flat. That was why people loved firemen. Because they knew how to hurry.

Three trucks and a pair of ambulances crowded the front entrance. The night guard came outside, followed by a half dozen cops who'd been hiding in a back room.

He stared at the condo's glass walls, trying to guess which unit

Brandi occupied. And wondered why a woman who had everything money could buy would get involved in something like this. It was one more piece of the puzzle that didn't fit.

He thought he saw her looking down from the top floor. The penthouse. He dialed her number.

"Hello?" she answered.

"Brandi?"

"Mr. Valentine?"

"Nice try," he said.

32

The Man in the Purple Suit

The Armory's parking lot was full, the faithful braving the weather to drink beer and watch wrestling. Valentine squeezed the Mercedes between two sorry-looking pickup trucks. It was nine-ten. Kat went on in twenty minutes.

He sat for a while and felt the car grow cold. The question was, would Kat help him? Although he wasn't well versed in the ways of modern love, he knew that an invitation from a woman was a big thing, and Kat *had* asked him to come see her wrestle. She liked him. If he played his cards right, he was sure he could end up sleeping on her couch tonight.

The ticket taker would not take his money. "Show started an hour ago," he said. "Have fun."

Valentine went inside and bought a bucket of popcorn. The Armory had always been a bastion of male aggression, and he was having trouble imagining Kat doing battle within its walls. Pushing open the double doors, he was greeted by a roar.

The auditorium was packed, the mostly male audience yelling itself hoarse. Up in the ring, a man in orange tights was being pinned by a cartoon character wearing a hockey mask. Valentine found a vacant seat in the last row and fell into it, his feet slipping on spilled beer.

The wrestlers were both giants. Orange tights' girlfriend, a slinky miss in a red gown, entered the ring holding a folding chair.

Soon her boyfriend's opponent was lying facedown on the canvas. The crowd stomped its feet and cheered.

Hockey mask staggered to his feet. Orange tights offered his hand, being a gentleman about the whole thing. The blue-haired woman sitting beside Valentine did not approve.

"Cold-cock the motherfucker," she screamed.

Hockey mask obliged and threw a punch at his opponent, missing by a country mile. Popcorn flew into the ring. He tried again, and got a little closer. More popcorn. The third time, it almost looked real, and a collective cheer filled the auditorium.

Somehow, the contest ended with everyone being friends. If someone had told Valentine the script had been written by a ten-year-old kid, he wouldn't have been surprised.

The old woman with the dirty mouth pulled out a program. Valentine said, "Who's on next?"

"Vixen!"

"She good?"

"As mean as a junkyard dog."

"Who's she fighting?"

"A big-titted slut named Judo Queen. Doesn't stand a chance."

"Who said Judo Queen's a slut?"

The old woman drew back in her seat. "No offense, mister. You related or something?"

Valentine started to reply, then heard cheers. Kat was coming down an aisle on the opposite side of the auditorium. She slipped through the ropes and began dancing around. She looked great, her mane of hair flowing seductively down her back, her lips painted red. The sacred crane was nowhere to be seen. *Atta* girl, he thought.

Vixen came next, drawing boos. She was accompanied by her manager, a massive guy wearing a purple suit. He looked like a grape, and Valentine laughed so hard it made his stomach hurt. By the time Vixen reached the ring, other people in the crowd were laughing as well.

"What's so funny?" the old woman asked.

"The guy in the purple suit."

"Fits pretty good, if you ask me."

Vixen disrobed. About five-ten, done up in leather, a cat-o'-nine-tails strapped to her waist. Not a girl you'd bring home to Mom. She strutted around the ring, getting the crowd to shout her name. *Vix-en! Vix-en!*

The referee slipped through the ropes. Right away, Valentine saw a problem. He was about five feet tall and a hundred pounds soaking wet. A snack for either one of these ladies. And Vixen had trouble written all over her.

A bell rang and the women started to tango. There was lots of pushing and foot stomping but no real fighting until Vixen grabbed Kat's hair and started yanking. Kat let out a yell, then put Vixen down on the canvas with a perfectly executed hip throw.

"Kick her in the face!" the old woman yelled.

"You're all heart," Valentine said.

Vixen got up slowly, mouthing off to Kat. They circled one another, the distance between them growing smaller. Vixen got her hands in Kat's hair, and Kat emitted a scream that sounded real.

The crowd stood. Valentine found himself standing with them. The old woman strode past him into the aisle.

"Make that bitch pay, Vixen. Make her pay!"

Kat and Vixen rolled around, kicking and screaming until Kat ended up on top, holding Vixen in a hammerlock. Valentine found himself yelling his head off. As the midget referee started to count Vixen out, he joined him.

"Three . . . four . . . five . . . six . . ."

Then all hell broke loose.

Vixen's manager jumped into the ring. Grabbing Kat by the hair, he yanked her up, allowing Vixen to escape. He jerked Kat up and down. Then Vixen started slapping her face.

Kat was crying. Blood appeared beneath her nostril. Valentine ran down the aisle toward the ring. As he slipped through the ropes, the referee ran over.

"You're not allowed up here," the referee said.

"So what's the grape doing?"

"He's her manager."

"Well I'm Judo Queen's manager. Feel better?"

"It's just a job," the referee said defensively.

"Yeah, and you stink at it."

Valentine walked up to Vixen's manager and socked him on the jaw. The grape hit the canvas, dropping Kat. Valentine tried to break her fall, then heard a scream. Vixen landed on his back and dug her long fingernails into his arms.

He wasn't keen on fighting women but didn't see that he had much choice. Shifting his weight, he flipped her over his back. She hit the canvas like a bag of cement.

He helped Kat to her feet. The midget referee raised her arm into the air. The crowd was close to rioting they were having such a good time.

"How's your nose?" he shouted over the din.

"It's fine," she said. "Haven't you ever seen food dye before?"

His mouth opened, but no words came out.

"You are one flaming asshole," she informed him.

◆

As it turned out, Kat and Vixen—whose real name was Gladys LaFong—were as tight as sisters. They had daughters in middle school together, and liked to share vegetarian recipes they found on the Internet. Gladys had been in the wrestling racket for five years. The grape, her husband, was Donny LaFong, the same Donny LaFong who'd played football for the Jets and fumbled the ball on a crucial play in the Super Bowl, putting him in the Hall of Shame with many other sports notables. In person, he was a hell of a nice guy, as Valentine found out when he tried to apologize.

"No problemo," Donny said, pressing an ice pack to his swollen jaw. "They don't call it the hurt business for nothing."

"I really feel bad," Valentine said, glancing over to the corner of the dressing room where Kat and Gladys were huddled. "I really messed your act up, huh?"

"Well, yeah, I guess so," Donny said, picking up a can of Bud with his free hand. "You want a cold one?"

"No, thanks. Is there someone I could call, explain what happened?"

"That's not how it works in the rassling business," Donny explained.

"What do you mean?"

Donny killed his beer and wiped his mouth on his sleeve. "They call you. The promoters. They pull the strings. It's their show, and we're the hired clowns."

"I'm really sorry," Valentine said for the fifth time.

"Don't worry about it."

Valentine put his hand on the big man's shoulder. "I was in the end zone when you ran that fumble in for a touchdown against Miami in the playoffs."

Donny flashed him his best aw-shucks smile.

"Thanks for remembering," he said.

Gladys and Kat were not nearly as forgiving. They sat with Donny's purple jacket spread between them, trying to stitch up the popped shoulders. Neither woman looked up when he came over. Valentine cleared his throat. "Hey, look, if there's any way I can repair what I did . . . please tell me."

Gladys refused to acknowledge him. Without makeup she was a plain-looking, freckle-faced woman in her late thirties with an honest face and a soft Virginia twang. Kat said, "No, Tony, there isn't anything you can do."

"Maybe I could call the promoter, explain what happened."

Kat pulled him out of the dressing room into the tunnel. The night's final match was wrapping up, and the crowd's cheers rocked the building. Pinching his arm, she said, "Do you have any idea the trouble you've caused? We're not allowed to improvise, Tony, it's in our goddamned contracts."

He swallowed hard. "I thought you were getting hurt. The way Donny was bouncing you around. I don't know . . . I just had to do something. I'm really sorry."

"Somehow, that doesn't make me feel any better," she said.

"Why not?"

"Because it's a pattern with you. Remember the night we met? You climbed into the ring and knocked me down. Okay, maybe I deserved it, but it still didn't make it right. You can't just go jumping into things and beat people up."

He started to reply, then stopped. He'd been knocking people down for most of his life, and had a sneaking suspicion that it was too late for him to stop.

"I'm sorry," he said.

"I think you've run out of those."

He kicked at the floor. "I need a favor."

She crossed her arms. "What's that?"

"Can I sleep on your couch tonight?"

Her hand slapped his face, the sound as loud as a popping balloon. He saw tears in her eyes. Storming into the dressing room, she slammed the door behind her.

♦

Valentine wiped freshly fallen snow off the Mercedes' wind-shield before climbing in. Sticking the key in the ignition, he played with the radio and finally found Sinatra singing "That's Life" on a jazz show on the public station. He jacked up the volume. The song ended sooner than he would have hoped.

Sinatra had a way of making the world a lot clearer, and it occurred to Valentine that he'd run out of options. Taking out his cell phone, he turned the power on. He needed to call a couple of attorneys and get one to take his case. With an attorney's help, he'd work out his story, then call Davis and negotiate his surrender. He was going to have to go on the defensive, his life about to become a living hell. He decided to call Mabel, desperately needing a friendly voice to talk to.

"Oh, Tony, I'm so glad it's you," his neighbor said.

"What's wrong?"

"I've got a woman named Lin Lin on the other line."

"Is this about Yun?"

"Yes. Three thugs abducted him. The thugs told Lin Lin to get ahold of you."

Valentine leaned his forehead on the cold steering wheel. "Did she say where they were taking him?"

"To a dojo, whatever that is. They told Lin Lin if she calls the police, they'll kill him."

"Tell Lin Lin I'm going to the dojo right now."

Mabel put him on hold. The parking lot was a zoo, with everyone trying to leave at once. Throwing the Mercedes into reverse, he backed out of the space, then threw the car into drive. With his hand stuck against the horn, he made his way to the front of the line. His neighbor returned.

"This has been an awful day," she said.

"What's wrong?"

"Cujo attacked me."

"You got the dog?"

"Yes. While I was fixing dinner, he tried to take a pork chop out of my hand. I hit him with a skillet right in the kisser and he started going at my ankles so I jumped up on the table so he couldn't get at me."

"Where are you now?"

"I'm still standing on the table."

"Why didn't you call the cops?"

"I did. There's a disturbance at the Seminole Indian reservation in Tampa. The operator said I would have to wait."

"Maybe you should call a neighbor," he suggested.

"Aren't you Mr. Helpful," she said, and hung up.

33

The Death of
Tony Valentine

The stairwell groaned beneath Valentine's size twelves. The building that housed Yun's dojo had been ancient when he'd first started taking classes. At the second floor landing he stopped. The door was ajar, and he pushed it open and poked his head in. The dojo was a large, high-ceilinged room with padded walls. A naked bulb shone over the locker room door.

Only bare feet were meant to walk on the dojo's parquet floors, and he left his shoes by the door. Crossing the dojo, he drew the .38 from his pocket. Opening the locker room door, he stuck his head in.

The room was long and narrow, with lockers on both walls and showers in back. His teacher sat bound to a chair. The Mollos stood behind him. Big Tony, his right hand in a cast, was holding a Louisville slugger. Seeing Valentine, he took a cut at Yun's head. His teacher ducked, the baseball bat whistling past his skull. Joey, his face swathed in white tape, called, "Strike one!" Little Tony pranced around like a demented court jester.

Valentine's heart started to race. "Is this necessary?"

"Top of the ninth, two out, tying run at third base," Joey said, egging his brother on. "Count on the batter is no balls, one strike."

"This is for breaking my hand," Big Tony said. He cocked the bat like Joe Morgan of the Cincinnati Reds, flapping his right arm as the pitcher started to throw the ball, his muscles twitching in anticipation.

"Don't do it," Valentine said.

"Give me one good reason why I shouldn't."

"I won't pay you."

That got Big Tony's attention. He lowered the bat. For the first time, Valentine became aware of Yun's breathing. It was abbreviated, his teacher slowing his heart beat in an attempt to stay calm.

"You brought the money?"

"Don't have it," Valentine said.

"Then how you gonna pay us?"

He took the Mercedes keys from his pocket, and let them dangle from his forefinger. "You can have my car."

Big Tony eyed the logo. "You got a Mercedes?"

"SLK 600 coupe."

"How many miles?"

"Sixteen thousand."

"Leather interior?"

"No, plastic. Of course it's got a leather interior. You ever driven one?" Big Tony shook his head. "It's almost as nice as getting laid."

"Put the gun in one of the lockers."

"Do we have a deal?"

Big Tony nodded.

"I didn't hear you," Valentine said.

"We have a deal," Big Tony said.

Valentine put the .38 in a locker and shut the steel door. He'd been tapping into Neanderthals' wavelengths for years, and knew how the Mollos thought. Before anything else, they wanted their money. He watched Big Tony untie Yun.

Yun joined Valentine by the door. Valentine tossed the keys across the room. Big Tony plucked them out of the air. He showed the keys to his brothers. And then he kissed them.

223

"What about the title?" Big Tony asked.

"I'll send it to you," Valentine said.

♦

The Mollos followed them out of the locker room, with Little Tony doing a cartwheel as he came through the door. Joey now had the bat and pointed it in Yun's face.

"You're one lucky Chinaman," Joey said.

Laughing, they disappeared into the stairwell. Valentine touched Yun's arm. "You okay?"

Yun rubbed his arm where it had been tied. "Whose car you give them?"

"Archie Tanner's."

"Oh, wow," his teacher said.

Blaring rap music disrupted their conversation. They went to the dojo's wall of windows and stared down. The Mollos had piled into the Mercedes and were hooting and hollering like teenagers. The car rocked up and down like a carnival ride.

"He got insurance?" his teacher asked.

"Of course he's—"

Valentine's eyes shifted to the other end of Ashton. Parked at the corner was a white van, its engine running. The driver's window came down. An arm emerged, holding what looked like a transistor radio.

The Mercedes pulled onto the street. Sitting in back, Little Tony had lit a joint. Big Tony turned, poised to take it from him. And that was the image that remained in Valentine's head when the car exploded.

A brilliant white flash followed, momentarily blinding him. His knees buckled. When he looked down at the street again, the Mercedes was in a thousand pieces. And the white van was gone.

◆

Ashton resembled a war zone. Little Tony lay on the sidewalk and was now much littler, the lower half of his body gone. Joey lay beside him, his torso consumed by flames. Big Tony lay nearby, his head the color of a roasted chestnut. He was still breathing. Valentine took off his overcoat, and slipped it underneath Big Tony's head. Then he died, and Valentine put his overcoat back on.

"You didn't tell me somebody was trying to kill you," Yun said.

"It's been that kind of week."

"Turned out okay," his teacher said.

"What do you mean?"

"This was your car. Cops come, I tell them one of these guys was you. Let them figure out which one. You dead, at least for a little while. That gives you advantage."

"Over who?"

"Whoever trying to kill you."

A police car's siren pierced the frigid night air. Being dead gave him another advantage as well. The police would stop looking for him. He touched his teacher's arm.

"I've missed you," he said.

"I miss you, too, Tony boy."

◆

Sprinting up the stairwell, Valentine hurried across the dojo to the locker room. Chances were, the cops would ask Yun to let them inside the dojo, just to poke around. He retrieved the .38 from the locker. Opening a window, he climbed out and jumped.

His knees did not approve. Soon he was hobbling down a deserted street. The sirens had awoken every stray dog in town. Their howling was spooky, like a chorus of lost souls that had decided to have a sing-along. A car snuck up from behind, its headlights capturing him in two perfect spheres of light. It was a checkered cab. He got in.

The driver was one of the legion of old-timers that served Atlantic City's streets with class and distinction. Flipping the meter on, he said, "Your wish is my command."

"Blue Dolphin motel."

"A fine establishment."

The driver drove two blocks north, then started to make a left off Atlantic. Valentine barked his displeasure. "Hey buddy, I grew up here. Where you going?"

"There was a shooting on Atlantic. The police have the block closed off. My dispatcher told me to avoid the spot."

"Where on Atlantic?"

"Right outside the Burger King."

The Burger King was across the street from the Drake. He'd told Anna to stay on the beach, and remembered all the junk food wrappers he'd seen in their apartment. He brought his face up to the bullet-proof glass. "Did your dispatcher say what happened?"

The driver looked at him in his mirror. "You a cop?"

"Ex."

"I thought you looked familiar. Dispatcher said some foreign guy walking out of the Burger King got shot by someone in a van."

"How did your dispatcher know it was a foreign guy?"

"That's what the dispatcher heard over the police dispatch. You want me to take you there?"

"I thought you said the street was blocked off."

"I know a back way," the driver said.

◆

Valentine found the Croatian's white van parked on a side street next to the Drake. He walked up the path to the motel's front office. Inside, he saw the manager reading the paper and smoking a cigarette. He went in.

Atlantic City being a gambling town, everyone had a price. For the manager at the Drake, all it took was a fifty dollar bill to reveal the Croatians' room number. They were staying in number 33, second room from the very end.

Valentine walked down the unlit path to the room. Knocking, he stepped to one side and drew his gun. Juraj Havelka cracked the door an inch. With bloodshot eyes he stared down the .38's barrel, then backed into the room.

"We have company," Juraj said.

Valentine shut the door behind him. Anna sat on the floor, watching the news on the TV. She slowly rose.

"They killed Alex," she said.

Valentine looked at Juraj. "Your brother?"

"Yes," Juraj said.

Anna put her arms around Juraj's shoulders. She'd been crying so hard that her eyes looked like busted panes of glass. "Alex and I went to get dinner. He was crossing the street with the food. A car pulled up with two men inside. There was a shot and Alex sank to the ground." She stared at the carpet. "I ran."

"That was a smart thing to do," Valentine said.

Her eyes met his. "Yes?"

"Yes."

"Please shut up," Juraj said angrily.

On the TV, a reporter appeared. He was standing on a street corner talking to Yun. Valentine moved closer to the set. The reporter said, "Can you tell us what happened here tonight?"

The camera panned to show the smoldering remains of Archie Tanner's Mercedes, the twelve-cylinder engine a molten mass. Big Tony and his brothers were covered in yellow tarps. Valentine pointed at the screen.

"That used to be my car," he said.

"They are after you, too?" Anna asked.

"Yes."

Juraj was unmoved by the pictures on the TV.

"Too bad my brother was not so lucky," he said.

34

The Last Time

Anna and Juraj were hungry, and they were broke. Valentine found an all-night convenience store, bought groceries, and delivered them to the Croatians' room a short while later. With the food came a stiff warning: Don't go out unless someone's dying, and leave the Do Not Disturb sign on the door.

Anna followed him outside. She was upset, and beneath the starless sky she explained why. "Juraj is convinced you are part of The Bombay gang."

Valentine lit up one of his last cigarettes and filled his lungs with the great-tasting smoke. Did being dead mean he could smoke and eat tons of fatty food, and not worry about it killing him? It seemed only fair, considering what he'd been through.

"Why's that?"

"When Juraj told you it was Alex who had been murdered, you did not act surprised."

"I wasn't."

She seemed confused, as if Juraj's accusations were suddenly hitting home. He wagged a finger in her face, the words spilling out in a mouthful of smoke. "What the hell is wrong with you and Juraj? You told me yourself you thought you were being set up by The Bombay. And now you're surprised that you're getting killed? You should have left town when you had the chance."

She stared at the frozen ground. Then her eyes rose to meet his. "Are you always so . . . I don't know the expression. Self-righteous?"

"If that's what you want to call it, yeah, I usually am."

"What gives you that privilege?" she demanded.

Valentine had to think about it.

"I guess because I'm usually right."

Anna marched down the path to her motel room. He finished his cigarette, then took a walk on the beach.

◆

His whole life, he'd been taking walks on the beach. After school, after work, and now, in retirement, whenever it suited him, which translated into almost every day. By the shoreline he found a dozen empty beer bottles, and he dug a plastic bag out of a trash can and gathered them up. He'd lived on this beach as a kid, and it made him sick to see the amount of cans and bottles and other trash strewn around. Was it his imagination, or did people not love things as much as they used to?

He walked down to the Blue Dolphin. Going to the fence that separated it from the beach, he stood on tiptoe and peered over. Coleman and Marconi were standing in front of the motel talking to the night manager. Dangling from Marconi's hand was a large plastic bag. Cops were genetically incapable of hurrying, and he grew cold watching them grill the manager.

He thought about his conversation with Kat the day before. The drug dealer killings Marconi had boasted about had happened three years earlier when he was still on the force. Five coke dealers had been shot in the head and robbed over a period of six months. One shooting had occurred in the parking lot of a casino where Valentine had been working.

The dealer had been dying when Valentine had reached the scene. He'd been no more than a kid. When Valentine had asked him to describe his assailant, the dealer had managed to stroke his face once, then gone to meet his maker. Valentine hadn't understood the kid's dying gesture—until now. It was an allusion to the invisible scar on Marconi's cheek.

Valentine watched Coleman and Marconi get into their car and leave. The manager went inside his office and turned out the light. Popping the latch on the fence, he slipped onto the property.

The plastic key to his room still worked. He entered the darkened room, kicking furniture as he let the shades down. His big toe caught a bedpost. He cursed silently.

Then he turned on a light and had a look around. Marconi and Coleman had rifled the drawers and selectively taken different pieces of clothing. In the bathroom, he found his toilet kit gone. Some pieces of clothing were still hanging in the closet, and he guessed the detectives had only taken items that fit them.

He sat on the bed. His head hurt, his feet were cold, and his stomach was aching for a hot meal. But more than anything else, his sixty-two-year-old body was nearing a state of total exhaustion.

He opened the window an inch, hoping he would hear any unwanted visitors approach. Then, taking off his clothes, he slipped beneath the bed's warm blankets and was soon sound asleep.

◆

He dreamed he was standing next to a construction worker. The construction worker had a jackhammer and was busting up a piece of pavement. He yelled in the man's ear but got nowhere, the jackhammer drowning out all sound.

He opened his eyes. Someone was banging on the door of the adjacent room. It was morning, the sunlight splashing on the walls. Rising, he grabbed the .38 off the night table and went to the door to his room. He cracked it open and looked out. And blinked. Kat Berman stood outside.

He shut the door. He slipped the .38 into the pocket of his overcoat, then threw on yesterday's clothes. Patting down his hair, he opened the door.

"Looking for someone?" he said.

"You," she said, smiling. "Actually, your son. I was hoping he'd tell me how to find you."

"Well, here I am."

She surprised him with a kiss on the cheek. "Can I come in?"

"Sure," he heard himself say.

When they were sitting on the couch in his room, she said, "I need to talk to you."

"Isn't that what we're doing?"

"Serious talk." Taking her handbag off the floor, she removed a liter of Fresca and two plastic cups. She poured, nearly emptying the bottle.

"Are we celebrating something?" he asked.

"We most certainly are. I don't drink booze, so I hope you don't mind the soda." She handed him one of the cups. "Cheers."

"Bottoms up."

She giggled, reading more into his toast than he'd intended. His face grew red and he shifted uncomfortably. What the hell was going on? Twelve hours ago, she'd been ready to neuter him. They finished their sodas in silence. Then Kat put her hand on his leg. And left it there.

"This morning, Gladys and Donny and I had a meeting with

the promoter who staged last night's show. Guy named Rick Honey. Rick produces wrestling shows for cable TV. Anyway, Rick sits us down in his office, acts like he's pissed. He used to be a wrestler, called himself Mr. Clean. So Rick says, 'Whose idea was it to change last night's script?' "

"I hope you told him it was mine," Valentine said.

"Of course not! Nobody tells the truth in this business, Tony. So Donny says, 'It was my idea, Rick. I thought the script stunk.' Now, Rick just stares at us for a minute like he doesn't know what to say. Then he reaches into his desk drawer and takes out some contracts. He tosses them on the desk, and he says, 'You know what these are?' We all nod our heads and Rick says, 'Before we talk terms, I want there to be an understanding. From now on, we stick to the script, okay?' Well, Donny and Gladys and I looked at each other, and I can't tell you how hard it was not to laugh!"

"Terms for what?"

"For me and Gladys to fight each other *five* times. Rick said the Armory got more calls after last night than any other wrestling match they've had. We were a hit."

"You're kidding me," Valentine said.

"No, I'm not. We stole the show."

He felt his spirits soar. He hadn't screwed up Kat's life after all. Maybe spilling his guts out to Father Tom at confession had done more good than he'd realized.

"What kind of money did he offer you?" he said.

"Five bouts, ten thousand dollars a bout."

Valentine took her hand and squeezed it. "That's the best news I've heard all week. I hope you said yes."

"There's a catch."

"What's that?"

She removed some legal-looking papers from her handbag and dropped them in his lap.

"The deal is for all four of us."

"I'm not following you," Valentine said.

"Donny told Rick you were part of the act."

"He did what?"

"Tony—don't get mad, please."

Valentine picked up the papers and held them up to his face. It was a contract, his name at the top of the page. His role as the jealous boyfriend was clearly spelled out. He would beat Donny up, only this time he'd get paid for it, two grand a pop. On the bottom of the page were the dates, the first show three weeks away at the Orlando Centroplex.

"This is crazy," he said, putting the contract down. "You should have told this guy the truth, Kat."

"But, we couldn't . . ."

"No—you didn't want to."

She started to reply, then dropped her head so her chin was touching her chest. "You're not going to do it."

"I'm not a wrestler," he said, feeling his blood boil in a different way now, unable to rein in his feelings. "I could have hurt someone. You said it yourself. Now you want me to do it professionally. For the love of Christ, what are you thinking, girl?"

"Oh, fuck it." Taking the contract from him, she threw it across the room. "You stepped into the ring, didn't you? My life was going along just fine until you came along. This is the chance of a lifetime Tony—of my fucking lifetime. But do you care? No! You just want to keep messing things up for me, don't you?"

"You know that isn't true," he said.

"Then why won't you do it? It would be fun, and three of the shows are in Florida, so you'd be in your backyard. And Donny and Gladys are a scream. Come on, Tony."

Because it's stupid, Valentine thought. So stupid that he couldn't see himself participating. The bottom of the social totem pole. But if he told her that, she'd walk out and he'd never see her again, and he didn't want that either.

"Can I think about it?"

"That is so lame," she said.

He blew out the air trapped in his lungs. "All right."

"Meaning what?"

He looked into her eyes. "For you, okay."

"Oh, Tony!"

She threw her arms around him and started kissing his face. Her breath was hot, her lips as sweet as confectionery sugar. Soon every part of his body was aroused, and he couldn't have turned back if he'd wanted to.

◆

The last time he'd made love had been eighteen months ago.

He'd done it with his wife on the couch in the living room of their new home in Palm Harbor. The couch had been delivered that morning, and its addition had made the house complete. It was the beginning of their new lives; like a pair of kids he and Lois had stripped off each other's clothes and done the wild thing.

It had been great. So much so, they'd gone to bed after dinner and made love again, then fallen asleep wrapped in each other's arms.

The next morning, he'd lain in bed and run his fingers through Lois's hair, hoping she'd wake up wanting to do it one more time. Only she hadn't.

The autopsy had revealed that his wife was suffering from degenerative heart disease. Lois had always been in touch with her body, and Valentine figured that she'd known something inside of her wasn't working right. Only she'd said nothing, wanting to get settled in before seeing a doctor.

Whatever the reason, she had spared him from news he felt cer- tain she knew was bad.

Later on, he'd realized a terrible thing. He'd instigated the sex, something he did from time to time, his choice of venues not always appropriate. Lois never complained, and sometimes had more fun than he did.

Only this last time, it had been all him, and he could not help but think that the exertion had added a strain to her already fragile heart, and that it had killed her.

Which made him what? A carnal killer? It ripped him apart to think that his cravings had destroyed the thing he loved the most in this world. The guilt had hung heavy on his soul, and made the idea of having sex impossible.

Until now.

◆

Had someone been staying next door, Valentine guessed they'd be banging on the walls about now, he and Kat having more fun than civilized people were supposed to have. It was sex with fireworks in the background, the kind of sex you heard about, read about, saw on the big screen, but never got to experience firsthand, the problem not with your plumbing or your mate, but just the situation itself. It was sex with a wild, unbridled glee tacked on to it, a smoldering fire suddenly doused with buckets of gasoline.

He tried not to think of Lois, and for the most part he succeeded. But her memory crept up a few times, and he found himself imagining her in the place she now inhabited, judging him. Any other time, it would have stopped him cold, only he was too far gone to care.

"What are you thinking," Kat whispered a half hour later.

The blankets were off the bed and the lamp from the night table lay on the floor. Valentine stared at the cheap popcorn ceiling, his lungs aching for a cigarette.

"I'm thinking I'd better up my life insurance if I'm going to hang around with you."

"Come on, be serious."

"I haven't felt this good in a long time," he admitted.

"Tell me something about yourself," she said a short while later. "Something no one else knows."

He turned on his side and looked at her. He didn't have a lot of secrets—what you saw was pretty much what you got—and had to think about it some.

"And don't make something up," she added.

"Okay," he said after a lengthy pause, "I'll tell you a story that I never told anyone."

"What's that?"

"I once let a cheater go."

"On purpose?"

"Uh-huh."

Kat propped herself up on an elbow. "I'm all ears."

"Back when Atlantic City first opened, the casino owners didn't know what they were doing. Hustlers liked the town so much, they'd called it a candy store.

"One night, I was standing in the blackjack pit at the Sands. A woman in a motorized wheelchair came in. She was about seventy, and her name was Justine. She told the pit boss she'd been in a car accident, gotten a settlement from the insurance company, and wanted to play some blackjack. The pit boss cleared a spot at a table, and Justine started playing all seven hands, a hundred bucks a bet.

"Woman was a real character. Chain-smoking, drinking whis-

key, calling the pit boss and the dealer 'Honey' and 'Sweetie.'
Everyone loved her, until she started winning."

"How much did she win?"

"After an hour, she had all the dealer's chips."

"How much was that?"

"Around twenty grand."

"Was she cheating?"

"Well, *I* thought she was."

"How come?"

"It didn't pass the smell test. If she'd only played one hand, I
would have said beginner's luck. But she played all seven. It felt
like a hustle."

Kat giggled. "The smell test. I like that."

He touched his nose. "Still works pretty good."

"So what happened?"

"The dealer gets more chips, and Justine goes back to work,
bam, bam, bam, and just beats him silly. And then she innocently
asks, 'Can I bet more?'

"She's already betting the table limit, so the pit boss asks the
shift manager. The shift manager wants to win his money back, so
he says sure. Then he turns to me and says, 'You agree?' Well, I
didn't agree. So I grabbed a drink girl—"

"Cocktail waitress."

"—sorry, and I took a glass of water off her tray. I'd come up
with a theory of what Justine was doing, and I decided to test it."

Their bodies had finally cooled down, and Kat covered them
with a blanket. "Which was what?"

"Blackjack is hard to play, especially if you're talking. And
Justine was talking to everybody. I couldn't figure out how she
was keeping track of all her cards. And then it hit me. She wasn't
playing her hands."

"Who was?"

"The wheelchair. There was a computer hidden in the motor. Justine was entering the cards on a keypad, then looking at a digital readout. So I went and spilled my water on her. The next thing you know, the wheelchair starts smoking."

"Is having a computer illegal?"

"It sure is."

"Then why did you let her go?"

"It was strange. I looked at her, and she looked at me. She was scared. I had a feeling it was the first time she'd ever broken the law. I said, 'Learned your lesson?' And she nodded. So I looked away, and she ran out of the casino."

"Did you get in trouble?"

"No. The computer melted, so all the evidence was destroyed. I later got grilled by my captain, but I got out of it."

"How?"

"I told him I'd doused her with holy water."

Kat punched him in the arm. "You're horrible," she said.

35

Tattoos

Valentine did not want to start their relationship with a lie, so he asked Kat to get dressed, then told her everything that had taken place in the past twenty-four hours, including how the Mollo brothers had been turned into cinders the night before. Brushing out her hair, she said, "Well, I guess they got what was coming to them."

He sat on the bed buttoning his shirt. Nothing he'd said had fazed her, and he guessed the great sex had something to do with it. It had certainly bolstered his own spirits.

The Saturn's engine was slow to turn over. Kat gunned the accelerator and the car rose from its slumber. "Normally, I don't bring guys I've just met to my house," she said, "but with you I'll make an exception."

Valentine thought she was joking. Then he remembered that Kat had a twelve-year-old daughter she was raising by herself.

"Thanks," he said.

◆

She lived in a rented bungalow in Stargate, a sleepy burg five miles south of Atlantic City. The town was still reeling from the last recession, the hundreds of millions being skimmed off the casinos by the state not filling a single pothole or planting a much-needed tree. The promise of a better tomorrow had never been kept, and probably never would.

Her house sat on a dreary street with tiny, fenced-in yards. She eased the Saturn up the concrete slab that served as her driveway and killed the engine.

"It's not much, but I call it home."

Valentine touched her arm.

"Let's get one thing straight," he said.

"What's that?"

"You don't ever have to apologize about your life to me."

She leaned over and kissed him. It felt just as good as the first time, and it didn't wear off until they were standing on the porch and she let out a shriek.

The front door had been kicked in and leaned precariously against the door jamb. Making her stand back, he drew his .38 and entered the house.

The rooms were small but clean. He saw no pulled-out drawers, or upturned furniture, or anything that might suggest vandals. A strange odor lingered in the air, the smell reminding him of burnt marshmallows.

Coming onto the porch, he said, "Looks okay," and she ran past him and headed for the bedroom, emerging moments later with a strongbox in her arms. She dumped its contents onto a couch. Money, most of it twenties, poured out.

Valentine helped her count it. Twelve hundred and forty bucks. He saw the anxiety vanish from her face.

"It's all here," she said.

"How about your jewelry?"

"I wear it," she said, "but the TV's still here, and the VCR and my computer." She started to stuff the twenties back into the strongbox. "I don't get it. Why didn't they take anything?"

"Beats me. What the heck is that smell, anyway?"

"I thought it was you."

"Me?"

"You didn't light a cigarette?"

Valentine shook his head. He had two cigarettes left and had decided that when they were gone, there would be no more. He cased the place again.

Kat's house was filled with old-fashioned bric-a-brac, just like his place in Florida, and he went around sniffing pots of flowers and other things known to occasionally produce a bad odor. The smell was strongest in the kitchen, so he checked the various appliances capable of starting a fire.

The stove was off, as was the coffee maker and toaster. Stymied, he rifled through the garbage can. Kat entered the room. "Why'd you turn off the radio?"

"I didn't," he said.

The radio, a white retro Sony, sat on the counter beside a Betty Crocker recipe box. He pulled it away from the wall, and found a dime-size hole in one its speakers. Squinting, he saw where the bullet had gone through the wall and made a peephole onto the backyard.

"I leave it on all the time," she said, peering over his shoulder. "There's a jazz station I like."

"WQRX?"

"That's the one."

"You dig Sinatra?"

"Doesn't everybody?"

Now he was truly in love. He put the radio back in its spot.

"Okay, Mr. Detective," she said. "Why would a burglar shoot my radio out?"

A burglar wouldn't shoot your radio out, he thought. Burglars came through windows, or back doors, and if they didn't find something worth stealing, left their mark in some way—like stealing a beer from the fridge, or pissing on a woman's underwear. That was the mentality of people who robbed houses, their patterns as predictable as the weather.

And burglars didn't enter houses with their guns drawn, as the intruders who'd entered Kat's house had done. Entering the kitchen, they'd been startled by a voice on the radio and had mistakenly shot it out.

"Wait a minute," she said, sitting behind the wheel of her car a minute later. "You're telling me these burglars were planning to kill me?"

"Yes."

"Why?"

He could think of only one logical answer.

"Because you know me," he said.

"Jesus, Tony."

He thought of the other people in his life who might be targets. Taking out his cell phone, he hit Power, and found that the battery had gone dead.

"Where's the closest pay phone?"

She drove to a 7-Eleven on the next block. The pay phone was in the back of the store by the bathrooms. Feeding quarters into the slot, he dialed Davis's cell number.

"Hello?" the detective said.

"Hey, Eddie," he said.

With horns blaring in the background, Davis pulled off the road. "Who the hell is this?"

"Tony Valentine," he said.

There was an uneasy silence. Then Valentine remembered: He was supposed to be dead.

"This is Richard Roundtree, isn't it?"

"Valentine! You're not dead?"

"Never felt better."

"There are three bodies down at the morgue . . ."

"It's a long story. Look, I need to ask you a question. Have you been home recently?"

"What?" the detective said.

"Yes or no?"

"No, not that it's any of your—"

"Go home right now and see if you weren't broken into."

"*What?*"

"You heard me." He read Davis the number printed on the pay phone. "Call me back and see if I wasn't right."

The phone went dead in his hand.

Kat came into the store, bought a bottled water, and struck up a conversation with the weirdo manning the register. The guy was downright scary-looking, his face pierced with black pins, his hair a mix of lollipop colors. She didn't seem bothered and happily chatted away.

Valentine loitered around the pay phone. Ten minutes later, the phone rang. Lifting the receiver, he said, "Was I right?"

"They shot my goddamned dog," Davis seethed.

"*What?*"

"Had this dog since I was in college. They busted down the back door, and Bruno must have attacked them."

"Any of your neighbors see them?"

"Yeah. They fit the description of Coleman and Marconi." Davis paused. "But you knew that, didn't you?"

"They were at the top of my list. Did your neighbors call 911?"

"Call 911? I live in a black neighborhood, Tony. Whatever Coleman and Marconi say happened, that's what the police are going to believe." He paused again. "You haven't explained why they're after me."

"Because they think I made the scam at The Bombay and then told you."

"You're saying I'm fucked," the detective said.

"Yes, I'd say you're fucked."

He could almost hear Davis thinking. "Maybe I'd better call in sick, and go hang at my girlfriend's."

"I would," Valentine said.

Davis recited his girlfriend's phone number. Valentine wrote it down on the palm of his hand, then hung up.

Behind the register, the weirdo had taken off his shirt and was displaying the colorful array of tattoos adorning his upper torso. Each was of a famous wrestler–the Hulkster, the Rock, Stone Cold Steve Austin–and the weirdo did tricks with his muscles that made them come to life, with Kat ohhing and ahhing at the appropriate moments. Valentine hooked his arm into hers and bolted from the store.

"Let me guess," she said when they were on the road. "You don't like body art."

"You didn't see me sporting any tattoos, did you?"

"Can't say I looked that hard."

"They're crude. Some religions think they're blasphemous."

"Name one."

"Okay. The Jews. I knew a Jewish guy who had a tattoo. He died, and his wife wanted him buried in a Jewish cemetery. So they cut his arm off."

She made a face. "I was thinking of getting one. Lots of women wrestlers have them."

He gave her a look that said this conversation would go no further. She stared at the road.

"So what did they do with the arm?" she asked a few minutes later.

"I guess they buried it in a Gentile cemetery."

"Very funny," she said, punching him in the shoulder.

36

The Four Kings Approach

Valentine needed a car.

Kat drove him to the Hertz lot at Bader Airport, and he rented a Mustang. As he turned the car on, Van Morrison's "Tupelo Honey" came blaring out of the radio's speakers.

He parked next to Kat's Saturn and got into her car. Kat was on her cell phone telling the principal at her daughter's school why she was pulling Zoe out. She hung up.

"What a pencil dick. Zoe's already missed so many classes, what difference will another day make?"

He took out his cigarettes. "Mind if I smoke?"

"Is that a little question or a big question?"

"What do you mean?"

"Do I mind if you smoke in my car, as in right now, or do I mind if you happen to smoke, as in all the time?"

He showed her the two remaining cigarettes in his pack. "I've got these to go, then I'm back on the wagon."

"Go ahead."

He lit up, then exhaled a dark plume. When the cigarette was nearly gone, Kat spoke.

"You haven't told me what you're going to do."

No, he hadn't. He'd told Kat what he wanted *her* to do, which was fly to Florida with Zoe and hole up in his house until this thing played itself out. It was the best he could offer, and he'd been relieved when she'd said yes.

"You don't want to know," he said.

"*Tony . . .*"

He filled his lungs with smoke. Knowing it was one of his last cigarettes made it taste that much better. He stared across the lot into the rental car office. "I need to find out how The Bombay's getting ripped off. Frank Porter knows, so I'm going to make him tell me."

"Make him how?"

"I'm going to use the Four Kings approach."

"It sounds ugly."

"You ever been to Fremont Street in Las Vegas?"

"I've never been west of the Mississippi."

The cigarette was nearly out. He smoked it until he tasted the filter, then snuffed it in the ashtray. "When people think of Las Vegas, they think of the Strip, and all the big casinos. But the original Las Vegas is on Fremont Street. Locals call it old downtown. The casinos here are old-fashioned joints.

"The Four Kings is one of the better ones, a member of the 'All Right to Be Bright Club.' The interior is light and tropical. Old-timers dig the food and the lounge shows. There are some high rollers, but mostly it's just the motor coach market.

"Anyway, the Four Kings has a strict policy about cheating. It's been in force for years, and every crossroader who's ever worked Las Vegas knows about it. If you get caught cheating, they drag you into the back room. And in that back room there's a wall. The wall was originally white, but it hasn't been painted in forever.

"The wall is covered in crossroaders' blood. By the time you leave that room, some of your blood gets added to that wall. That's the deal. If you're new, it's usually just a punch in the mouth. But if they've seen you before, watch out. The Four Kings approach."

"That's brutal," she said.

"It is. And you want to know something?"

"What?"

"It works. The Four Kings has been ripped off the least of any casino in Nevada, probably any casino in the world. Don't get me wrong: I'm not advocating beating up criminals. I'm just telling you what works with crossroaders. You have to threaten them, and then you have to be willing to back it up."

"Is it really necessary?"

He took her hand with both of his. "They killed my best friend, and they tried to kill me. And now they're after you and Eddie. You're goddamned right it's necessary."

He followed Kat to her daughter's school. Soon Zoe came out. A skinny waif, too much makeup, and a boy's haircut made up the package. She got into the Saturn and immediately started arguing with her mother.

Valentine followed them to the exit for the New Jersey Turnpike. The Saturn went up the long entrance ramp, then stopped. He saw Kat turn and wave good-bye. He waved back.

◆

How Frank Porter had saved his house in Pheasant Run from his ex-wife was one of the great mysteries of New Jersey.

Frank had bought five acres of wooded paradise twenty years before, then saved his dough and built his dream house, a two-story A-frame with a wood deck sitting off the second story. Designed like a Swiss chalet, the house was a favorite gathering place and had hosted many Sunday afternoon football parties.

Valentine inched the Mustang up the long, sloping driveway.

Halfway up, he pulled off the road and got out. The underbrush was heavy, and the car got swallowed by the forest.

He knew Frank's schedule about as well as his own. Today, a Friday, was one of Frank's off days. Usually, he stayed at home, tinkering in his shop or working in the yard.

The climb up the gravel driveway got his heart going. The wind was blowing through the trees, creating a thousand whispers. It was strange, but he did not feel apprehensive. The tip of the A-frame appeared above the treetops. Then the rest of the house took shape. Up in Frank's study a light was on.

He went around back and entered the two-car garage.

The door leading into the house was unlocked, and he cracked it an inch. Strains of B.B. King floated through the downstairs. A long time ago, Frank had played a mean blues guitar, then one day upped and quit. New priorities, Valentine remembered him saying.

He walked through the laundry room and into the kitchen. The kitchen had an island in its center, and on it sat a large coin counting machine, with thousands of dollar coin-wrappers arranged neatly behind it.

He walked down a hall and entered Frank's study. The TV set was on, *Baywatch* competing with B.B. Frank was riding a stationary bike while talking into a cell phone. Their eyes met. Valentine made a hurry-up motion with the .38.

"Got to go," Porter said into the phone. Then he climbed off the bike. Unshaven, wearing a jogging outfit with sweat pancakes staining both arms, he looked a hundred years old.

"Put the cell phone down," Valentine said.

"You think I'm going to make a move?"

"You heard me."

"Sure. Just don't shoot me."

Porter's desk sat next to the bike. He placed the cell phone on a stack of books, and Valentine saw his fingers imperceptibly twitch. The .38's burp was louder than he expected, like a firecracker exploding in his hand. The bullet tore through the books. Porter jerked his hand into the air.

"Oh, Jesus," he cried.

Valentine walked around the desk. Hidden behind the books was a .357 Magnum. He made Porter sit on the couch, then pulled up a chair. Porter buried his face in his hands.

While Valentine waited, he stared at the wall behind them. It was covered with autographed sports junk: footballs, baseballs, group pictures of every Super Bowl winner of the past ten years. The last time he'd been in Frank's house, none of it had been there.

"Tell me why you did it," Valentine said.

Porter reached for the box of Kleenex sitting on a side table. He stopped when he saw the .38's barrel move.

"Real slow," Valentine said.

He tugged a Kleenex out of the box and blew his nose. "That's a good question. The money, I guess. That, and it was a sure thing."

"How is stealing a sure thing?"

"It is when you're stealing from a crook."

"You mean Archie?"

Porter nodded. "Brandi approached me last summer. She said Archie was skimming money off The Bombay. I said, 'So *what?*' and she said, 'He's vulnerable. We can rip him off, and he won't call the cops.' So I said, 'Who's we?' and she said, 'Everybody on the graveyard shift.'"

"So you were the last in."

Porter blew his nose again. "Yes. I don't know if I would have gone along if so many people weren't involved. But I did."

"How does the Desert Storm gang fit into this?"

Porter looked surprised. "You did your homework."

"Answer me."

"The Desert Storm gang is the core of the group. It includes
Sparky, Brandi, Gigi, and Monique. They do the legwork, like getting the money out of The Bombay and laundering it. They also
keep everyone else in line."

"And they're the ones making the bombs."

"Yes."

"Whose idea was it to make the Croatians into patsies?"

"Mine. Just in case something went wrong, we could point the
finger at them."

"Was it your idea to buy a white van that looked like theirs?"

Porter nodded. "But then they started bleeding us, so I had a
bright idea. I wanted to see if Archie really was scared of the
police, so I hired Doyle, knowing he'd sniff out the Croatians
right away. Doyle did, and I told Archie."

"And Archie told you to keep the cops out of it."

"Uh-huh."

Valentine rose. "Get up."

"Where are we going?"

"To have a talk with the district attorney."

Porter remained sitting. "You're not going to help me out?"

"No."

"I thought we were friends . . ."

"Get up," Valentine repeated.

A funny look flickered across Porter's face. Like he was adding
up his options. Then his hand dove under the cushion. Valentine
shot him in the chest.

Porter flew over the chair, his legs going straight up into the air.
An automatic pistol fell out of the cushion and onto the floor.
Valentine crossed himself, then walked around the chair.
Kneeling, he pulled back Porter's sweatshirt. He was wearing a

Kevlar vest, the slug lodged in the indestructible material.

There was a bottle of Evian in the drink holder on the bike. He

poured it on Porter's face. His friend blinked awake.

"Two guns. You expecting someone?"

Lying on his back, Porter nodded.

"Double-cross your partners?"

His friend didn't say anything.

"I'd like to meet them."

"No, you wouldn't," Porter said.

◆

He marched Porter downstairs to the basement and tied him to
a support beam with a piece of rope. "I want to know how
Archie's skimming The Bombay."

Porter was sweating profusely. "You and everybody else."

"You don't know?"

He shook his head. "It's Brandi's ace in the hole. If the gang
gets busted, she'll turn state's evidence and use it as leverage."

"She tell you that?"

"Fuck, no," Porter said, "I figured it out myself."

"One more question."

"What."

"Who killed Doyle?"

Porter looked at the concrete basement floor.

"Don't ask me that," he said.

Valentine considered pistol-whipping him. Or beating him
up. Only this was Porter, a guy he'd known for over twenty
years.

Instead, he went upstairs and searched the house. In the master
bedroom he found a suitcase packed with tropical clothes. On the
dresser, a ticket to Guatemala and a passport.

He dumped out the suitcase and ripped open its walls. Stacks of hundred dollar bills spilled out. He marched down the basement stairs clutching the money to his chest. Opening the furnace, he fed a stack to the flames.

"Tony, please don't do that," Porter begged him.

"Who killed Doyle?"

Porter stared at the money, then back at him.

"I want the name of the person who detonated the bomb that killed my partner," Valentine said.

"They wouldn't tell me who did it."

Valentine fed the rest of the money to the flames.

◆

Porter's driveway was over a quarter-mile long, most of it on an incline. Valentine walked to where his rental was parked and slipped into the forest. Finding a stump, he sat down, then laid the double-barreled shotgun he'd found in Frank's closet on the ground.

Twenty minutes later when the white van appeared at the bottom of Porter's driveway, he was deep in thought.

Of the scores of hustlers he'd busted over the years, only a handful had ever tried to kill him, and that was to avoid going back to prison. But the majority hadn't put up a fight. He supposed it had to do with the fact that they were professional criminals, a group that, for the most part, had few illusions about life. Amateurs were different when it came to crime. They had dreams, and were often willing to kill to keep those dreams alive.

The van came up the hill at a fast clip, its occupants hidden behind the tinted windshield. When it was a hundred yards away, he picked up the shotgun, and stepped into its path.

The squealing of brakes echoed across Pheasant Run. He raised the shotgun and aimed at the windshield. Then hesitated. The van retreated, its back end swerving first to the left, then to the right. Lowering the barrel, he shot out both front tires.

The driver lost control. Valentine watched the van veer off the drive and go crashing through the forest. Flipping on its side, it started to roll. He entered the forest to the sound of screams.

Two hundred yards off to his left, the van lay upside down, its tires spinning furiously. The windshield had imploded and thousands of silver dollars had spilled out, engulfing the car's occupants.

The coins were so thick he had to clear a path. Seeing a hand, he dug until he was looking at an upside down face. It was Monique. Her mouth was open, her eyes lifeless.

He dug some more and found Gigi behind the wheel, her pretty face sheeted in blood. Her eyelids fluttered.

"Help me," she whispered.

Valentine checked her pulse. It was good and strong. He was no doctor, but had a feeling she'd make it if an ambulance got to her before the bitter cold did her in. Her eyes opened wide.

"Please," she whispered.

Kneeling, he brought his lips next to her ear.

"Who killed Doyle Flanagan?"

"I can't . . ."

"Tell me."

"Will you help . . ."

"Tell me."

She whispered a name in his ear. Rising, he started to walk out of the forest and back to his rental.

"Please . . ." she called after him.

The wind whistled through the trees, their branches carrying the words to a song. *She's as sweet as Tupelo Honey. She's as sweet as honey from a tree.* He knew every word by heart, because Doyle had sung that song every day of his life. He felt his hands start to tremble and realized it had nothing to do with the cold.

37

Bally's

"You know what a pack rat Doyle was," Liddy said.

Valentine stood in the foyer of Liddy's house, staring at a pile of Doyle's stuff in the middle of the living room floor that she was about to throw away. It was stuff he could relate to. Old record albums, bundled copies of *Life* magazine, and an old wooden tennis racket in a frame.

"I want you to go out of town for a few days."

Liddy frowned. "I'm not ready for that, Tony."

"I think you'd better. I found out who's ripping off The Bombay."

She sat down on the couch, a pained look on her face.

"Is it bad?"

"Yes," he said.

Liddy had a cousin in Vermont. She wrote the phone number on a piece of paper and gave it to him. Valentine promised to call as soon as he could. She walked him to the door. Then said, "Wait," and returned a few moments later holding a fax. "The dry cleaner found this in Doyle's jacket."

He slipped his bifocals on. It was a purchase order for fifty Series E Micro-Processor–Controlled Slot Machines from Bally's Gaming in Nevada, the largest manufacturer of slots in the world.

"Can I keep this?"

"Of course."

He stuffed the fax into his pocket and gave her a hug.

◆

He drove to the Philadelphia airport and dropped his rental off. He found Kat sitting on a bench next to the Delta ticket counter, her daughter in a nearby arcade playing video games.

"I need a cigarette," he said.

Next to the arcade was a special glassed-in room for smokers. He'd always looked down his nose at the people who sat in such places, puffing away furiously, and now he found himself sharing a bench with a couple of diehards. Kat sat beside him, holding his hand.

Zoe sauntered in. "Are you my mother's new boyfriend?"

Valentine hemmed and hawed. The French probably had some cute word for his relationship with Kat, but the English language was void of such niceties.

"That's me," he said.

"Aren't you a little old?"

"Zoe!"

She stared at her mother. "You know what they call these rooms?"

"No, honey, I don't."

"Nicotine aquariums."

She kept up the monologue all the way to the Delta ticket counter. Valentine inquired about the next flight to Tampa. The ticket agent said, "How about right now?"

Valentine looked at the big board above the agent's head. The noon flight to Tampa hadn't left. The agent explained the situation.

"The plane needed some repairs. Nothing serious. I can still get all three of you on."

"I also need to go to Palm Beach," Valentine said.

"That's the Tampa flight's final destination," the agent said.

Valentine laid his credit card on the counter.

"How much luggage?" the agent asked.

"None," he said.

♦

"Why are we going to Florida without any luggage?" Zoe wanted to know when they were seated in the very last row. The plane had been sitting at the gate for hours and was filled with the living dead.

Kat patted her daughter's arm. "Well, honey, Tony asked me so suddenly, I just didn't have time to pack."

The pilot came over the PA and announced that it would be another ten minutes before they left. A collective groan filled the cabin. Kat and Zoe started to spar, the little girl masterful at pushing her mother's buttons. Borrowing Kat's cell phone, Valentine ducked into the lavatory. He dialed Mabel's number.

"Oh Tony, you're not going to believe what happened," his neighbor said.

"What?"

"I took your advice and called my neighbor. He came over and rescued me from Cujo. Actually, he just opened the back door, and the dog ran out.

"Well, everything was fine until an hour ago. I was in the kitchen fixing a cup of tea. I was standing at the stove when I heard this sound. Like a rat gnawing at wood. It was coming from the back door, so I ducked down. Then I heard a voice. It was a man and he was swearing under his breath, saying motherf***ing this

and motherf***ing that, like it was the first word he'd ever
learned. And then it hit me. It was a burglar. Well, you'll never
guess what happened next."

"A cop showed up."

"Be serious!"

"Your neighbor came to your rescue."

"Strike two."

"For Christ's sake, what happened?"

"Cujo rescued me. He was in the backyard and came flying
through the bushes. He attached himself to the burglar's butt, and
they went dancing down the street."

There was a knock on the bathroom door. He opened it. Zoe
stood outside, her legs crossed.

"You gonna stay in there all day?"

"Sure am."

Valentine shut the door. Then said, "Mabel, I wanted to tell
you something."

"What's that?" his neighbor said.

"I met a woman, and she's coming home with me. I wanted
you to know."

For a moment he thought Mabel had hung up on him.

"Does that mean I can't work for you anymore?" she asked.

Valentine felt a lump in his throat.

"No, of course not."

"I need to do something with my life," Mabel said. "I admire
you for doing something with yours. I just hope this situation
won't turn into one where I can't work for you anymore."

"It won't," he said.

"Is that a promise?"

"Yes."

"Thank you," she said. "Should I meet you at the airport?"

Valentine smiled into the phone.

"That would be great."

The pilot came over the PA and told everyone to get into their seats. Zoe was still outside when he unlatched the lavatory door.

"Asshole," she muttered, hurtling past him.

He took his seat and buckled up. Kat was looking out the little window at a man on the tarmac waving orange flags at the pilot. She glanced his way. "You were gone awhile."

"Sorry. You and Zoe patch things up?"

"I missed you," she said.

She leaned across the empty seat and kissed him like the world was about to end and this one had better mean something. When she pulled away, he was seeing stars.

"I missed you, too," he said.

38

Palm Beach

Mabel was at the gate when they disembarked. She was wearing Terminator shades, and at her side was one of the scariest-looking dogs Valentine had ever seen. Pure black, about seventy pounds of muscle, with a black tongue that stuck an inch out of its mouth, its hackle sticking straight up.

"How did you get that monster in here?"

"I told the airport people I was legally blind," she said.

"A dog," Zoe squealed with delight. She grabbed Valentine's sleeve. "You didn't tell me you owned a dog!"

Before any of them knew what was happening, the child from hell was rolling around on the floor with the dog from hell.

"Zoe, stop this nonsense this instant," Kat said, leaning over to scold her. "You're embarrassing yourself, and me."

"I cleaned up your house a little, turned down the beds," Mabel informed him, angling to get a better look at Kat. "You really do need to get a housekeeper."

Valentine saw no reason to delay things. He tapped Kat on the shoulder and said, "Kat, I want you to meet Mabel Struck."

Kat stood up and stuck her hand out. The braid in her hair had come undone, and her black mane lay seductively on her bosom. Valentine heard a loud click as Mabel's jaw came unhinged.

"Tony's told me all about you," Kat said, pumping Mabel's hand.

"No kidding," his neighbor said.

"Said he couldn't run his business without you."

His neighbor was smiling mischievously, taking the whole thing better than Valentine had expected. Like she was *proud* of him.

"So how did you two meet?" Mabel asked.

"Well, you're not going to believe this," Kat said.

"Try me."

"Tony came to my gym and started a fight."

"He did *what?*" Mabel said.

"It's a long story, but we got it worked out."

"A fight, as in he hit you?"

Kat giggled. "Tony bloodied my nose."

Mabel stared in horror at him. *"You beast!"*

The flight to Palm Beach was boarding. Mabel's eyes were burning his face. And Zoe's. And every other person milling around the gate. Which was why Valentine got himself on the plane as fast as humanly possible.

◆

Only in Florida could you rent a sporty BMW with nine hundred miles on the odometer for forty bucks a day.

He crossed the bridge into Palm Beach, his headlights shining on the array of brightly lit yachts and sleek cabin cruisers dotting the Intercoastal waterway. Rich men's toys with names like *Uptick* and *Margin Call*, the crews dressed in gleaming white uniforms, mopping down teak decks beneath a gibbous moon.

On the island, traffic was heavy, the road reduced to one lane because of construction. He inched down the main drag looking for County Road. He found it when he thought he was lost, and hung a left that took him into a residential area with Mediterranean-style houses with barrel tile roofs. Expensive, but nothing fancy.

Past the entrance for the Breakers Resort, the scenery changed. Houses grew into mansions with six-foot stucco walls that hugged the narrow beach. The speed limit dropped to twenty-five miles per hour, and he inched past driveways lined with gleaming Rolls-Royces and expensive Italian sports cars.

He remembered Archie's mansion from a magazine article. Archie had built a monstrosity that blocked his neighbors' view of the ocean. He found the place with little trouble, Archie's initials adorning the front gate. He drove into the servant's entrance and parked behind a white caterer's van.

He waited for someone to come out and tell him to beat it. When that didn't happen, he got out of the rental, and stuck his head through the azalea bushes.

Light streamed out of every window of Archie's place. He shifted his gaze to the limo parked by the front door. The plates were government issued, and the driver wore a uniform.

Rifling through the caterer's van, Valentine found a white waiter's jacket and put it on. It didn't clash with his pants, and he grabbed a serving tray and balanced it on his palm.

Going into strange places had never bothered him. Back when he was in uniform, he'd investigated a department store robbery. The thieves had walked into the store, hoisted a twenty-foot canoe onto their shoulders, and walked out. It was all a matter of attitude.

He opened the back door and walked into the kitchen. The room was huge, with two refrigerators, two stoves, and two of everything that most people only needed one of. It was also empty. From the back of the house, a man's angry words punctuated the air. He took a plate of pastries off the counter and balanced them on his tray, then followed the voice down a cavernous hall-way.

He passed the living room. A trio of musicians played in the corner. At the hallway's end, he found the help hovering outside a closed door. He edged closer. "What's going on?"

"The governor's on a rampage," a Cuban woman in a maid's uniform whispered. "He's going loco."

Everyone was grinning, enjoying this little perk to their day. Through the door he heard the governor say, " . . . and look where your plan's gotten me, Arch—just look! I've got a shit storm on my hands that gets bigger every time I turn on the television. The Indians haven't been this mad since we stole Manhattan from them. And you want me to do what?"

"Wait a few days, let it blow over," Archie said.

"It's not going to blow over," the governor bellowed. "Death by delay doesn't work with the media. I'm the Bad Guy of the Month, and if I don't do something fast, I'm going to become an ugly footnote to the Year in Review."

"You can't give in," Archie said. "Casino gambling is your sal-vation. Hundreds of millions in taxes. This thing will blow over. They're just Indians. No one cared about them before, and no one's going to care about them next week."

"How many million?" the governor said.

"Three hundred million a year, easy."

"You can generate that much in taxes?"

"More," Archie said emphatically.

"That's a lot of money."

The governor was caving in. Next they'd be drinking a toast. Valentine grabbed the door handle and twisted it. The help scat-tered.

He entered with the tray hiding his face. Five people sat at an ornate dining room table. Archie, Brandi, Florida's baby-faced

governor, and two of his handlers. Dinner was over, a turkey's car-
cass in the table's center. It was the Indians who'd introduced the
Pilgrims to turkey, not that Valentine thought any of these people
would see the significance.

"Here's dessert," Archie said. "Pastries flown in from La Bonn
in Paris. Governor, you've never tasted cream puffs like these."

The governor smiled beatifically. It was obvious that he really
liked cream puffs. Valentine placed the tray down. Then took out
his business card and dropped it on the governor's plate. The governor stared at the card, then up at him.

"Who the hell are you?"

"Name's Tony Valentine. I'm a private investigator."

"And?"

"Archie is running a crooked operation. I thought you'd like to
know before you make any agreements with him."

Archie rose from his chair. He was wearing a tuxedo and had
tucked the tablecloth into his trousers. He swiped at it angrily.
"He's a crazy old man. Don't listen to him."

"You know this person?" the governor asked.

Archie sputtered. "He was doing a job for me. But he went
nuts. Just last night—"

"Archie," the governor said.

"Yes?"

"Do you know him?"

"Yes, governor."

"Sit down." The governor turned to Valentine. "Where's your
proof?"

Valentine pointed at Brandi. "Ask her."

All eyes fell on Brandi. Her wardrobe tonight was particularly
stunning. A simple black dress and a choker of glistening diamonds. She looked at the governor and nodded.

"Archie's running a skim," she said quietly.

"As in skimming money, and not paying taxes?"

"That's right."

"How long has this been going on?"

"Since he's owned The Bombay," she replied.

"How long is that?"

"Twenty-three years."

One of the governor's handlers stood up. He had ex–Secret Service written all over him. Early fifties, crew cut, a face as blunt as a nail. He whispered in the governor's ear.

"How much money are we talking about?" the governor asked.

"Twenty million," she said. "Maybe more."

The governor leaned back in his chair. The media often portrayed him as being stupid, but Valentine had never bought that label. Thickheaded, yes, but not stupid. The governor whispered to his handlers. It was the ex–Secret Service guy who answered him.

"Sounds like real trouble."

"And I'm stepping right in the middle of it."

"With both feet," the ex–Secret Service guy said.

The governor balled up his napkin and tossed it onto his plate. He rose from the table. "Thanks for dinner."

Archie looked a heartbeat away from a stroke. "For God's sake, governor, let me explain."

"No," the governor said forcefully.

"What about our deal?"

"No deal," the governor said.

◆

The governor and his handlers left. Archie fell into his chair. The blood had drained from his face. He wiped at the corners of his mouth with his napkin. Then he stared at Brandi.

"You've ruined me."

Brandi stared down at the uneaten food on her plate.

"Why?" he said.

Brandi's Gucci purse sat on a table by the door. Valentine dumped its contents onto the table. Among her things was a pearl-handled revolver and pair of dog tags. He picked up the revolver and pointed it at her.

"Because she hates you," Valentine said. He pulled up a chair and sat next to her. "The part I couldn't figure out was why. But then it occurred to me that a lot of things haven't made sense over the past few days."

He put the barrel of the revolver under Brandi's chin, and made her look at him. "Like the raid on the Micanopy casino. Running Bear released dozens of alligators and chased the FDLE agents away. Those alligators didn't appear out of thin air. Someone alerted him.

"Or the Indian tribes around the country staging protests. I've done work for the Indians. As far as I know, they don't have any kind of communications network. Which meant someone alerted *them* to what was going on with the Micanopys. And that someone was you."

Brandi nodded, her eyes never leaving his face.

"What I couldn't figure out was your motive. But then I remembered our little chat in Sinbad's. You said you came from a mixed family. Stupid me. I thought that meant one of your parents was white. I was wrong. One of your parents is Indian."

"My mother was a Seminole," she said quietly.

"Not a Micanopy?"

"That would explain a lot to you, wouldn't it?"

"It would be a start."

She smiled thinly. "The Micanopys are like family to me. They were the first reservation to have casino gambling, and they let other tribes work in their casinos. My mother worked there, my father worked there, and so do my cousins." Her eyes shifted, and she stared at Archie. "I wasn't going to let you destroy them."

"That explains the stealing," Valentine said. "But it doesn't explain the killing."

"That was Coleman and Marconi's idea," she said, still staring at Archie. "Once things started to unravel, they decided to get rid of anyone who could implicate them."

He twitched the gun's barrel and saw her wince. Her eyes shifted to his face.

"That's not what I meant. Gigi told me you were the one who pulled the switch that killed Doyle. I want to know why."

Brandi's features turned hard as stone. She no longer resembled the beautiful woman sitting in the chair a moment ago.

"He got in the way," she said.

Valentine punched her in the face.

◆

Valentine stuck the revolver beneath his jacket and watched her slide out of her chair and onto the marble floor. Kneeling, he pulled back one of her eyelids. She was out cold.

Archie came over and stood next to him.

"You said she was stealing from me. How?"

"Slots," Valentine said.

"Is there anyone else involved."

"A whole shift. Plus surveillance. And probably others."

The casino owner made a fist and punched his other hand.

"What about my bodyguards? And my staff down here? Is there anyone I can trust?"

"No," Valentine said. He gathered Brandi up and tossed her over his shoulder. "Let's go."

"Where are we going?"

"Back to Atlantic City."

◆

They entered the kitchen with Archie telling the cook and kitchen staff she'd passed out from something she ate, and how dare they serve such crummy fucking food. Out in the driveway, Valentine opened the back door of the BMW.

"I don't think that's a good idea," the casino owner said.

"Why not?"

"Because she's a black belt in karate."

Valentine popped the BMW's trunk and looked for air holes so she wouldn't suffocate. Then he lay the unconscious woman into the tight space. Throwing the waiter's uniform into the bushes, he got behind the wheel and waited for Archie to belt himself in before starting the car.

It wasn't easy, but he managed to do the speed limit through the tony neighborhood while staring in his rearview mirror. No one from Archie's mansion followed them. Soon he reached the middle of Palm Beach's downtown. He stopped at a light. He was sweating, and he jacked up the air conditioner.

He stared at the line of chauffeured cars parked in front of Tom and Jack's fashionable eatery. A decorative sign heralded the restaurant's stone crab special. A pound of giant claws for only seventy-five dollars.

"You know what bugs me, Archie?"

The casino owner was also sweating. He shook his head.

"You turned these people against you. Your employees weren't thieves when they started to work for you. You *made* them into thieves."

Archie stared straight ahead. And said nothing.

Valentine approached the bridge that would take them over the Intercoastal waterway and back to the real world of fast food and normal-priced cars. On the middle of the bridge a red light began to flash. The traffic stopped in both directions.

He threw the rental into park, then watched the drawbridge go up. A yacht motored through, the ship's captain playfully tooting his horn. A loud *Bang!* made both men jump.

Valentine didn't move, his eyes fixed on the dime-size hole that had appeared in the BMW's windshield. He watched the glass crack in a thousand places, then realized what had happened.

Someone was shooting at them.

Dropping down, he stared at the white-haired geezers in the Jaguar in front of them. They looked harmless, and he glanced in his rearview mirror at two kids necking in a Jeep.

Where had the shot come from?

He felt a second bullet whiz by his ear. Spinning around, he saw where two black holes had appeared in the backseat. Then understood.

Brandi had another gun.

He had his door open when he felt Archie's hand touch his waistband.

"No!"

Holding the pearl-handled revolver with both hands, Archie fired through the backseat's upholstery, not stopping until the gun's chamber was empty. Valentine slapped his hands over his ears.

Then the bridge lowered and traffic started moving again.

39

The Squarest Guy in Atlantic City

Long-term parking at West Palm Beach airport was deserted. Valentine parked under a halogen light, then pushed a button that popped the trunk. Then he and Archie got out and had a look.

Brandi lay on her back, her lifeless eyes staring into space. Six bullets had penetrated the trunk and riddled her body. As they stared, flies appeared and became stuck in puddles of blood that coagulated around their legs. Valentine waved them away and started to shut the trunk. Then he noticed the tiny revolver clutched in Brandi's right hand. A two-shot.

They walked over to a stand to wait for the shuttle that would take them to a terminal. During the ride over, a portion of the windshield had disintegrated, and he hoped it wouldn't be too long before airport security would be around to have a look.

"It was self-defense," Archie said.

Valentine thought about the two-shot. Archie had probably bought it for her. Which meant he knew she was out of bullets.

"Bullshit," he said.

Archie clutched his arm. "Listen to me, you stupid guinea fuck. *It was self-defense.* Say otherwise, and I'll make sure the district attorney presses charges against you for shooting up The Bombay."

Valentine pulled his arm free. Porter had said that Brandi hadn't told anyone how Archie was skimming The Bombay. It was her trump card, and it had died with her.

A jet took off from a nearby runway. Then a tram came by, and they got on it.

◆

Twenty minutes later, they were sitting on a runway in Archie's private Lear jet. Archie swore the pilot could be trusted–"He's worked for me for ten years"–but that hadn't stopped Valentine from searching the cockpit for weapons.

Soon they were airborne. Archie got up and fixed them drinks, his fingers dropping ice cubes on the floor. He handed Valentine a Diet Coke in a plastic cup, then took the seat directly across from him. Killing another human being did something even to the worst people, and his face had taken on a gallows pallor. Valentine sucked down his drink in one long swallow.

Twenty-five minutes later, Jacksonville came into view. North of the city, paper mills spewed pillars of soot, the smoke dotting the night sky in lazy exclamation points. Valentine got up and poured himself another soda. Then he took a cell phone off the minibar and tossed it to Archie.

"You need to call the New Jersey attorney general. Have him call a homicide detective named Davis. I've got a number where Davis is hiding out. Davis is the only policeman in Atlantic City he should call."

"Davis is square?" Archie asked.

"He's square. Tell the attorney general to pass this message along. When the police raid your casino, Davis needs to watch where the employees run to. Wherever they run to, he needs to get to as quickly as he can."

Archie made the call. The attorney general was in bed and barked his displeasure loudly enough so Valentine could hear. Archie gave him the full story. Hanging up, he said, "He's calling Davis right now."

"Now you need to call the Palm Beach police and tell them about Brandi's body in the rental at the airport."

Archie stared at the phone, then tossed it aside.

"Let her sit for a few hours."

"Call them."

"Forget it," the casino owner said.

Valentine was too tired to argue. Leaning back in his chair, he closed his eyes. He felt his body melt into the soft cushions.

He thought of Brandi's corpse in the trunk of the rental. It was a hot night in Palm Beach. A few hours would be ghastly. Suddenly his eyes snapped open. Then he undid his seat belt and stood up.

Maybe it was the fact that he'd slept so little over the past few days. Or just witnessed another life senselessly wasted. Or maybe it was the sad realization that he'd never pick up the phone and hear Doyle Flanagan's voice again . . .

Whatever it was, it put a crack in his inner resolution. Placing his hands around Archie's throat, he started to choke him, spilling Bloody Mary on the casino owner's ruffled shirt and tuxedo jacket. He tried to scream, and Valentine squeezed as hard as he could.

He had no idea killing someone could be so much fun.

40

Big Mac, Large Fries

Bruno, Davis's German shepherd, had been in K9 for ten years. Then they'd retired him. And because the police were senseless, he was supposed to be taken to the pound and put to sleep. It was what happened to a lot of K9 dogs.

Davis had been the one who'd taken Bruno on his final car ride. On the way, he'd gone to his house and put the dog inside the garage. Then he'd driven to the pound and explained to the man on duty how Bruno had escaped when he'd let him out to pee.

"Happens a lot with K9 dogs," the man had said.

Which had made Davis feel better, knowing he wasn't the first cop who'd broken the rules to save an animal that had been more loyal than most of his partners. When he'd gotten home, Bruno had greeted him like there was no tomorrow, like he'd known the score.

Which was why finding the dog shot dead with a piece of pant leg in his mouth had snapped a chord in Davis. He would never own another dog like Bruno. It was that simple.

The attorney general's telephone call had come at a few minutes past eleven. Hanging up, Davis had gotten his Sig Sauer, then kissed his girlfriend good-bye. Getting in his car, he'd driven to his own house, which was only a few blocks from his girlfriend's. He'd pulled up behind Coleman and Marconi's unmarked Chevy and killed the engine.

Coleman and Marconi had been parked beneath a streetlight in front of Davis's house since eight, waiting for him to come home. Davis flashed his brights, then got out, holding the Sig Sauer loosely by his side.

Coleman and Marconi stepped out of the Chevy. They'd also drawn their weapons, the barrels pointed at the ground.

"Hey," Marconi said, like nothing was wrong.

"Hey," Davis replied.

They'd had a beer together once. Marconi had told him about getting bit in the face, and all the taunting at school. Davis had felt sorry for him and paid for their drinks.

"Which one of you shot my dog?" Davis asked.

The detectives stared at him.

"Say what?" Marconi said.

"You heard me."

Coleman made a move. Davis shot him and Marconi before either man could get off a round. Something he'd practiced for years, but never figured he'd have to use. Or ever wanted to.

The detectives lay bleeding in the street. Lights went on up and down the block. Davis went over and disarmed them, then pulled back both mens' pant legs. A white bandage was taped to the side of Marconi's left ankle. A spot of blood had seeped through the dressing.

"Figures," Davis said.

◆

Valentine awoke as the jet started to land, his ears popping. He saw Archie sitting across from him, talking on a cell phone. Why was it only in dreams that he did the things he wanted to?

They landed at Bader Field, the snow-covered landscape a grim reminder of winter's presence. The jet taxied to the runway's end where three unmarked police cars waited.

As Archie stepped off the plane, a detective offered him a coat. Davis, dressed in blue jeans and a North Carolina University sweatshirt, approached with his credentials in hand. "We raided The Bombay twenty minutes ago and started arresting your employees. The TV reporters showed up not long after. I figured you'd want to speak to them first."

"Couldn't you have arrested them at home," Archie said, stamping his feet on the frozen ground. "Did you have to turn it into a fucking three-ring circus?"

"I'm sorry, Mr. Tanner, but I'm not in public relations."

"Don't get cute with me," Archie said. "Where the hell is the attorney general, anyway? Did the governor send any of his people? *Where is everybody?*"

Valentine glanced at the men sent out to meet Archie. All cops. The governor and the attorney general hadn't sent anyone because being associated with Archie was about as wise as shaking hands with a leper, a fact that everyone on the tarmac seemed to appreciate except Archie.

"I *made* the governor of this fucking state," he spouted indignantly. "Did any of you know that? I bankrolled his last campaign and put him into office, the ungrateful rat bastard."

There was not enough ground for the cops to stare at. Only Davis seemed unmoved by Archie's tirade, his broad shoulders holding firm against the punishing wind.

"I'm sure you did," the detective allowed.

"You dissing me, detective?"

"Just telling you the way things are," Davis replied. He pointed to the three cars parked beside the runway. "Let's go."

♦

Had Valentine not known better, he would have thought the president was in town. Hundreds of police sawhorses surrounded The Bombay, choking traffic for blocks. Behind the blockade, Atlantic City's finest were conducting the largest single bust in their history, with hundreds of handcuffed prisoners waiting in line to be carted off to jail.

The local media had set up camp, the talking heads basking in artificial light as they told their stories. Seeing Archie step out of a car, they converged like sharks, only to be repelled by Davis and the other detectives. Archie ducked into The Bombay with Valentine by his side.

The casino was a shambles, with chairs and gaming tables smashed to bits. Slot machines had been destroyed, roulette wheels cracked in half, the legs taken off craps tables and used to bash in the casino's expensive decorations. Instead of going quietly, Archie's employees had wrecked the joint.

A gang of dealers and pit bosses had barricaded themselves in the Hard Count room. The police had tried to talk them out, and when that hadn't worked, brought in a battering ram to knock down the door. Valentine watched the police do their thing. Had he missed something when he'd looked at the Hard Count room through Porter's computer? He tried to imagine what.

Then the door came down.

"Kill them," Archie shouted.

The police nearly did just that. Using their billy clubs, they beat the dealers and pit bosses senseless.

When the employees were subdued, Valentine went into the room. The scales and coin-counting machines had been smashed. Buckets of coins had been dumped on the floor. He knelt down and picked up a handful. It was both Funny Money and the real stuff.

Then he noticed a sign on the wall. It read THIS SCALE, FUNNY MONEY ONLY. *How simple,* he thought.

Then he heard someone say his name.

Davis stood in the doorway, grim-faced. Valentine followed him out of the Hard Count room. In the casino, the dealers and pit bosses had been handcuffed and were being led away in a line. Archie was with them, kicking his employees and cursing.

◆

Outside, it had started to snow, the flakes swirling around Davis's Thunderbird in miniature cyclones. The detective drove away with his windshield wipers on their highest setting.

Valentine assumed they were going to the police station. Davis would want to sit him down in front of a tape recorder and explain what had happened so the prosecutors would be clear on exactly what crimes had been committed. It was a common procedure, something he did all the time.

Only the exit for the police station came and went. When Davis put on his indicator five miles later, Valentine didn't have a clue where they were headed.

The Thunderbird skidded down an icy road. Through the whirl of snow, Valentine saw a pair of familiar golden arches. It was the McDonald's where Doyle had bought the farm. A pair of police cruisers were parked in front, their bubbles acting like strobe lights in the storm.

"The manager called it in twenty minutes ago," Davis explained. "He asked that we keep it quiet, seeing that Doyle got murdered here last week."

Davis pulled into the lot and waved at one of the cops. The uniform walked over, blowing steam off his coffee. He had the face of a fifteen-year-old. Lowering his window, Davis said, "Tell me you didn't touch anything."

"No, sir," the uniform said. "We left it just like we found it."

Davis edged the Thunderbird around back and parked. He removed a flashlight from the glove compartment and led Valentine across the lot to where Frank Porter's mini-Mercedes was parked.

The flashlight's beam found Porter sitting behind the wheel. On his lap sat a cardboard tray. In it, a Big Mac, large fries, and a thick shake. Still clutched in Frank's hand was the gun he'd eaten for dessert, the slug having passed through the back of his skull and painted the rear window. The burger was half-eaten, and Valentine wondered what had caused Frank to lose his appetite and decide to end things. What sudden insight had made him wake up and realize the horrible things he'd done?

He went to the bushes and threw up.

"Jesus!" Davis exclaimed.

"What?" he gasped.

"He *moved*."

Valentine took the flashlight from Davis's hand. Opening the driver's door, he shone the beam onto the dead man's face. Porter had fallen onto the wheel and appeared to be grinning. Valentine closed his eyes with his fingertips. The flashlight caught a piece of paper sticking out of Porter's pocket.

"Go ahead," Davis said.

Valentine held the paper so they could both read it.

To Whoever finds this note:

Please tell my friends that

I know what I did was wrong. I
just didn't know how to stop it.

F. P.

Valentine put the note back into Porter's pocket. Then whispered in his friend's ear.

"You stupid bastard," he said.

41

Balzac

Sitting in front of the Blue Dolphin in Davis's Thunderbird, Valentine counted the dead on the fingers of both hands. Doyle. Sparky. Rolf. Juraj's brother, Alex. The fun-loving Mollos. The Mod Squad. And now Frank. He shook his head in disgust. They were all dead, and over what? A few million bucks? It was chickenshit when you cut it up among a hundred people. Prison was no picnic, but murdering so many people to avoid it? That seemed like a crime all by itself.

"What happened to Coleman and Marconi?" he asked Davis.

"I shot them," the detective said. Then added, "They're both expected to live."

"Make you feel any better?"

The detective gave it some serious thought, then shook his head. Valentine started to get out of the car and felt the cold rip through his overcoat like a knife. Davis touched his sleeve.

"How long are you going to be?"

"Give me a half hour."

"How about ten minutes?"

It was 3 A.M. and Valentine was ready to collapse.

"What's the rush?"

"I've got the district attorney waiting, Tony. He's got a hundred people in jail and he doesn't have a case. That's the

rush."

Certain things never changed. Taking the fax from Bally's Gaming out of his pocket, Valentine tossed it onto Davis's lap. "Okay, here's your case. Last summer, some Bombay employees talked Archie into running a promotion called Funny Money. There was only one catch. Archie would have to rearrange the casino.

"Arch bought the idea. He let everything get turned upside down. What Arch didn't know was that the employees put fifty slot machines on the floor that he didn't own. *They* owned the machines, and that's the bill for them.

"In the act of rearranging the casino, a number of surveillance cameras were put on double-duty. When the employees wanted to empty their slot machines, Frank Porter switched the double-duty camera so those machines weren't filmed.

"Getting the money out was simple. The coins were put into buckets, with Funny Money coins going on top, just in case a DGE agent happened to be around. They were dumped on a tray in the Hard Count room that was for Funny Money only. Then they were wrapped and taken out of the casino." He paused. "Think you can remember all that?"

The detective nodded his head.

"Good-bye, Eddie," he said.

♦

He entered the motel office, wallet in hand. The manager was asleep in his chair. He slipped two hundred-dollar bills into the sleeping man's pocket, then went to his room and threw his things into his suitcase.

Out of habit he checked under the bed and found Kat's red lace Victoria's Secret underwear. Just holding the garment in his hand made his heart race. The phone on the night table rang. He answered it.

"Oh Tony, how could you?"

It was Mabel. "How did you find me?"

"I called the Atlantic City police, who called Detective Davis in his car, who told me where you were," his neighbor replied.

She was turning into one hell of a detective.

"How could I what?" he asked.

"Get into a relationship with a woman with a twelve-year-old."

He stared at the undergarment clutched in his hand.

"Beats me," he confessed.

"Gerry called while I was at the airport picking you up. I saved his message on voice mail."

"Is he okay?"

"Listen to the message yourself. Oh, and one more thing."

"What's that?"

"You owe me," his neighbor said.

A dial tone filled his ear. Dialing voice mail, he punched in his seven-digit code and heard his son's voice ring out.

"Hey, Pop. I figured I'd better touch base, give you an update. We arrived in Zagreb last night. You wouldn't believe the mess the city's in. Yolanda convinced me to go to the U.S. Embassy, and ask about this person you wanted us to find. Which is what I did.

"Well, you really struck out, Pop. This person isn't some big crime boss like you thought. It's a Catholic nun running a mission. She's the local Mother Teresa. Yolanda and I visited her this morning. She feeds half the town's poor people. Said her brothers in the United States send her money.

"We couldn't get a flight out until tomorrow, so Yolanda

offered our services to the mission. They've got a small hospital, and Yolanda is treating a bunch of sick kids." His son paused. "Guess what they've got me doing."

"Try me," Valentine said.

"Cleaning bed pans. *Yeeech!!!* Okay, it's not that bad, and the patients are really appreciative, even if I can't understand a word they're saying. So, that's the story. I'll call you when we reach Spain. Oh, yeah, Yolanda says 'Hi.'"

Valentine replayed the message, letting the words form a picture in his head that he hoped to take with him to his grave. Which was of his son helping people.

Then he put on his overcoat and took a walk.

♦

His first stop was the pay phone on the corner next to his motel. He'd been thinking a lot about Sparky Rhodes, wondering if anyone had discovered his body. He doubted it, and he started to dial 911, then decided he'd better not. All 911 calls were recorded, and he didn't need someone recognizing his voice and dragging him into another investigation.

Dropping fifty cents into the machine, he called information instead. The line rang ten times before a female operator answered.

"What number please?"

"I need you to call the police."

"Excuse me?"

"You heard what I said. Tell them there's a dead man lying in a basement." He gave her Sparky's address, then said, "Please tell the police there's a cat in the house."

"A cat," the operator said.

"Yes. An old black cat. She'll need a home."

"I'll be sure to tell them," the operator said.

"Thank you," he said.

♦

His next stop was the Drake. He found Juraj and Anna standing by the empty swimming pool, the orange tips of their cigarettes glowing mysteriously in the dark. Anna came toward him.

"Don't you ever sleep?" Valentine asked.

"We were lying in bed when we saw the news on TV," she said. "There was a film of you and Archie Tanner going into The Bombay. It took us a while, but then we realized what you had done."

Valentine waited. Anna threw her arms around him.

"Thank you. From the bottom of our hearts, thank you."

That was more like it.

"You're welcome, Anna," he said.

She gave him a kiss as good as any of Kat's, a kiss from the soul. It was great until Juraj decided he wanted to kiss him too, and planted his lips on both of Valentine's cheeks, then gave him an old-fashioned bear hug.

The Croatians walked him down to the shoreline. Valentine wanted to tell them how lucky they were—he was not in the habit of letting hustlers go, even well-meaning ones—but he sensed they already knew that. They said another round of good-byes, with Anna giving him another kiss. Valentine pinched her sleeve as Juraj walked away.

"You're going to keep cheating casinos, aren't you?"

"No," she said.

"Don't lie to me, Anna."

She crossed her arms defiantly. "No!"

"Anna . . ."

"All right, *yes*."

Taking two crisp twenties from his pocket, Valentine shoved them into her hand.

"What is this for?" she asked.

"If you're going to keep playing the five thousand dollar tables, make him get a decent haircut."

◆

He walked the beach he'd grown up on. The tide was low, the waves a bare ripple across the black sea. A brightly lit cruise ship was anchored offshore, and he stopped to stare. There was a late-night party going on, everyone having a swell time. He felt himself shudder.

Hindsight being twenty-twenty, it hadn't taken him long to realize what he'd done. He'd solved a crime that hadn't occurred. No one had missed the money. Not Archie, or the Division of Gaming Enforcement or the Casino Control Commission. And if no one missed the money, then who cared?

The money. That was what it always came down to in Atlantic City. The money. It flowed back and forth, changing hands every day, but in the end, it stayed in the casino's coffers, because the casinos set the odds, and the casinos never lost. Somehow, Porter and the rest of The Bombay gang had forgotten that.

He slipped off his shoes and socks and let the waves slap his toes. The water was freezing cold, but that was okay. He wanted to feel connected to something besides here, and the icy waves sure did the trick.

He stared across the ocean, trying to imagine himself cleaning up after sick people. It had to be the worst job in the world, yet

Gerry had made it sound okay. Like he was getting something in return.

There was a message there somewhere, he thought.

◆

Back at the motel, he found Davis hanging out by the manager's office. He started to walk away. The detective followed him.

"You always so antisocial?"

"I'm done," he said. "Leave me alone."

The detective kept following him. "You ever read any Balzac?"

"Who?"

"He was a nineteenth-century French novelist."

"No, I never read him."

"I did. In high school. One line in a book stayed with me. *Behind every great fortune, there is a crime.*"

The cold was making Valentine's ears ring. "So?"

"When we raided The Bombay, you told me to watch where the employees ran to. Well, they ran to *two* places. The employees in the casino ran to the Hard Count room. But a bunch of employees in the back ran to a storage room."

Valentine stared at him. "Did you find anything?"

"Yeah. Cases and cases of champagne sitting out in the open. While behind locked doors, a few thousand cartons of cigarettes."

"So?"

"Case of champagne costs what—a thousand bucks? Carton of cigarettes costs twenty. Why keep the cigarettes locked up, unless they're hot. So I had a check run on them."

Valentine stuck his hands in his pockets, remembering it like it was yesterday. He'd pulled Archie over for speeding and found the trunk of his car stuffed with bootleg cigarettes.

"And?"

"They're hot," the detective said.

"Did you jam him?"

"About twenty minutes ago," Davis said. "You should have seen Archie squawk."

It had been one of the saddest weeks of Valentine's life, yet he found himself smiling. Selling bootleg cigarettes in New Jersey is a felony: Archie Tanner would do hard time *and* lose his casino license. Valentine couldn't help himself, and he pinched Davis on the cheek.

"You are one smart kid," he told him.

42

Three Weeks Later

Valentine stood before a full-length mirror, grimacing.

The dressing room's concrete walls shook. Outside, the Centro-plex's standing-room-only crowd was getting ugly. They were not used to waiting, and Valentine could hear calls for blood, the faithful stomping their feet. His own feet felt frozen to the floor.

The dressing room door opened and shut. Kat edged up beside him, looking worried.

"Tony, you okay?"

No, he wasn't okay, he was light years from okay, only that didn't matter. He'd said yes, signed the stupid contracts, let them dress him up like a clown. Ha, ha, only now it didn't seem so god-damn funny.

"Tony, please say something."

Valentine kept staring at himself. He did not look right, or even *real,* his hair done up in a ridiculous bouffant like an Elvis imper-sonator, his costume a canary yellow sports jacket, yellow pants, and a shimmering yellow tie. First there was Donny the grape, now Tony the banana.

"Tony?"

The dressing room door opened. Donny and Vixen popped their heads in. They were both freaking out.

"They're rioting out there," Donny said.

"Come on Tony," Vixen said, "you can do it."

Valentine stared at his ridiculous image in the mirror.

"It's just opening-night jitters," Kat reassured them. "Give us another minute, okay?"

They left and the dressing room fell silent. Kat got close enough so they were able to share the mirror's reflection. Her eyes met his in the glass.

"You don't have to do this," she said.

"Yes, I do."

"No, you don't."

"But I'll let you down."

She kissed him on the cheek. "I can live with it."

"You sure?"

"Yeah."

Valentine breathed a sigh of relief. He'd been dreading the thought of stepping into the ring and making a fool of himself in front of ten thousand beer-guzzling lunatics. Dreading the notion of doing something different, for once in his life.

In the mirror he saw sadness in Kat's eyes and realized she was lying. Lying because she cared more about his feelings than her own. Lying because she loved him.

He slapped her on the ass. Kat jumped an inch off the floor.

"But I *want* to," he said.